befe
Avoid

F

F

WHEN THE MUSIC STOPPED

London, 1910. Twins Lester and Lillia Holdsworth are destined for the stage. Lester is a brilliant pianist; Lillia a magnificent opera singer. But their cruel father has other ideas for their future. Lester is sent to a military academy, while Lillia must marry Lord Dalton – a pompous friend of her father's looking for a young wife to give him an heir. Their plans to defy their father's wishes are put on hold when war breaks out. Lester flies planes for the Royal Flying Corps and Lillia trains as a nurse. They wait – like the rest of Europe – for the war to end and the music to start again.

WHEN THE MUSIC STOPPED

WHEN THE MUSIC STOPPED

by

Beryl Matthews

Magna Large Print Books
Gargrave, North Yorkshire,
BD23 3SE, England.

British Library Cataloguing in Publication Data.

A catalogue record of this book is
available from the British Library

ISBN   978-0-7505-4704-8

First published in Great Britain by Allison & Busby in 2017

Published in Large Print 2019 by arrangement with
Allison & Busby Ltd.

Magna Large Print is an imprint of Library Magna Books Ltd.

Printed and bound in Great Britain by
T.J. (International) Ltd., Cornwall, PL28 8RW

Chapter One

London 1910

As the last glorious notes of the aria from *Madame Butterfly* faded away, Lester lifted his hands slowly from the piano and smiled at his twin sister. 'You hit every note perfectly, Lillia, now let us try one from *La bohème* this–'

'Enough!' General Holdsworth stormed over to the piano and slammed down the lid. 'This house is bedlam with you two in it! Come to my study immediately.'

The twins watched their father march out of the room and sighed in unison.

'Here we go again,' Lester murmured, standing up and taking his sister's arm. Side by side they followed their father.

He was waiting just inside the door and slammed it shut as soon as they were in. The twins winced as a precious vase rattled on the mantelshelf, but they were used to his rages. He had no interest in music and they were sure he must be tone deaf not to appreciate it.

When he remained standing they became wary, knowing they were really in for an unpleasant episode this time.

'You are both eighteen now and it's time to think about your future. I have made a decision.'

'But we know–'

9

'Be quiet, Lillian! Lester – next week you go to military academy and train to become an officer.'

She heard her brother's sharp intake of breath, and wondered what fate was planned for her.

'Lillian – Lord Dalton has done us the honour of asking for your hand in marriage. I have accepted, for you cannot hope to make a better match.'

Now she was furious and felt her brother grasp her hand as they both glared at this parent who was so unlike them. And why did he insist on calling her Lillian? It was irritating. Lillia was prettier and she liked it.

'We have both been awarded a place at the Royal College of Music, and term starts in September,' Lester protested.

'You can forget all that music stuff and nonsense,' he shouted. 'I have already told them you will not be attending. You will both do as I say, and I will not hear a word of protest from either of you. You need to be separated!'

The twins were too stunned to move or speak as their world crumbled around them. Lester – a soldier? Lillia – married to a middle-aged bore of a man? As brother and sister, they had been companions from conception. They knew each other's thoughts, and if one were sick or in trouble, the other felt that as well. The pain of dismay now swamped them.

'You may go and begin making preparations for your new lives.'

They practically ran back to the music room, shut the door and locked it. Then they faced each other, white with despair.

'How did our lovely, quiet and sophisticated mother ever come to marry a man like that?' She clenched her fists as tears of fury filled her eyes. 'He cancelled our places at the college. How could he do that? Doesn't he know how hard we have worked for those places?'

'To him, music is just noise.'

She nodded and wiped her eyes. 'What are we going to do? If we still had our places at the college, we could have defied him and gone there anyway, but he has made sure we can't do that.'

'I don't see we have any options but to let him believe we are going along with his arrangements.'

'Oh no, I will *not* marry Lord Dalton! He's old – and a politician! You know what I think of politicians!'

'Exactly.' A slow smile appeared on his handsome face. 'Make him withdraw his offer.'

'How...?' her eyes opened wide as it dawned on her what he was suggesting. 'Of course! You are so clever. All right, so I can possibly get out of my predicament, but what about you? The army is not for you. If you go we shall be parted, and I could not bear that.'

'It had to come one day,' he said kindly, 'and it will be hard for us, but it is what we must do. One day our careers would have taken us in different directions anyway.'

'But the prospect of our chosen careers has been taken away from us!' she declared angrily.

'A temporary setback only. You work on convincing Lord Dalton you will make him a most unsuitable wife, and I will go to the military

11

academy until I can find a way out.'

'How will that be possible?' she asked.

'I will have to convince them I will never make a soldier, let alone an officer. The next few months are going to be difficult, but we must succeed, and then we will try for another place at the college. We won't give up.'

'Of course we won't!' she rushed over to her twin and hugged him. 'I shall find it very hard without you, and you must write every day – please.'

'I will. Now, we must consult Mother and see if she has a way to deal with this. When did she say she would be returning?'

'Tomorrow. I'll wager he's done this while she's been away and without consulting her. She couldn't overrule him because I believe she is frightened of him, and that's why she visits her friend so often. How did we ever come to have a father like this?'

Lester shook his head in disbelief. 'We certainly haven't inherited anything from him, thank goodness. I often wonder where our love of music comes from. Although Mother enjoys music she has no talent for it and doesn't even play the piano.'

'We must be throwbacks from someone in our past, and we are the only twins in the family. We are unlike any other family member with our dark hair and green eyes. We really don't fit, do we?'

'We must try and find out more about our ancestors sometime,' Lester remarked, thoughtfully, lifting the lid of the piano and sitting down, his hands running lovingly over the keys.

She settled down and waited for her brother to

start playing. When the first notes of a piece by Rachmaninoff filled the room, she sighed with pleasure. She could listen for hours to her brother playing. There was something quite magical about his touch. She could play, but was lacking that something special he possessed. How could that dreadful man send him to become a soldier? There was only one place her brother belonged, and that was seated at the piano.

He looked across and smiled. 'Do you want to sing?'

She shook her head. 'No, just play.'

The next morning there was no sign of their father, much to their relief. They waited anxiously for their mother to return and rushed to greet her the moment she stepped inside the door.

'We must talk with you, please,' Lester told her. 'It is most urgent!'

The pleasure of seeing her children again quickly faded from Sara's face. 'Come to my sitting room. Have a tray of tea sent up,' she asked the butler.

'At once, madam.'

Their mother removed her travelling cape and tossed it on a chair when they reached her room, and then she faced her children. 'Do sit down, my dears. I know you are bursting to tell me something, and from your expressions it is clear I am not going to like it. But I will not hear a word until I have had a cup of tea.'

The twins sat side by side and waited until the refreshments had arrived and their mother was on her second cup.

She replaced the cup carefully on the tray, sat back and said, 'Lester, now you can tell me what has happened.'

When her son had finished the story of what their father had done, she stood up and walked over to the window. There was silence.

'What can we do?' Lillia asked. 'What he has planned for us is dreadful.'

Their mother spun round, her face milky white and she was trembling with rage. 'It is terrible! You are both musicians of extraordinary talent. That is what you were born to do!'

'Not according to him.' Lester stood up and guided their mother back to her chair, while his sister poured another cup of tea. 'We didn't mean to upset you so, but we desperately need your advice. Is there any way out of this? We do have our inheritance from Uncle Bertram. I know it doesn't come to us until we are twenty, but is there some way it could be released sooner?'

She shook her head. 'I'm so sorry, my dears, but it was under your grandfather's control, and after he died I discovered he had used it to finance something your father was involved in. There isn't anything left.'

'That can't be so!' Lillia said angrily. 'It was willed to us!'

Lester laid a hand on his sister to calm her down. 'We understand it was out of your control, Mother.'

'The sad truth is we are only just managing to maintain our lifestyle.'

'But you had a fortune in your own right.' Lester was dismayed by this news. He had always believed their mother was wealthy. 'Where has it all gone?'

Sara was too distressed to speak for a moment.

'He took it!' Lillia exploded. 'Did that man find a way to help himself to your money?'

'Once a woman marries everything she owns becomes her husband's. You know that, darling. There wasn't anything I could do about it.'

'All that is going to change when women get the vote!' She stormed around the room. 'It's time our voices were raised against such injustice.'

'If you raise your glorious voice, it will certainly be heard.' Lester dredged up a sad smile, and turned calmly to his mother. 'It appears we are not in any position to defy him.'

'None I can see at the moment. I am dreadfully sorry. If I could put things right for you I would, but you know well enough that he is not a man you can reason with. If your uncle was still alive I could have gone to him for help, but there is no one I can turn to now. I can't bear to see your lives ruined like this.' Sara's voice broke and she turned away to hide her anguish.

Seeing how distressed their mother was, Lillia calmed down and went to her side. 'Have no fear for us. The fulfilment of our dreams will be delayed, but we will find a way out of this.'

'Once you are married to Lord Dalton there will be no way you can pursue your career in music.'

'I won't be marrying him!' A determined gleam came into her eyes. 'I know of a way to make him withdraw his offer.'

Sara knew her daughter well. She was a prima donna to her soul and had the ability to make things go her way. The only person she had never been able to manipulate was her brother. If she said the marriage offer would be withdrawn, then there was a fair chance that it would be. She turned to her son. 'Do you have a plan as well?'

'We were hoping there would be a way out of this without resorting to underhand tactics, but it is clear there is no easy answer. We have discussed this and now know we will have to take action. Lillia is going to prove she will be a most unsuitable wife, and I will show I will never make a soldier, let alone an officer.'

Kneeling beside her mother, Lillia took hold of her hands. 'How did you come to marry a man like this? He is way below your class.'

'I was faced with a desperate situation and had no choice. One day, when you are older, I will tell you why we are in this sad situation, and I pray you will not hate me for what I have done.'

'Mother!' they both declared. 'You could never do anything to make us stop loving you! Can't you tell us now?'

She looked at her children and gave a sad smile. 'You still amaze me when you speak together as one person. This is not the right time because it will only add to your burdens, but when the time comes I will tell you the whole story. Until then, I must ask you to be patient and do as he says. Believe me when I stress that we do not have a choice at this time.'

'We will do as you say.' Lester went over to his mother and kissed her cheek. 'We'll try not to do anything to make your life even more difficult than it is, but we must deal with this in our own

16

way. Don't come to our defence or show dis-approval at his decisions.'

'No, my dears.' Sara shook her head. 'I cannot stand by and see your talents wasted.'

'That is exactly what you must do,' her daughter told her. 'We will face his wrath, but we will not see it turned upon you. This is our fight and we are determined he will not win – indeed, he must not win!'

'She is right,' Lester agreed. 'We are not helpless children any more, and with our chosen future in the balance we will fight him – whatever the consequences might be. And when we are famous we will be able to look after you.'

'Can you not go back to your friend for a lengthy stay?' her daughter suggested.

'Certainly not! By suggesting that I do nothing you are asking too much of me. You are my children and this is not your fight alone – it is ours. I have always been careful to tread softly so you could have a happy upbringing, but I have stayed in the background too long. Now, tell me what you are going to do, for I am sure you have discussed this very carefully before approaching me.'

Without going in to details he said they simply had to convince everyone they were not suited to the roles their father had planned for them, and when he had finished he was pleased to see the colour return to their mother's face.

She leant forward. 'If you can do something without him being aware you are opposing his plans, then it might work, but you will both need to be very convincing.'

Lillia struck a pose of pure innocence and fluttered her eyelashes. 'We are accomplished performers and all he will see are two dutiful children obeying his orders without protest.'

Sara smiled briefly at her daughter and then was serious again. 'I may be able to support you, but what about you, Lester? You will be on your own, and once you are at the military academy it will be difficult for you to get out again.'

'Have no fear; something will come along to make that possible. I can take care of myself. One thing I do ask though: please don't let him touch my piano while I'm away.'

'He cannot. That was a gift to us before you were born and I have made sure it is in your names. He knows this well enough and dare not dispose of it.'

The twins were stunned and said in unison, 'Who gave it to us?'

'That again is something I cannot tell you. But rest assured that the piano is safe.'

'You are making my head swim with these mysteries,' her daughter declared.

Sara smiled. 'When you are both rich and famous, I will tell you all.'

Chapter Two

The time came for Lester to leave for the military academy and Lillia was distraught, but her brother had admonished her to make their parting calm. Their father must not have the slightest hint that they were unhappy with his arrangements. They hugged, smiled and wished each other happiness and success in their new lives.

Lester walked out of the house with a spring in his step as if eager to be on his way and waved as he disappeared up the road.

Their father grunted with satisfaction and without a word returned to his study. Only then did Lillia and her mother allow the tears to fall.

'What am I going to do without him?' she whispered.

Sara led her daughter towards the music room. 'You are going to play the piano and sing at the top of your voice.'

'I could not!'

'Yes, you can, my dear. Let him know there will still be music in this house. If he thought that by sending Lester away the music would come to a stop, then you can prove him wrong. Sing something from *La bohème* for me, it is so beautiful and I never tire of hearing you sing.'

She sat at the piano and stifled a sob. She understood what her mother was saying – and she was quite right – but it was so hard without the other half of her. Their talents were different. Lester couldn't sing and she didn't have his skill at the piano, but together they made a whole.

'Play, my dear,' her mother urged gently. 'You can do it. Remember it's what Lester would expect of you. He will find a way to play the hand he has been dealt, and you must show your father, who is now probably gloating in his study, that you will not be beaten.'

Straightening on the stool, she began to play

19

and sing softly at first, then as the music took over her notes rang out loud and clear.

'Beautiful,' Sara sighed as the last notes faded and smiled at her daughter. 'I should think they heard that all the way to Covent Garden.'

Determination shone in her green eyes. 'One day they will hear me sing, but I have a great deal of work to do before I am ready to take to the stage. I am only eighteen and will need a few years to mature. I will not get that chance if I am forced to marry Lord Dalton. It is essential that I remain unwed, and it is the same for Lester. We have quite a fight on our hands, Mother.'

'And one I have no doubt you will win. I will help you both all I can. You have talents that need to be nurtured until they are honed to perfection, and that is something Gilbert is determined will not happen. Whatever hardships we have to face in the future, this is a fight for the three of us. I have already warned Lester that once his father realises he is being defied things could get unpleasant, and you may hear things that will shock you. Your brother has already told me he doesn't care what is said, but could you deal with society's censure?'

'Yes,' she declared firmly. 'I don't care what people say about us; I just want to sing. Father can slander us in any way, even turn us out of our home, but we will survive. And we will take care of you.'

She smiled. 'That's what your brother told me, but let us pray that doesn't happen.'

For the rest of the day Lillia kept her mind focused on her brother and, much to her relief, she did not pick up any indication that he was troubled. They were so in tune with each other she knew she must remain calm. Although they had been parted, they were still working together to thwart their father's plans. They were not alone either, because their mother was on their side, as she always had been.

Dinner that evening was difficult for her without Lester sitting opposite her, but she remained bright, refusing to let her distress show.

'Lord Dalton will be calling on you tomorrow afternoon, Lillian,' her father announced. 'I shall expect you to be courteous and show pleasure at the honour he is bestowing upon you by his interest. He doesn't like silly females, so engage him in intelligent conversation.'

'Yes, Father.'

'Sara, you will chaperone them but remain unobtrusive.'

'Of course, Gilbert. Will you be joining us?'

'I have business to attend to, but I am relying on you to see this first meeting goes smoothly. It will be a step up to have a lord in the family.'

Ah, that is what this is all about, thought Lillia. He is trying to climb the social ladder.

'Lord Dalton must already be impressed with her to have declared his interest.' She smiled at her husband. 'And I have no doubt he will soon be even more certain of her suitability once he gets to know her.'

'She is presentable enough, I agree, and young enough to give him the heirs he needs.'

She went cold with horror, but somehow managed to keep a smile on her face. These men were proposing to trap her in a loveless marriage for the sole purpose of producing heirs! Well, that wasn't going to happen. Neither would she see her brother's talent squandered just so this soulless man could have another officer in the family. He had already been elevated above his station by marrying their mother who came from the impeccable Kirkby family.

The moment their father retired to the smoking room to enjoy a cigar and several brandies, she spun to face her mother, absolutely furious. 'How dare he do this? I won't have it. If he tries to force this marriage on me I shall leave home. I can always get work somewhere. The music halls would probably give me work. I will not become a brood mare for anyone.'

'Keep your voice down, my dear,' her mother urged. 'Stay calm. You said you had a plan to make Lord Dalton withdraw his offer. Put it into action at once and I will support you. Will you tell me exactly what you are going to do?'

'It is for the best that you don't know, then you can say with complete honesty that you had no idea I had done this.'

Sara studied her daughter and frowned with worry. 'Don't do anything foolish.'

'Have you ever known me to act foolishly?'

'No, I haven't, but you have never had to face anything like this before. It would ease my mind to know what you are planning.'

Lillia's smile was devilish. 'It will soon become clear, and I think you will approve.'

'I say, this is exciting, isn't it?'

Lester glanced around the room containing six

beds and grimaced at the young man standing beside him. 'Exciting isn't the word I would use. My name is Lester.'

'James.' The young man held out his hand. 'From your reply I take it you are not happy to be here.'

'Correct.' Lester shook hands with James and smiled. 'This isn't what I had planned for my life, but it was forced upon me.'

'Ah, a strict parent?'

He nodded. 'But I'm here now and will have to see how it goes, but I doubt I'll make a soldier.'

'You stick with me. I come from a long line of military officers and will help you along if you need it.'

'That is generous of you, but I fear you could come to regret that offer.'

James laughed. 'I revel in a challenge. Come on; let's explore the place before we start being ordered around.'

They found the classrooms, dining hall, library and the main lounge. This last room was the most interesting to Lester because there was a grand piano pushed into the corner. He walked straight over to inspect it. It was good, but not the quality of the one he had at home. The anguish he felt at that moment was intense and he couldn't mask it from his expression.

'I say,' James came and stood beside him. 'You're looking at that instrument as if you know something about it. Do you play?'

'I know a piano of quality when I see one,' he answered, avoiding the question. He turned away to hide his sadness. 'It doesn't look as if it's played very often.'

James shrugged. 'I wouldn't know. I never could get past the scales.'

'What are you doing in here?' a stern voice demanded.

They spun round to find an officer standing in the doorway, and James answered, smiling. 'We've just arrived and thought we'd better find our way around, sir.'

'This room is off limits to you. Go back to your quarters and wait for someone to come and escort you to the dining room.'

Lester's spirit sank even lower. This was the only place they had seen a piano and it was out of bounds to students. It was going to be hard to endure this torture, he thought, as they hurried back to their sleeping quarters. To be separated from his sister and his piano was more than he could stand; not to mention their twice-weekly lessons with Professor Elland. But endure it he must! He knew his sister was suffering in the same way and he had to be strong so they could defeat their father's plans. From the moment they had begun to show interest in music he had resented it for some reason, and when they had won places in the Royal College of Music he had gone into a rage. They had ignored him and continued making plans for a future in music. That future had now been ripped away from them, and if he was gloating over the success of his devious plans then he was in for a shock. His sister was going to have to use all of her dramatic flair to make Lord Dalton withdraw his offer of marriage, and he had every confidence in her, but how on earth was he going to get out of this? He had shown complete unconcern to his sister and mother, but in truth he really didn't have any idea what he could do.

'Don't look so downcast,' James declared when they reached their room. 'We'll have a lot of fun, you'll see.'

'Sorry.' Lester dredged up a smile, not wishing to put a damper in this likeable young man's enthusiasm. 'I've got a sister – we're twins – and this is the first time we have ever been parted.'

'Twins! I say, I've heard that twins know if the other one is ill, and often they know each other's thoughts. Is that true?'

'It is like that with us.' Lester laughed at the boy's rapt expression.

'That's a bit inconvenient, isn't it?'

'Not really. We're used to it.'

'Is she pretty?'

'No.' Lester considered for a moment, then said, 'She's beautiful.'

'You would say that!' James grinned. 'At the end of term the families can visit. I'd like to meet her.'

'I'll make sure you do.'

'Terrific! I'll introduce you to my folks. My father's a general.'

'So is mine.'

'What?' James stared at him aghast. 'And you don't want to be a soldier? What did you plan to do with your life?'

'Be a musician.'

'Ah, that's why you were looking at that piano so fondly. There's no future in that. The army is a much better career choice.'

'I expect you're right, but is the army ready for an officer with the soul of a musician?'

'There's room for every kind of talent,' James assured him. 'There are military bands. At the end of term you can declare your interest in music and there might be a place for you in a band.'

'I'll consider it.' Lester stood up as a sergeant arrived to take them to the dining room.

'You do that!' James slapped him on the back, still smiling brightly. 'There are still four to arrive for our quarters. Wonder what they'll be like? If they're all as nice as you, we'll be all right. Lots of fun ahead. Let's go and see what the food is like.'

The dining room was only half full as there were still a lot of boys to arrive and James was soon talking to everyone there. Lester watched his new companion with amusement and couldn't help joining in the laughter, but he was unable to match their enthusiasm. However, James had planted a seed in his mind about the military bands. If all else failed it could be a way of still being involved with music. He managed to keep smiling as the pain tore through him again at the thought of spending his life in that way. No, it wasn't an option he could really consider, but he would have to wait a few weeks before trying to leave.

Chapter Three

It had been a busy morning, but Lillia was excited and satisfied with what she had achieved. If the threat of marriage to a politician had not occurred, she doubted if she would have taken this step even though she agreed wholeheartedly with the aims of the organisation, but she was glad she had done so. The women were showing a determination to win their battle whatever the consequences or danger to themselves, and she approved of such an attitude.

'Lord Dalton has arrived,' Sara declared as she entered her daughter's room. 'That dark green gown is a perfect choice. It is elegant and brings out the unusual colour of your eyes. Are you ready for the meeting?'

'Quite ready. We mustn't keep him waiting.'

She tried to wipe the look of distaste from her face as they made their way downstairs. She curtsied gracefully to Lord Dalton, keeping her eyes lowered as if nervous. Refreshments were served while they talked about various society occasions being planned, and she answered when spoken to, showing an interest she didn't feel, and appalled by the thought of being married to someone like this. Not only was he forty-five, but he was self-opinionated and pompous. How dare he try to snare himself a young wife! She was finding it increasingly difficult to be civil to him but it

27

was too early to put her plan into action.

Sara, always aware of her daughter's moods, stepped in to ease the rapidly building tension. 'My daughter has a charming voice, Lord Dalton. Perhaps you would like to hear her play and sing?'

'I would indeed. A talent like that is always useful when entertaining guests.'

Sara stood up and they made their way to the music room.

'What would you like to hear?' Lillia asked him, smiling as if eager to please.

'I am sure you have a repertoire suitable for entertaining. I leave the choice to you.'

She nodded and settled at the piano.

'Do not sing too well,' her mother said softly as she leant over to put music on the stand.

The thought of doing that appalled her, but she knew it was necessary. She began to play popular pieces heard in the drawing rooms, keeping the volume of her voice subdued and slightly off key. After two such songs she changed to her great love – opera. She had been taking instruction for the music from *Madame Butterfly* with Professor Elland and Lester, and they had both complimented her the last time she had sung it for them. Tears came to her eyes knowing what she was about to do to this beautiful music.

Her mother gently applauded when she had finished and Lillia quickly wiped the moisture from her eyes before turning to face Lord Dalton.

His expression was unreadable and she felt that her terrible performance hadn't had the desired effect. He appeared more amused than shocked, and when he smiled before turning to Sara, she knew this wasn't going to be the way to change his mind.

'Thank you for entertaining me,' Lord Dalton said, obviously not the slightest bit concerned about her lack of talent.

'She has had excellent tuition from Professor Elland from a very early age, as has her brother. They are both talented musicians.'

Lord Dalton swiftly changed the subject. 'I understand your son is following in his father's footsteps and is now at a military academy.'

'That was his father's wish,' she replied, hiding her feelings with a slight smile.

'Of course.' He then turned his attention back to Lillia. 'I have enjoyed our meeting today. Would you join me in a drive tomorrow afternoon? The weather is holding fair.'

'Thank you, sir. That would be very pleasant.'

'Excellent!' He was still smiling as he stood up. 'I must take my leave and return to Parliament for an important debate, but I look forward to our next meeting.'

They watched him leave, and then Sara shook her head. 'I fear he is even more enamoured with you. I was sure he would begin to have doubts when he heard your singing was not up to the standard of your reputation.'

'We know now that that was the wrong approach, and I suspect he is puzzled, knowing who my tutor is.'

'That could be so.' Sara took hold of her daughter's arm. 'Let us retire to my sitting room and

29

try to decide what we can do next.'

Her mother's expression was grim the moment they were alone. 'I will not have you throwing your life away by marrying that man. He is too old for you and you are too young. You seemed certain he could be made to withdraw his offer, but how is that to be achieved? I have to stop this, my darling! I would live in a hovel and take in washing before I see my children treated in this abominable way!'

Alarmed by her mother's declaration she rushed to her side. 'You must not do anything to anger Father. That was only the first meeting and we now know Lord Dalton will not be frightened off easily. There is another way, and I believe it will be much more effective.'

'Then tell me, for I cannot allow this to go any further.'

She realised that if she didn't explain then her mother would defy her husband, and no doubt face dire consequences from him. Before her brother left they had discussed the situation and had both agreed they must not allow their mother to suffer because of them. She most certainly would if she tried to stand between them and that man. At a very early age they had become aware that this was not a happy marriage. Sara and her husband had separate rooms and seldom went out together; indeed, they spent as little time as possible in each other's company. They had found it impossible to become close to him and he had never shown the slightest interest in their up-bringing. She explained her plans and waited anxiously for her mother's response.

'You have actually met them?' Sara gasped.

'I went to see them this morning.'

'I see.' There was silence for a while, and then a slight smile touched her mother's lips. 'When are you meeting them again?'

'Tomorrow morning.'

'I would like to come with you.'

'I am sure they would be happy to meet you,' she told her mother, taken aback by the request. She had expected disapproval from her mother.

Slowly, a rare smile spread across Sara's face. 'That is so clever of you, my dear. I do believe you might have found the one thing a politician will not tolerate in a wife. Are you actually a member?'

'Not yet, but I was told I would be very welcome to join their ranks. I am aware this could cause a great deal of trouble, and that is the reason I was reluctant to tell you about my involvement.'

'I am pleased you have. I have been very worried that I might not be able to stop this marriage. Lord Dalton and Gilbert are powerful men and not easy to defy, but this situation is so grave we have no choice in the matter. I shall join in the struggle for women's rights. With both women in the family involved we should have Lord Dalton leaving at speed. I know for a fact that he is stoically against women meddling in politics – his words not mine.'

'Are you sure you want to do this?' she asked her mother. 'Father will be furious when he finds out.'

'I no longer care what he thinks. My children have become wise adults, quite able to take control of their own lives. It is time for me to do the

31

same. I have one last thing to do for you, and that is to see he doesn't succeed in his desire to ruin your futures.'

'We have never understood why he dislikes us so much. Most parents love and support their children. His attitude towards us has always perplexed us, and as we have grown older it is as if he cannot bear the sight of us.'

'You remind him of everything he is not.'

'I don't understand why he should feel that way. Everyone has different qualities and talents. He must have been an exemplary soldier to have reached the rank of general. Surely that is something to be proud of? Why should it be of concern to him that our talents lie in the realm of music?'

'I cannot answer that. I have never been able to fathom what is in his mind.' Sara stood up. 'Let us see what tomorrow brings. Now it is time to change for dinner.'

The moment they walked into the dining room Lillia could see that her father was in a good mood because he actually smiled at her.

'Lord Dalton told me he was pleased with his visit today. He said you conducted yourself perfectly. That was well done, Lillian.'

'Thank you, Father,' she said, pinning a look of pleasure on her face. 'We are going for a drive tomorrow.'

'Yes, so I understand. Lord Dalton has already decided that you will make him a suitable wife and I have suggested your nineteenth birthday for the wedding. It will be a lavish affair and will need time to plan.'

'Wouldn't the summer be better?' Sara suggested. 'March can be a cold month.'

He waved a dismissive hand. 'Lord Dalton has too many commitments during the summer. He agrees that March will be perfect.'

With the subject dismissed the rest of the meal was taken in silence and Lillia concentrated on her food, although she had quite lost her appetite. It was September now and that didn't give them much time. These two men thought it was all settled, but they were in for a shock. Lester had insisted they have an escape route if their plans to extricate themselves from this situation failed, and after a long discussion they had one. They would have to leave home and go out on their own, but it would only be used if there was no alternative because it would involve hardship and poverty. If they had to put such a desperate plan into action then they would, but their mother must not know anything about it. Their music came above every other consideration, and as her father was in a good mood she had to make sure her lessons continued.

'May I continue with my singing lessons until the wedding? Lord Dalton did appear to enjoy listening to me.'

He frowned and then nodded. 'Only two hours a week.'

'Thank you,' she said meekly, hiding the gleam of triumph in her eyes by looking down. She had been worried that he had already cancelled those with the professor, and Lord Dalton had obviously kept quiet about her off-key performance.

The next morning Sara and her daughter went to the meeting place used by the Women's Social and Political Union. They were preparing for a demonstration that afternoon in Hyde Park and Lillia would have loved to take part, but she had agreed to a drive with Lord Dalton. There would be other times, she thought, as she watched her mother in deep discussion with some of the women. She had never seen her so animated. It was as if this crisis with her children had woken something inside her, and for the first time a fighting spirit had emerged. It was clear there would now be some changes made in their house, which until now had been completely controlled by her husband.

'Thank you for bringing your mother to meet us,' Agnes, the organiser of this group said. 'She is very knowledgeable about politics and you will both be a great help to us.'

'I'm sorry I can't join you in the demonstration today, but we have a problem to resolve. Once that has been dealt with we will be able to come here more often.'

'That will be excellent, and do not apologise. This has been arranged at short notice, but we will be well supported.' She gave a wry smile. 'We like to take everyone by surprise if we can.'

'I'm afraid we must leave now.' Sara came over to them smiling with excitement. 'Thank you for making me so welcome, and I will come to your next meeting.'

On the way home Sara smiled at her daughter. 'I wonder where Lord Dalton intends to go for a ride this afternoon. Hyde Park perhaps?'

'That would be perfect!' she laughed, 'but I

doubt that. Although the ladies have arranged this in a hurry, he probably knows about it already.'

'Yes, he's bound to have been told. Never mind, we shall have to bring the subject into the conversation.'

'I intend to.' She suddenly became pensive and tears filled her eyes.

'What is the matter, my dear?'

'Lester isn't happy. I can feel it. The moment we have frightened off Lord Dalton we must get him out of that place!'

As expected, Lord Dalton didn't take them through Hyde Park. Instead they had a leisurely drive around the Palace of Westminster while he explained the history of Parliament.

This was a good opportunity for Lillia to talk about politics.

'What are your views on giving women the vote?' she asked casually.

'I am against it, of course.'

'Do you not think that women should have a say in the running of their country?'

'Certainly not! That is a ridiculous idea, and it is not something you should be filling your head with.'

'And why is that?' she asked with a look of innocent enquiry on her face. 'The decisions you make in government touch all of our lives, not only men.'

'A woman's place is looking after her home and family, not interfering in something they have no intelligence for.'

She bristled and heard her mother's sharp

intake of breath from behind them. 'Are you implying that women are only fit for bearing children and allowing men to dominate them?'

He frowned at her vehemence. 'I wouldn't put it quite that way, but women have their role in life, and men theirs. That is the way it has always been – and will stay.'

'I must disagree, sir. What about Elizabeth I? She ruled and men did her bidding. And she is not the only woman we have had on the throne.'

'Men advised and guided Elizabeth, and by the time Victoria came to the throne she had no power over Parliament. These women of the WSPU will never win the vote for women. They are making a nuisance of themselves and looking foolish in the process.'

'Do you think they are foolish, Mother?' she asked.

'After our meeting with them I am of the opinion that they are highly intelligent ladies. It may be a long, hard struggle facing them, but they will eventually win. Women successfully manage households and staff, dealing with the many problems arising. They could make a valuable contribution to running the country – given the opportunity.'

'Exactly!' She turned back to Lord Dalton, a wide smile on her face. 'We must agree to differ on the subject, sir.'

He was looking from one to the other in astonishment. 'I understood you were interested only in music. You have met some of the women?'

'We have,' Sara told him.

'I see. Well, you would be wise to disassociate

yourselves from them immediately. If they continue to persist in their illegal activities there will be serious consequences. They could even be facing a prison sentence.'

'The ladies I spoke to are quite aware of that, and it will not stop them,' Sara told him. 'They are prepared to face any hardship for their cause.'

'Then they are even more misguided than I imagined,' Lord Dalton retorted. 'And I will hear no more of this subject.'

'Would you not wish me to show an interest in your work as a politician?' Lillia asked.

'Not by holding such radical views. Mrs Holdsworth, I am relying on you to put an end to this foolishness at once. When we are married your daughter will have no time for such nonsense.'

They pulled up outside the house and Sara asked, 'Will you come in for refreshments?'

'I cannot stay today. I have a box at the opera for Saturday evening and will call for you at seven o'clock. I know you will enjoy that.'

'I will indeed, and thank you for an interesting drive, sir.'

He actually laughed. 'Interesting – yes it was. Until Saturday then.'

Once inside the house, mother and daughter looked at each other in dismay, and Lillia said, 'I don't believe our views on women's rights put him off at all.'

'I'm afraid they didn't. That man has a sense of humour, which is surprising, and he is a fighter. He is absolutely certain he can change you once you are married, and is not concerned with what he considers foolish views.'

'Views he feels can easily be crushed once I am under his control.'

'That is so. I am beginning to think this offer should have been refused immediately.'

'It is too late for that now.' She followed her mother to their sitting room, deep in thought. When she had planned this with Lester it had seemed so easy to make Lord Dalton withdraw his offer, but it wasn't working out that way. *Oh, Lester, I need you! I am becoming very concerned.*

Chapter Four

It had been four weeks of purgatory for Lester. He managed the parade ground by concentrating on the rhythm of marching feet and he never missed a step, but not having a piano was tearing him apart. All he could do was picture a keyboard and go through the music in his head. He was also worried about his sister. It was evident from her letters that Lord Dalton was still determined to make her his wife. In an effort to protect their mother from the wrath of her husband they had made the wrong decision. They should have refused to go along with his plans the moment he had told them. But they hadn't, and now their situation was dire. His sister had been unable to make Lord Dalton withdraw his offer, and he was doing better at the military academy than expected. He was already being complimented on his progress, and he wasn't even trying to excel.

'Holdsworth!'

He leapt to his feet, along with the other boys when an officer entered their sleeping quarters.

'Come with me.'

When Lester glanced quickly at James and frowned, his friend just grinned.

The officer was already marching away and Lester had to run to catch up with him. What on earth did they want with him at this time in the evening? Lessons had finished for the day. He remained silent as they made their way to the main building.

'Captain Andrews wants to see you.' The officer stopped by the door leading to the lounge they had been thrown out of on the first day, and then he turned and walked away.

Still puzzled, Lester opened the door and walked in to find the room bustling with activity, preparing for a function of some kind. His attention immediately fixed on the piano. It had been pulled out from the corner and polished until it gleamed in the lamplight.

'Are you Holdsworth?' a harassed looking officer asked.

'I've been told to report to Captain Andrews, sir.'

'That's me,' he snapped. 'I understand you might be able to play the piano.'

'Yes, sir.'

'Our pianist has been taken ill. Show me if you are any good.' The officer marched over to the piano and lifted the seat of the stool. 'Damn! There doesn't seem to be any sheet music here.'

'I can manage without, sir. What would you like

39

me to play?'

'Anything you can manage.' He glanced at his watch. 'Guests will be arriving any time now and Brigadier Stansfield expects music.'

Lester settled at the piano and ran his hands over the keys, his heart racing with pleasure. At last! He began playing and was immediately at one with the music. At the end of the piece he waited until the last notes had faded, and then glanced up at the captain. It was only then he realised there was complete silence in the room, and the officer was staring at him in disbelief.

'I was told you knew something about music and might be able to play. I was not told that you are an accomplished musician. Do you have a large enough repertoire to play for us during the evening?'

'Yes, sir.'

He gave a huge sigh and actually smiled. 'Excellent! I'll tell you when to start, and take a break for refreshments when you need to. Well done, boy. You have just saved the evening for me.'

'My pleasure, sir.'

Lester remained seated at the piano while he watched as the final arrangements were made to the lounge. As the room cleared of workers he fixed his gaze on the officer, waiting for the order to begin playing.

Captain Andrews strode over to him, looking relaxed now. 'First guests are arriving and you can start playing. Something quiet at first, and when the room fills up you can change to more elaborate pieces if you so wish.'

'Thank you, sir. I will gauge the atmosphere of

the room and play what is appropriate.'

'I'm sure you will.' He glanced at the door. 'Here they come!'

For the next hour Lester curbed his eagerness and kept the music soft and gentle. He would get his chance to play some of his favourite pieces later in the evening.

'Captain Andrews said you might like a drink, sir.' An orderly was standing by the piano holding a tray. 'There's champagne, whisky or beer.'

'Water, please.'

'Water?'

'If that's possible.' Lester looked up and smiled.

'It's an unusual request at such a gathering as this, but I'll get you a glass of water at once.'

'Thank you.'

'How do you do that?'

'Do what?'

'You've been talking to me and haven't once looked at the keys or missed a note.'

'Hours and hours of practice.'

Shaking his head the orderly hurried off to get Lester his drink.

Captain Andrews took a moment from his duties to watch and listen to the music coming from the corner of the room. They were well into the evening and the boy hadn't stopped once. As the noise in the room had increased, the music had changed. Quite a few of the guests had gravitated to that part of the room and were obviously enjoying the skill of the pianist. They were also giving him requests and he was playing everything without any hesitation. His hands were now flying over the keys and he appeared totally unaware of his surroundings. Remarkable.

'Where did you find that pianist?' Brigadier Stansfield asked as he came to stand beside the captain.

'He's a student here, sir.'

'What? You can't put someone with such talent in a school like this. He needs to be in a music college! It's criminal. Look at him. Even at that young age he's an exceptional musician.'

'I agree, sir, but perhaps this is what he wants to do. He has been earning praise from all the tutors here.'

The brigadier watched Lester for a while, deep in thought. 'He reminds me of someone – can't think who at the moment, but it will come to me. What's his name?'

'Holdsworth. His father is a general.'

'Never heard of him, and if I had a son with that talent he would be studying in London or Paris. He doesn't belong here! Bring him to me at the end of the evening. I'll use your office.'

Lillia dropped the book she was reading and looked up, a wide smile on her face.

'What is it?' her mother asked.

'Lester is playing the piano and he is so happy! I can sense it!'

Gilbert Holdsworth glared at her. 'Stop that nonsense! You can't possibly know what he's doing. He's miles away.'

'We are twins and aware of each other's emotions,' she pointed out.

'Now you see why I had to part them,' he said

42

sharply to his wife. 'Your children are not right in the head and, hopefully, their new lives will knock some sense into them.'

'They are different and talented, but they are also exceptionally intelligent. There isn't anything wrong with their minds; it is just that you have never taken the trouble to understand how unique they are. You should be proud of them.'

'Unique! Oh yes, they are certainly that!' He threw his paper down and stood up, his face red with fury. 'And I don't need to hear your opinion. After all, you don't have anything to be proud of – do you?'

Lillia watched him storm out of the room, furious by the way their mother had been insulted. 'What did he mean by that?'

'Don't let it upset you. Rudeness comes naturally to him.'

'We have always known that, but he is becoming more open with his dislike for us. What is the matter with him?'

Sara thought for a moment, and then turned to her daughter. 'I have a feeling that he is uneasy about something, but I cannot fathom what is troubling him. Perhaps he has problems with his business.'

'What exactly does he do? You've never mentioned it and, to be fair, we've never asked.'

'That is because I don't know. Whenever I asked I was told he buys and sells.' Sara shrugged. 'But what kind of merchandise I have never discovered. All I know is that he has used our family money to support his activities. There is hardly anything left he can now use and that could account for his bad mood.'

'There is still the house. I know it belonged to your family, but could he sell it?'

'I was worried about that after the way he has tried to put a stop to your musical careers. I visited the lawyers who have handled the Kirkby family affairs for a long time. They looked into the matter very carefully and discovered a clause in your great-grandfather's will that would make it difficult for anyone other than of Kirkby blood to take possession of the house. Gilbert could, of course, challenge that in court, but I don't think he would risk the publicity such an action would bring. The lawyers are almost certain he could not win the case anyway.'

'Does he know?'

'Yes, the lawyers have informed him of the situation.'

'Ah.' She sighed with relief. 'That could account for his temper.'

'It could be a part of it. This also means that sometime in the future I could sell the house and pay for your tuition.'

'No, Mother! We would never let you do that. You have sacrificed enough for us. We will manage somehow.'

'I know you say that but things are not going well, are they? Lester is still at the military academy and Lord Dalton appears to be even more determined to make you his wife.'

'The outlook at the moment is gloomy but we will get through this. Things will get better. You'll see.'

She smiled sadly at her vibrant daughter. 'I wish

I had your courage,' she said softly. If she had, would she have defied her father all those years ago? No, that would not have been possible. The consequences would have been too great.

'Holdsworth. You can stop playing now.'

Lester reluctantly removed his hands from the keys and bowed his head.

'Everyone has gone and you didn't even notice, did you?'

He looked up at the officer. 'No, sir. This is the first time since arriving that I have had access to a piano. I am grateful. Thank you.'

'I am sure there will be more opportunities. Now come with me. Brigadier Stansfield wishes to see you.'

'Sit down, young man,' the brigadier ordered when they entered the office. 'You stay as well, Bob.'

Robert Andrews sat beside Lester and stretched out his long legs, wondering just what Alexander Stansfield was up to. Whatever his interest in the boy was he obviously intended to include him as well.

'You are an accomplished pianist,' Alex began. 'I play, but not with your skill and flair. It was a pleasure to listen to you this evening.'

'Thank you, sir.'

'What the devil are you doing here?'

Bob watched Holdsworth frown at the abrupt question.

'It was my father's wish.'

'But is it yours?'

'No, sir,' Lester replied honestly. 'We had won

places at the Royal College of Music, but our father has no interest in music.'

'We?'

'I have a sister, and she's a singer of great promise. Opera is her love.'

'Sister? Who has been your tutor?'

'Professor Elland, sir.'

'What are your Christian names?' Alex demanded with a look of surprise on his face.

'Lester and Lillia.'

Alex swore under his breath and surged to his feet, taking Bob completely by surprise. He had known Alex for ten years, and this kind of emotional reaction was not like him.

'You are twins!'

'Yes, sir.'

'Professor Elland is a family friend and has often spoken with pride about his twins, as he refers to you. What are your father's reasons for sending you here?'

'To become a soldier?' The corners of Lester's mouth twitched as he made that sound like a question.

'And do you believe you can?'

'Not if I can help it, sir.'

Bob chuckled at the blunt reply and noticed amusement spread across Alex's strong features.

'If your plan is to fail then you are not making a very good job of it. I understand you are already receiving praise from your instructors.'

'Quite unintentional, I assure you. I will have to try harder because that is the only plan I have.' Lester tipped his head to one side as he looked at the officer, feeling quite at ease with this man. He had the air of calm strength about him and gave the impression of someone you could turn to in times of need. 'You wouldn't like to throw me out for insubordination, would you, sir?'

'Unlikely. I have only taken charge here today – and I am very tolerant.'

'Ah, I'm sorry to hear that. I'll have to find another way.'

They were all laughing now and the atmosphere was relaxed.

'You haven't answered my questions about your father's motives. You don't have to say, of course, but I would like to know.'

'I can't tell you what is in his mind, but for some reason he is determined to stop us having a musical career. He has no interest in music and considers we make the house like bedlam.' Lester paused and clenched his hands tightly together and his concerns poured out. 'He was also determined to separate us. We've never been apart and I'm worried about my sister. He's accepted an offer of marriage for her from Lord Dalton. She has a plan to make him withdraw the offer, but it does not appear to be working any better than mine.'

'Is there no one you can turn to for help?' Bob asked, touched by the boy's anguish for his sister.

'No, sir. Our mother has always protected us as much as she can, but in this case she is helpless against such a tyrant. We will not allow her to do anything that would make her life even more difficult.'

'I see your dilemma,' Alex remarked gently. 'But don't give up hope.'

'We won't do that, sir.' Lester relaxed and smiled

again. 'Something will happen to turn the tide for us.'

'I'm sure it will.' Alex nodded to Bob. 'I want you to give Lester written permission to play the piano when the lounge is not in use.'

'Oh, thank you, sir!' Lester was on his feet, his face alight with pleasure.

'Only when your lessons are over for the day. After all, we wouldn't want you to fail, would we? Off you go and get some sleep, and thank you for a very entertaining evening.'

'It was my pleasure, sir.'

When the door closed behind the boy, Alex sighed deeply. 'Did you notice he called his father a tyrant?'

'I did, and I got the impression he was here only because they are trying to protect their mother. You know their tutor then.'

Alex nodded. 'Joshua Elland is one of the best musical tutors to be found anywhere. And his praise for the twins' talents is the highest. He must be devastated to have lost them. I'll go and see him, and in the meantime I want you to find out all you can about General Holdsworth. I'm damned if I can place him.'

'What are your intentions, Alex? We can't interfere in a family matter.'

'I know that, but he is a pupil here and therefore his well-being must be our concern. I just want a clearer picture of his home life and upbringing. When I was talking to him I had the feeling that he would make a fine army officer, even though he doesn't want to be here.'

'I agree. He is showing great promise without

even trying.'

'But he is a musician at heart, so we have a problem on our hands.' Alex smiled wryly at Bob. 'I knew this job wasn't going to be easy. Fancy a drink before turning in?'

'Good idea.'

Chapter Five

'You've been a long time,' James whispered when Lester crept back to the room. 'Did you play for the top brass?'

He nodded as he removed his shoes, trying not to disturb the other boys. 'And I've been talking to the new man in charge – Brigadier Stansfield.'

'I know him.'

'He's very tolerant, he told me.'

James stifled a laugh. 'He's got a sense of humour. You didn't believe that, did you?'

'Not sure, but time will tell. How do you know him?'

'He's a friend of the family.'

'He seems a decent man. He's going to let me play the piano when the lounge isn't being used.'

'My goodness, you must have made an impression.'

'Will you two shut up!' one of the other boys muttered. 'We are trying to sleep.'

'Sorry.' Lester quickly undressed and dived into bed, then reached over and prodded James in the next bed. 'Did you tell them I could play

49

the piano?'

James nodded, white teeth showing in the gloom.

'Thanks.' Lester settled down to sleep.

They were on their lunch break the next day when Captain Andrews came into the dining room and approached Lester.

'When you have finished your meal Brigadier Stansfield wants to see you.'

'I'll come right now, sir.' Lester was immediately on his feet, hoping the call was to give him the pass for the lounge. 'Is he in the same office?'

'No, we used mine last night. I'll show you where he is.'

Lester heard the murmur of interest from the other boys as he walked out with the officer. James was about to be bombarded with questions, but he didn't care what they said about him. He was desperately hoping that his stay here was going to be short.

'Did you sleep well? We kept you late last night.'

'Very well, sir.'

'Good. What is your mother's name?'

'Sara.' Lester gave the captain a puzzled glance.

'That's a charming name. And what is your father's full name?'

'General Gilbert Holdsworth. I don't know if he has a middle name.'

The officer stopped by a door, rapped sharply and then opened it. 'Holdsworth, sir.'

The brigadier looked up from the papers he was studying. 'Thank you, Captain. Did you get what you needed?'

'Yes, sir.'

'Good. Come in, young man and sit down.'

Hoping he was going to get his longed-for pass, he sat down and waited.

'I have been receiving messages all morning from the guests to say how much they enjoyed the music last night. Everyone was impressed with the quality of your playing.'

Lester bowed his head in acknowledgement of the compliment. 'It was a pleasure to play for them, sir.'

'I have a favourite Chopin piece that I have never been able to master.' He handed over some sheet music. 'Would you show me how it should be played?'

'When would you like to hear it?' Lester asked, quickly scanning the score for 'Étude Op. 10 No. 12 in C Minor'.

'Right now.'

He looked up in surprise. 'My lunch break is almost over.'

'I have arranged for you to have an extra hour. Consider it as a practice hour. Come on.'

There were only two people in the lounge and they watched with interest as Lester settled at the piano.

The brigadier sat where he had a good view and nodded, indicating that Lester could start. 'Play my piece first and then anything you like. I'll tell you when it's time to return to your class.'

That time came all too quickly for Lester, and when he looked up he was surprised to see at least a dozen people in the room. They applauded and he stood up, bowing with a flourish and laughing

51

with pleasure.

'How I wish I could play like that,' Alex said as he came over to Lester. 'That was splendid.'

'I am pleased you enjoyed it, sir, but I need time and good tuition before I reach the standard I am aiming for.'

'Perfection?'

'I'm not sure such a thing is possible,' Lester laughed, 'but I intend to get as close to it as possible.'

'You are asking a lot of yourself.'

'I know, but the challenge drives me.'

'I have a feeling you will succeed.'

'Listen to me in ten years' time and see if your instinct is correct, sir.' Lester glanced at the clock. 'Thank you for this hour. I really appreciate your interest.'

Bob walked over to join them and handed Lester an envelope. 'Here is your pass to use the lounge and a list of the times it could be empty. If you come here when there are more than four people relaxing here, you must ask for their permission to play the piano. Should they object you are to leave at once. Is that clear?'

'Perfectly. I assure you I will not abuse the privilege.'

'See you don't or it will be withdrawn. Now you must hurry to your next class.'

They watched as Lester strode from the room and Bob shook his head, his fair hair falling over his forehead. 'I hope you know what you are doing, Alex. If the other boys feel you are showing undue favouritism it could make life difficult for the boy. Remember, whatever his talent, he is still a student here. I'm responsible for seeing discipline is maintained.'

'He's tough enough to take it with good humour – both mentally and physically. You can stop worrying, though. I have only taken him out of class this once because I needed to find out just how good he is.'

Bob sighed. 'And now you know you are going to interfere.'

'I am, indeed. Have you managed to find out anything about General Holdsworth?'

'Not yet.'

'Then get to it as soon as you can. His army records should be easy to trace even if he has retired from the service.'

'I'll do that now. What are you going to do next?'

'This evening I shall visit my friend Joshua Elland. He should be able to tell me exactly what the situation is with this family.'

The door to the practice room was slightly open, and Alex settled down to wait for Joshua to finish the lesson. The voice he could hear was good and powerful. As it soared effortlessly to the top notes, Alex drew in a deep breath and revised his opinion. It was better than good, but Josh clearly wasn't satisfied and was pushing her hard.

When they came out of the music room, Alex was surprised to see how young the pupil was. He hadn't imagined that from the maturity of her voice.

'Alex!' Joshua beamed with pleasure. 'Lillia, come and meet my good friend Brigadier Stansfield.'

She stepped forward smiling, and Alex felt a jolt of recognition as he looked into a pair of clear green eyes. 'It was a pleasure to listen to you, Miss Holdsworth. You are so like your brother.'

'We are twins. Do you know Lester?' she asked eagerly.

'I've met him at the academy.'

Her smile fled and was replaced with worry. 'Is he all right?'

'He is doing well. You don't need to be concerned about him.'

'That isn't easy, sir. This is the first time we have ever been apart and I miss him dreadfully.'

'It must be difficult for you, but his tutors speak highly of him and he has made many friends. He is a very charming young man.'

'That is kind of you to say so. I still worry, though. It has been a pleasure to meet you, sir. Goodnight, Professor.'

The moment she left, Joshua turned on Alex. 'I heard you have been given a new posting. Is it at the academy? Do you have my boy there?'

'I do, and that is why I am here.'

'Oh, thank the Lord. This is a terrible situation. We must help him!'

'Calm down. He's all right and seems to be a sensible boy. In fact, from what I have seen of him he will make an excellent officer.'

'That cannot be allowed to happen. Rarely does talent of the kind the twins possess come along in a lifetime. I have nurtured them since they were five years old and watched their abilities blossom. Lester has been snatched away from me and I have that delightful girl only twice a week! That is not nearly enough, and that unfeeling man is proposing to marry her off to Lord Dalton.' Joshua's face crumpled with despair. 'This cannot be allowed to happen,' he repeated. 'Lillia is destined for the operatic stage, and Lester – the prospect of what he can become takes my breath away. The world must not be deprived of my children's talent!'

Touched by his friend's obvious distress, Alex made him sit down. 'I've heard him play and he is good...'

'Good? Don't be so insulting! You have a better ear for music than that. You are in a position now to help him. I beg of you, my friend. I am helpless – helpless,' he moaned.

Alex poured them both a stiff drink from the cabinet in the corner of the room and handed one to Joshua. 'I'm not sure how much I can do, but you can start by telling me all you know about the family.'

'I know little of the father. He is illusive and not very sociable. Mrs Holdsworth, on the other hand, is a charming lady and loves her talented children dearly. She is clearly devastated by this turn of events, but like the rest of us feels powerless to act against such an unpleasant husband. The twins are very protective of her and will not allow her to do anything to anger him. How such a cultured woman came to marry a man like that is a mystery. He doesn't like music!'

'That is a crime, indeed,' Alex remarked dryly. 'One wonders how the children came to be so musical.'

'Ah, that is another mystery. They have inherited nothing from their father, which is a good thing.' Joshua gave his friend a calculated look. 'Now you are in charge of the academy would you let me come once or twice a week to continue Lester's tuition? I assume you do have a piano of suitable quality there?'

'We do, but I'm afraid I can't let you do that. The boy is there for training to become an officer in the army. I can't interfere with that or show him too much favouritism. I have already overstepped the line by allowing him to play the piano in the officers' lounge.'

'Thank you for that! Without a piano that boy will fret.' Joshua tipped his head to one side. 'Are you sure you couldn't bend the rules just a little more and allow me to come there?'

'Absolutely not. However, at the end of term we have an open day when the parents are allowed to visit. You can come as my guest.'

'And will this special day be held in the lounge?' Joshua asked sneakily.

Alex laughed. 'It will – and perhaps the twins will entertain us with a song or two?'

'They will! Thank you, thank you.'

'Now that is settled, get your coat and hat and I will take you out to dinner.'

Lillia was even more worried about her brother after hearing Brigadier Stansfield's opinion that Lester was doing well at the military academy. That wasn't the plan at all. He was supposed to fail. She wasn't doing any better either. Even her involvement with the WSPU hadn't made Lord Dalton change his mind about making her his wife. He appeared to think it was a joke.

When she walked into the house a maid was waiting for her inside the door.

'Lord Dalton is waiting to see you. He's in the lounge, Miss Lillia.'

She muttered a rude word under her breath and was in no mood to be civil to him tonight. 'Where is my mother?' she asked.

'Mrs Holdsworth has retired early with a bad headache,' the maid answered.

'I'll go and see her as soon as I've got rid of His Lordship.' Now she was worried about her mother. It was unlike her to take to her bed, especially with a guest in her house.

'Ah, there you are – at last!' Lord Dalton said as she entered the room. 'I have been waiting for almost an hour.'

'We were not aware you were calling tonight. Mother is unwell, and I had my music lesson with Professor Elland.'

'Surely that is unnecessary now. You are quite proficient enough.'

'Proficient enough for what, sir?' She was at the end of her patience with this pompous man.

'For entertaining guests, of course.'

Something inside her snapped, and without her mother or Lester to hold her in check, she spoke her mind. 'I have been training since I was five years old, and I do not intend to waste all that hard work singing in drawing rooms! My aim is the concert stage and opera house.'

'You can forget those foolish notions,' he told her. 'Once we are married your job will be to help me with my career and entertain my guests.'

'Married, sir?' She shook her head. 'My father

arranged that with you. I have not been con-
sulted, and I have never received a proposal of
marriage from you.'

'If you are the dutiful daughter I have been led
to believe, then you will do as your father orders.'
He was getting angry now.

'Then you have been misinformed. I am far
from a dutiful daughter. I can be disobedient and
wilful, with an explosive temper. I will also make
my own decisions in life – and that is not to
become a brood mare for an aging politician! I
will save you the embarrassment of having to
propose to me because I will certainly refuse!'

'How dare you speak to me like that? You need
a good thrashing to bring you into line.' He
stepped menacingly towards her.

'If you raise a hand to me, sir, you will regret it.
I am not a weakling, and am already taller than
you. I am also sure society will relish the story of
your violence.'

He stepped back, his expression thunderous as
he glanced towards the door, then he pushed past
her and stormed out of the house.

The full import of what she had just done hit her
with a force that took her breath away. Such an
outburst would have serious repercussions, not
only for her, but for their mother as well. They had
appeared to go along with this scheme in order to
save their mother from any unpleasantness, but
she had just thrown all their good intentions away.
There was going to be trouble now.

Turning to leave the room she was surprised to
see their butler, Adams, standing just inside the
door. 'Has my mother sent for me?' she asked as

calmly as possible.

'I heard raised voices, and as you were alone with the gentleman I came in case you needed assistance.'

She took a deep breath. 'It was an unpleasant scene. How long have you been there?'

'Some time, Miss Lillia.'

He had obviously heard everything. 'I am afraid I lost my temper, and without my brother's calming presence I fear I have caused a lot of trouble.' Her eyes misted over with tears and she wiped them away with a sweep of her hand. 'I do miss him so much. If he had been here this would never have happened.'

'We all miss him. This house isn't the same without your music and laughter. If you and Mrs Holdsworth need help at any time you can come to me or Harry, the footman. We will do what we can for you.'

'That is very kind of you and comforting to know. Now I must see how Mother is.' She dredged up a smile to show that his kindness was appreciated, although she doubted there was little they could do without putting their jobs in danger. Anxious to see how her mother was, she hurried out of the room and up the stairs.

When she reached her mother's room she was surprised to see the maid sitting outside the closed door. 'Why are you here, Mary?'

'The butler has given orders that Mrs Holdsworth is not to be left alone. One member of staff must always be close at hand.'

Alarm swept through her. Why would he issue such an order? Was she suffering from more than a bad headache?

Lillia slowly pushed open the door. There was only one dim light in the corner of the room, leaving the bed in deep shadow. She carefully made her way over and sat on the chair beside the bed. 'Mother,' she whispered, 'are you awake?'

'I am.' The reply was faint.

'I have never known you suffer with severe headaches. The doctor should be called.'

'That is not necessary. I shall be well after a good night's rest. How did your lesson go?'

'Very well. The professor is hard on me, but it is for my own good. I met a Brigadier Stansfield there and he knows Lester. He spoke highly of him. He was a pleasant man – for an officer.'

'Don't judge them all by your father, my dear. I was told Lord Dalton was here. Did you see him?'

She had been hoping to avoid this but she couldn't lie to her mother. 'I did, and I lost my temper and told him I would never marry him. He was angry when he left. I am sorry to be causing you so much trouble. I tried to be civil to him – I really did...'

There was a muffled sound from her mother and she leant over the bed in alarm. 'Are you all right?'

Sara turned her head and looked at her daughter. 'We do not have trouble, my dear. We are now facing a serious crisis.'

Gasping, she switched on the bedside light. 'Oh, what has happened? Your face is all bruised.'

'If I told you I walked into a door, would you believe me?'

'I would not!' she replied adamantly. 'Not with Adams insisting a member of staff must always be near you. He did this, didn't he?'

'You are not the only one who speaks their mind now and again. We had a terrible argument.'

'And he used his fists!' She was incensed. 'He can torment Lester and me as much as he likes, but when he shows violence towards you he has overstepped the bounds. Where is he? I will deal with this.'

'No, my dear, you must not confront him while he is in such a rage. He is out, anyway, and I doubt will return for some time. Now, let me sleep.'

She bent and kissed the top of her mother's head, devastated that she had been treated so cruelly. No matter what she had said, something had to be done to make sure this never happened again. She was the only one here, so it was up to her.

Chapter Six

It was midnight before she heard her father return. Unable to sleep she had not retired for the night but had waited in her room, furious that their mother had been treated so harshly and longing to have Lester by her side again. Her mother had told her not to confront the general, but rest was impossible until this crisis had been dealt with.

The moment she reached the bottom of the stairs the butler appeared. 'Where is he?' she asked.

'In the library. I believe he has had a little too

much to drink. Is there a message you would like me to deliver?'

'Oh, I have a message, but he will hear it from me.'

'Perhaps the morning would be a better time?' Adams suggested.

She shook her head. 'This can't wait.'

Adams reached the library door before her, rapped sharply and stepped inside. 'Miss Lillia wishes to see you, sir.'

'Not at this time of night. Tell her to leave it until morning.'

Stepping round the butler who was blocking the doorway, she walked up to her father. 'This will not wait until morning. I have come to warn you never to raise your hands to our mother again. If you do we will see you have cause to regret your brutality.'

He glared at her in disbelief. 'What happens between your mother and I is none of your business. You are just a child and your threats are powerless. Now get out of here before I lose my temper and throw you out of my house.'

'It isn't your house,' Lillia told him triumphantly. 'It legally belongs to the Kirkby family and you cannot touch it. If anyone is to leave this house it will be you.'

'Is that what your mother told you?' he asked, stepping menacingly towards her. 'That ancient agreement is worthless and can easily be swept aside. I can do whatever I like.'

That news had shaken her. He seemed so positive, but she could not back down now. 'If you try to take complete possession of this house then we will drag you through the courts until every aspect of your life and brutality is public knowledge.'

'You are too young to do that, and your mother never would!'

'That is not so, Gilbert,' said a soft voice from the doorway.

Sara came in and stood beside her daughter. 'I have allowed you to do as you please while the children were growing up. I wanted them to have as normal a life as possible. You gave me that chance and I was happy to remain the docile, obedient wife. However, circumstances have changed. The twins are older now and quite capable of making their own decisions. You have unwisely decided to disrupt their lives, and I can no longer stand by and see that happen. If you take any further action against us we shall fight you, very publicly through the courts, if necessary.'

'You couldn't do that,' he snarled. 'Don't forget your past will also be revealed, and it is I who will be hailed as the generous, kind man.'

'That could well be true, but I care nothing for my reputation. What happened in the past is no longer of importance. The only thing that matters to me is that two talented children, who have no blame attached to them, are allowed to pursue their chosen careers.'

Lillia's head was buzzing as she listened to this extraordinary conversation. What was all this talk about reputations and the past?

'You have made a grave mistake, Gilbert,' Sara continued. 'If you had not interfered you could have continued to live the comfortable life you have had since marrying me. I have always felt that I owed you that, but from this moment on your authority over us is at an end.'

He was obviously shocked and Lillia was sure the glass in his hand was shaking. It was remarkable to see him at a loss for words. Her mother then took hold of her arm and guided her out of the room.

Adams and Harry were both waiting outside the door and remained there while they made their way up the stairs. The general did not attempt to follow them, though.

'What was that all about?' she asked her mother the moment they were in their rooms. 'He looked stunned.'

'No more questions tonight.' Sara sighed. 'We both need sleep, my dear.'

'Of course.' She kissed her mother's cheek. 'Thank you for coming to my aid, for I fear I was going to lose that battle of wits.'

'You disobeyed me and I was forced to do something I have been trying to avoid. I owe your father a debt and I did not wish to make an enemy of him, no matter how difficult the marriage has been.'

She was upset now. 'I am so sorry. I know you told me not to confront him, but...' She gave a shaky sigh.

'You have always faced problems head-on, and have the tendency to speak without thinking. I was well aware that you would not sleep until you had given vent to your feelings. Don't be upset,' Sara said as her daughter's eyes filled with tears. 'It is how you are, and it was brave of you to defend me.'

'Have I made things worse?'

'You have brought things to a head sooner than I would have wanted, but perhaps that is not such a bad thing.' Sara smiled and squeezed her daughter's hand. 'Now go and get some rest, my dear.'

She made her way to her room, chastened that she had acted without thinking – again! She must write and tell Lester everything that had happened tonight.

When she went down to breakfast the next morning she was delighted to see her mother already there and looking her usual composed self. Makeup had been carefully applied to cover the bruises on her face.

'Did you sleep well?' Sara asked her daughter.

'Not really,' she replied, serving herself a good helping of food from the various dishes, and then sitting opposite her mother. 'Everything was running through my mind. Lester will want every detail of what has happened. Can we tell him he can come home now?'

Sara poured herself another cup of tea before speaking. 'I have been giving this a lot of thought and, reluctantly, I have decided it would be wiser for him to stay where he is for the time being.'

'But why?' She was astonished and disappointed. 'Surely there is no reason for him to remain there? He didn't want to go. He only agreed to it in order to protect you from Father's wrath. His sacrifice hasn't prevented that happening so why are you saying he must stay there? I don't understand.'

'If you will stay calm and listen, I will explain.'

She waited for her agitated daughter to be still, and then continued. 'Gilbert has apologised to me for his conduct yesterday, and I believe he is truly sorry.'

Lillia gave a snort of disbelief and opened her mouth to express her disgust.

'Don't say anything,' Sara warned. 'I accepted his apology, in the hope that he will not pursue the subject of the ownership of this house, as he had threatened several times. It is unlikely he would win such a case or risk the publicity, but should he succeed in having it transferred to him then you and I can go and stay with my good friend, Isobel, for a short time while we look for suitable accommodation. To take two of us would not be easy for her – three would be impossible, and I could not ask it of her. It would be better if Lester remains where he is until we know exactly what is going to happen. It would be wise to be prepared for any eventuality.'

She was devastated as she realised how precarious their situation could be, and even harder to bear was the thought of continued separation from her twin.

'I know this is not what you want to hear, my dear, but it is for the best. You said that the army officer told you he is doing well and has made friends, didn't he?'

She nodded.

'Then let him stay there while we deal with the situation here. Don't tell him what has happened. Keep your letters cheerful, without a hint of the crisis we might be facing. Do you understand the necessity for such secrecy?'

'I do,' she admitted reluctantly, concerned that he may pick up her feelings through their twin connection. 'If he knows what is happening he will return home immediately.'

'Exactly, and there isn't anything he can do. In fact, if he comes back it will only make matters worse. Your father tolerates you, but he dislikes Lester intensely.'

'I didn't know that.' She was shaken by this news. 'I cannot recall Lester ever doing anything to cause such dislike. He has always been polite and courteous towards him. I am the one who is often rude and disrespectful.'

'You are twins but your temperaments are opposites. Lester is thoughtful, calm and controlled; you are emotional and explode at times. Those different traits make you suitable for the professions you have set your hearts on.'

She smiled then. 'Lester always says I make a perfect prima donna, and I suppose his character helps him to be an excellent pianist.'

'Without a doubt.'

'I do so wish we could bring him home. I find our separation very hard.'

'I know you do, my dear, but this may be a blessing in disguise. It has made me realise that I have made a grave mistake in your upbringing. You should have attended school and mixed with other children instead of being tutored at home. Music and each other has been your whole world.' Sara shook her head. 'That is so wrong.'

'How can that be?' She was completely confused. 'We have been happy. It was what we wanted.'

'And there lies the problem. Tell me, how many friends do you have?'

'Friends? I have never needed friends, and neither has Lester.'

'I have been lacking in my duty as your mother to allow this to happen. Your father saw this and stepped in to do something about it.'

'Are you now saying that what he did was right?' she asked, astonished by what she was hearing.

'His intentions were good; the way he went about it was wrong. I am aware that this is not going to be easy for you to accept, but you must both now make separate lives for yourselves. It can be a harsh world out there at times, but you have to be able to cope with the good and the bad on your own. I feel confident that Lester can do that, but I worry about you. You are ill-equipped to deal with the real world, and that is my fault. I would like you to think about taking up an interest of some kind, or even a profession you could become involved in until you reach your goal as a singer.'

'But I have an interest and a proposed profession – singing.'

'You need something else.'

'Are you suggesting I give up singing?' she asked, thoroughly bewildered.

'No, I would never do that. You are good and the professor says you show great promise, but it will take time for you to become established as a performer. During that time I want you to have something else in your life. You need to start to mix with people from all walks of life.'

'I have started to do that with the WSPU.'

'Their aims are commendable and I whole-

heartedly agree with them, but there is no telling where their civil disobedience will lead. Do you want to end up in prison? Such a disgrace will certainly harm your desire for a singing career.'

'Oh no, I couldn't risk that.'

'Can you think of anything you would be interested in? A milliner, perhaps?'

'I only want to be a singer...' She burst into tears. 'And I want my brother back.'

Sara gathered her heartbroken daughter into her arms and let her cry out her grief and confusion. This was the most vulnerable of her children and she had to find a way to help her live an independent life. Without Lester's calm strength to lean on, his sister was in for a rough time. Distressing as it was, it had to be done.

As soon as the sobs faded, Sara smiled at her. 'Do you feel better now?'

'Yes. I am sorry, but I am very confused and frightened.'

'I know you are, but will you promise me you will try to think of something you could do away from music?'

'I promise.'

Sara kissed her daughter on the forehead. 'Go upstairs and wash your face, then we will go for a walk.'

How could she have been so foolish to allow this to happen? Sara watched her daughter leave the room, her heart heavy with sadness and regret. Of course she knew what had happened. When the twins had begun to show musical talent at such a young age she had been overjoyed, and this had blinded her to everything else. The best tutor had been engaged, and over the years she had watched their talent blossom. It had meant so much to her Especially Lester's growing mastery of the piano. Many times she had sat in the music room and watched him with tears in her eyes as the memories swept in. Not once had it occurred to her that her children were isolated. That was not only a mistake; it was selfish of her. As they grew older she should have been urging them to go out, make friends and learn what life was all about outside of the music room. It had taken her husband's action to wake her up to what she had allowed to happen. Now her beloved children were suffering because of her selfishness, and she was causing them more confusion by insisting they remain separated. The next few months were going to be difficult for all of them, and she prayed it wasn't too late.

She stood up, holding on to the back of a chair to steady herself. The first thing she must do was put things right with her husband. Things were going to be difficult enough without having his anger and resentment hanging over them.

She found him in the library and when she entered he looked up from the papers in front of him. 'May I have a moment of your time? I need to talk to you.'

He put his pen down, sat back and nodded.

Sara sat at the other side of the large oak desk. 'I don't know what your motives were for separating the twins, but after much thought I have come to realise that it had to be done. Indeed, it should have been done a long time ago. They have been on their own too much with only music and each other for company. It was wrong of me to allow that to happen.'

'That's a surprising admission.'

'It is, I agree, but I wish you had discussed your plans with me first.'

'And what would you have said?' he asked sarcastically.

'I would not have agreed, of course, and would have urged you to let me find another way.'

'It would have been impossible to leave such a decision to you. From the moment they were born they have been your whole life. And you have not been a very good wife.'

'You knew from the beginning that there was no love, affection or even friendship between us. Be honest, Gilbert, you married me for the money and position such a union would bring you. I know that, and for the sake of the children I have allowed you to take whatever you needed without protest. Now I am going to ask you not to contest the ownership of the house or try to raise money against it.'

His gaze narrowed. 'I need money and where is that to come from?'

She stood up, walked over to a glass cabinet and opened the doors. 'This contains many valuable items, and you have my permission to sell any or all of them as you need to. That could keep you supplied for some time.'

'And after that?'

'I will see that you have whatever you need. I don't want us to be enemies. Let us work together for the sake of all of us.'

He studied the contents of the cabinet, assessing the value of the exquisite Chinese and Japanese items, and then nodded. 'I agree. Will you tell me what you intend to do about the children?'

'Lillia will not marry Lord Dalton, but I am already urging her to find something of interest other than music. I would like Lester to remain at the academy, but that will have to be his choice. I will not force either of them to do anything that makes them unhappy.'

'I am surprised you are not doing everything possible to bring the boy back home, but I will tell you that I do not want him here permanently. If he will not stay where he is, then you must find him accommodation elsewhere. As for the girl there is now no question about her marrying His Lordship. She has already dealt with that by telling him exactly what she thinks of him.'

Sara looked at her husband, an amused glint in her eyes. 'She is apt to speak her mind when she is angry.'

'As I have often discovered, but she is less trouble without her damned brother always at her side.' He closed the cabinet doors and faced his wife. 'Let us try at least to be civil to each other.'

'I am sure we can manage that if we both adhere to our agreement. I will keep you supplied with money even if it means we end up with a house stripped of its more valuable contents. If Lester agrees to stay where he is, will you allow him to come back here during term breaks?'

He nodded. 'That will be acceptable.'

Sara left the library reasonably satisfied. She was going to have to talk to Lester and explain the situation. Gilbert was determined not have her son back in the house again permanently and that was troubling. She had won a small reprieve but it was not a happy situation. They had to discuss this and find a way round it. The immediate problem had been dealt with – for the time being anyway.

Chapter Seven

The finishing line was in sight and Lester increased his stride, determined to beat James. His friend grinned at him, matching his pace. After a final spurt they crossed the line with James one stride ahead, and they collapsed on the ground laughing, having thoroughly enjoyed their little battle over the five mile run.

'Dead heat.' James slapped Lester on the back as they clambered to their feet. 'And we've beaten everyone else.'

'You were just ahead of me, but I'll beat you next time,' he declared, still breathing heavily.

James said teasingly, 'You're quite an athlete for a musician. Are you pleased you came here now?'

'I haven't decided yet.'

'Don't try and fool me,' James told him. 'I've watched you over the last few weeks and you are enjoying yourself. Go ahead – admit it. And then when lessons are over for the day, you sneak off to play the piano.'

'I don't sneak off. You all know where I'm going.'

James studied his friend carefully. 'When we first arrived I was afraid you were going to leave as soon as it was possible, but since they have allowed you to play the piano you have appeared much happier. We've never heard you play. I'll have to ask the brigadier if we could have a musical evening for the whole academy. I'll offer to arrange it.'

'That would take a lot of organising, and who are you going to get to perform at this concert? One pianist is not enough.'

'I'm sure you could entertain us for the evening. There's talk by those who have heard you that you are quite good.'

'That's kind of them,' Lester laughed. 'My tutor, Professor Elland, wouldn't think much of that remark.'

James's mouth dropped open. 'I know him. He's famous and considered the finest tutor there is, and he only takes students who are not only talented, but gifted musicians. How long have you been with him?'

'He took us as students when we were five years old.'

'What? You and your sister?'

Lester nodded. 'I could get a tune out of a piano as soon as I was able to sit on the stool, and I think Lillia was singing from the moment she was born.'

'My word. I had no idea you were both that talented. We've really got to have a concert.'

At that moment the captain strode over to them. 'Well done. It's good to see friendly rivalry. Now, get to the baths. There are only a few stragglers left.'

'Yes, sir.' James nudged Lester. 'Beat you to the baths.'

After they had all cleaned up and had their meal, everyone was in high spirits because they had been given a rare afternoon off to do whatever they liked. The boys were lounging around talking or reading.

Lester had received a letter from Lillia so he settled down to read it, eager to find out how she was getting on now the threat of marriage had been dealt with. When he'd heard about his sister's outburst he hadn't been surprised. Subtle hints had not driven Lord Dalton away, and knowing his sister, she wouldn't have been able to remain docile for long. Thankfully there hadn't been any serious reaction from their father, which was very surprising. When his mother had asked him if he would stay at the academy for a while longer, he had agreed. He missed them dreadfully, but as far as he could gather from their letters things were a little easier without him there. He had always known that he was the main focus of his father's dislike, although he had never understood why this should be. One day he would confront him and ask for an explanation. He began to laugh quietly as he read his sister's letter.

'What's amusing you?' James asked.

'Our mother has suggested that my sister find something of interest to do other than music. She has sent me a list and asked me to choose for her. It reads: music, singing, dancing, tightrope walking, acting, singing, dancing, hat making, music, dressmaking, singing, opera, nursing, singing. Guess which subject she has underlined?'

'I wonder what she would like you to choose,' James replied dryly, and both boys burst into

75

laughter. 'I thought music was all you were both interested in, so why is your mother urging her to find something else to do?'

'She has realised we have had only one interest in our lives and need to get out and mix with other people. That is the only way we are going to learn to cope with life. A few weeks ago I wouldn't have agreed with her, but I do now. Music had become our whole life and we were content with each other's company. If we had remained that way we would never have had the experience to face the struggles and disappointments that will certainly occur in pursuing our musical careers.'

James studied his friend thoughtfully. 'I'm not sure that is true. You didn't want to come here, but you have settled in with us without any great problems.'

'That has surprised me,' Lester agreed, 'but my sister has a very different character to me. She is emotional and speaks and acts without thinking. All of her self-control goes into the mastery of singing.'

'Ah, then she does need something away from music where she has to obey orders like we do here. She did have nursing on her list and that would be perfect. I have a cousin who has gone into that profession and she loves it.'

'I don't believe for one moment she was serious. She would consider that as unlikely as tightrope walking. My sister was undoubtedly joking when she suggested that.' Lester shook his head and then grinned. 'If the patients took too long to recover they would receive a severe reprimand from her.'

76

'Oh, I am looking forward to meeting her. Go on, suggest she takes up nursing.'

An amused glint shone in Lester's eyes. 'I think I will, but be prepared because she is liable to storm up to me and demand to know if I have lost my mind.'

'In that case you had better not tell her until after the end of term parade. Suggest it during the Christmas holiday. I say, why don't you spend Christmas with us? I'll ask Mother to invite you.'

'She doesn't even know us.' Lester stood up, shaking his head. 'See you later.'

'Where are you going?' James slapped his hand to his head as he watched his friend walk away. 'Daft question.'

'I had no idea there would be so much paperwork attached to this job.' Alex threw down his pen. 'How are the arrangements going for the reception, Bob?'

'There's only one outstanding thing I need to know and that is who will stand with you when you take the salute at the parade.'

'We'd better have James Anderson's and Lester Holdsworth's fathers.'

'Right. I'll draft the letters to them.'

Alex sat back and sighed. 'Can't say I'll be sorry to have a break. We've been so busy; this term has flown by. Come on, I need a beer.'

The two officers stopped by the door of the lounge when they heard the music, and Bob shook his head. 'I gave that boy a free afternoon and instead of enjoying himself with his friends he plays the piano.'

'It's what he wants to do – no, it's what he needs to do. Every time I hear him playing I'm convinced he shouldn't be here, but he has settled in and is doing well. He seems to be quite popular with the other boys as well.'

'I've been keeping a close eye on him,' Bob admitted. 'I was expecting to have trouble with him when I found out he was here against his will, but he's a good student. Over the weeks it has also become apparent that he has leadership qualities. He will make a good officer.'

Alex pushed the door open a little. 'Just listen to that. How can a father put a son with that talent into the army? I haven't had time to ask what you've found out about Gilbert Holdsworth.'

'The only general by that name would now be 110 years old.'

'That can't be right.' Alex closed the door again. 'There must be a mistake in the records.'

'No, I've checked very thoroughly. I've got someone doing another search but they haven't found anything yet. We are trying to discover if any records are missing.'

'That would account for it, I suppose.' Alex didn't look convinced. 'We will meet him at the end of term and that will give us a chance to talk to him.'

'Yes, we'll find out more then.' Bob rested his hand on the door. 'Let's get that beer. The boy won't know we're here. He is oblivious to everything when he's playing.'

'Thank goodness it isn't snowing,' James declared as he gave his uniform buttons an extra polish.

78

'You'll rub holes in them if you don't stop. You look perfect.'

'Are you sure? I mustn't disappoint my father. Is yours here yet?'

Lester shook his head. 'He isn't coming.'

'What? But he made you come here, so he can't miss this, surely? I say, does that mean your sister isn't coming?'

'She's already here with our mother.' Lester grinned at James. 'Don't worry. I'll introduce you.'

'My parents can't wait to meet you.' James shoved his friend out of the door and winked at him. 'I've had a word with Mother.'

Once the parade was over they went to the lounge where family and friends were waiting for them. The moment Lester entered his sister rushed towards him and wrapped her arms around him. 'I've missed you so much,' she told him with tears in her eyes.

He gave her a big hug, laughing with joy to see her again. The separation had been hard on both of them, but it had shown him that it was necessary for them to live separate lives. They would have had to part in the future to pursue their different careers so they needed to become independent and live as two – not one. The pain they were suffering now would help them in the future.

She stepped back and studied him critically. 'You've grown and are taller than me now.'

He measured them with his hand above her head. 'Only by about an inch. Did you ask if you could run across the room in such an unladylike manner?' he teased.

She laughed and shook her head and he realised just how much he had missed that sound. Even her laughter was musical. Their mother was waiting patiently to greet him and he smiled with pleasure as he kissed her cheek.

Someone else stepped forward, making him exclaim in surprise. 'Professor Elland. It is good to see you,' he said, shaking his hand.

'Have you been practising?' he asked immediately.

'They have kindly allowed me to come in here and play. I have managed a couple of hours most days.'

Joshua looked crestfallen. 'That is not enough, dear boy.'

'I know, sir, but it is all I can fit in. This room is out of bounds to us really, but they have given me special permission to come in here when it isn't busy. I am grateful for their kindness.'

'Yes, yes, of course. A few hours is better than nothing,' he agreed, but still didn't look happy.

James was across the room trying to attract his attention and he beckoned him over. His friend said something to his parents and they all came over.

Introductions were made and the group were soon talking and laughing together. Lester was amused to see that James could hardly take his eyes from Lillia.

'I am sorry your husband couldn't come,' General Anderson told Sara. 'He missed a fine parade. The boys drilled quite expertly.'

'They did, indeed,' she replied. 'My husband had a commitment he could not break.'

'Understand. Great shame though. We would

have liked to meet him.'

Brigadier Stansfield joined them at that moment and he smiled at Lester and Lillia. 'If you are ready I would like to announce our musical interlude.'

'Please do, sir.' The twins made their way over to the piano with Joshua right behind them.

They had corresponded about their short programme so she sat beside the piano and listened to her brother playing the opening piece. When the applause had died away she stood up, resting her hand on the piano and nodded to Lester to let him know she was ready.

Her clear, powerful voice filled the room making James lean forward in his seat, enraptured. The twins entertained for the allotted hour and brought their performance to a stirring close, then they stood up and bowed in acknowledgement of the tumultuous applause.

James was on his feet like everyone else, stunned. He turned to Sara. 'I say, Mrs Holdsworth, that was splendid. It is the first time we have heard Lester play. He's taken a lot of teasing from us about his need to play the piano, but we had no idea about his skill – and your daughter is beyond compare.'

'You have very talented children,' General Anderson added.

'Indeed.' James's mother also complimented Sara. 'Do you have any plans for Christmas?'

'I expect we shall have a quiet time as usual.'

'Our boys have become firm friends and we would be honoured if you and your family would join us for Christmas.'

'That is very kind of you...' Sara hesitated. Gilbert had said he didn't want Lester in the house, although he had made a concession about the Christmas holiday. However, this would be a perfect solution and it would be lovely to spend time in a happy atmosphere, but...

'I say, please do come,' James pleaded. 'We have a large house with plenty of room – and we do have an excellent grand piano.'

Everyone laughed at his desperate urging, and James's mother scolded her son. 'James, you must give Mrs Holdsworth time to decide.'

'I do beg your forgiveness, but it would be splendid if you could manage to join us.'

'Well ... I am not sure my husband would be able to come, and we always invite Professor Elland.'

'Bring him with you.' General Anderson had the same glint of humour always present in his son's grey eyes. 'I am sure he would like to spend time with his pupils.'

'I would.' Joshua bustled up to them. 'I must. Their performance was good, but it needs more work.'

'I would have said it was flawless. You must be proud of them,' Mrs Anderson told him. 'We would be very pleased if you could also spend the holiday with us.'

The pleading look Joshua sent to Sara made her say, 'Then we do accept your very kind invitation.'

'Excellent!' The Andersons were all clearly delighted, and James hurried off to fight his way through the crowd surrounding the twins.

Chapter Eight

The Andersons lived in a beautiful mansion on the outskirts of Winchester and Sara loved the house the moment she walked inside. It was larger than their London house but, unlike the air of discord prevalent in their residence, this place immediately engulfed them in a feeling of happiness.

James was excited to see them, and as soon as introductions were over he took the twins to the music room, stating that it was at their disposal at all times. No one would be offended if they wanted to work with their tutor while they had the chance.

'We've had the piano tuned for you.' He beamed at his friend. 'Try it.'

'But we have only just arrived.' Lillia looked doubtful. 'It would appear very rude of us to shut ourselves away in here so soon.'

'No one will mind and I know they will love to hear you play and sing.'

Lester didn't need any further urging. It was a fine instrument – almost as good as the one he had at home. He played a short piece and nodded with approval, and then he winked at his sister and played the introduction to a carol.

Giving a gurgle of laughter, Lillia pulled James and the professor to stand with her by the piano. 'We will all sing together.'

General George Anderson strode into the entrance hall of his house to greet Alex Stansfield and his parents, Charles and Jane. 'We are delighted you could join us.'

'Thank you for inviting us.' Alex tipped his head to one side and smiled. 'I hear your musicians have arrived.'

'Isn't that a happy sound? All the youngsters have joined in.' George laughed and then immediately became serious, leading Alex to a side room. 'Want a quiet word with you before we become immersed in the festivities. Gilbert Holdsworth hasn't come, and that's a damned shame. I wanted to meet him. His wife is a charming, well-bred woman and I can't understand why he isn't here spending time with his delightful family. Not right.' George shook his head. 'It's as if the man doesn't want to meet any of us. What do you know about him?'

'Nothing. I've had my captain searching army records, but the only one we've found by that name would now be over a hundred years old. Bob's still looking to see if some records have been lost.'

'Hmm, unlikely. I'll see if I can unearth anything. Now, come and meet everyone and then we can join in the carol singing.'

Everyone in the house had gravitated to the music room and was singing at the tops of their voices. Alex laughed with amusement when he saw Joshua standing by the piano and conducting the singers as if they were an orchestra. It was a delightful scene and when he looked at Sara's happy

84

face he knew what George had meant. How could any man leave his beautiful wife and lovely children to spend Christmas away from him? At that moment he felt a pang of regret that he had never married and had children of his own. The army was his life. It was a choice he had made, but when Sara turned her head and smiled at him, he wondered if it had been the right decision. Returning the smile, he stepped towards her. If her husband was foolish enough to abandon her at this time, then he would happily keep her company for the next few days.

Ruth stood in the entrance hall and peered round the pile of parcels she was carrying. She grinned. 'Uncle George, they've come!'

He dived to catch two parcels as they toppled from the heap. 'We told our guests not to bring presents – we have plenty for everyone.'

'I'm not a guest,' she replied, loading him up with more packages. 'I'm your niece so that makes me family. The blue presents are for the men, gold for the women and pink for the children. Help me put them round the tree and then I want to meet these wonderful musicians I've heard so much about.'

'Don't you want to change first?' he asked as they arranged the colourful boxes with the enormous pile already around the tree.

'I'll do that later.'

George shook his head as he watched her run towards the music room, determined not to miss the fun. She was incorrigible, and he adored his independent niece. Her character had shown up when she was just a baby. If anyone tried to help her when she had been trying to walk she would scowl and push them away, making it very clear that she was going to do this on her own. The child had grown into a lovely young girl who knew her own mind. When she had announced that she was going to become a nurse, no one had tried to stop her.

He stood up and went to join the carol singers, a smile on his face. Ruth should have been a boy. What a fine soldier she would have made.

His wife, Emma, caught him before he made it to the music room. 'As soon as there is a pause in the singing, would you tell them that refreshments are in the dining room? Many of our guests must be hungry after their journeys. James didn't give me a chance to see if they wanted anything. The moment Sara and her children arrived he whisked them off to the music room.'

'I know, and as soon as his friend started playing everyone else rushed in there. We are going to have a musical Christmas, my dear.'

'Do you think the twins would entertain us one day?'

'I am sure they would. From what James has told me, music has been their whole life. He felt Lester was distressed when he arrived at the academy, but he settled in and did well after Alex allowed him access to the piano in the lounge. It was kind of Alex to allow him to do that.' He paused for a moment. 'It's a shame General Holdsworth couldn't come. I would have liked to meet him.'

'So would everyone,' his wife replied.

George shrugged and opened the door. 'I'll

break this up so our guests can have something to eat and drink.'

'Hello. I'm Ruth.' She held out her hand to Lillia. 'James is my cousin.'

'Lovely to meet you.' She juggled with a plate she was holding so they could shake hands. 'Have you met my brother yet?'

'I haven't been able to get near him. Every female in the house wants to talk to him.' She grinned. 'He's so handsome and I bet he looks wonderful in uniform.'

'He does, but he shouldn't be training to be a soldier.' Her eyes showed her concern as she looked across the room at her adored twin, but she quickly put a smile back on her face. 'You look smart in your uniform as well.'

'I've just come from the hospital and haven't had time to change yet. Let's find a place to sit so we can talk, and as soon as your brother is free you can introduce me to him. I'll just get some more food – I'm starving.'

Lillia waited while Ruth piled a plate with delicacies. She was curious to find out why a girl from such a wealthy family should be working as a nurse.

They found a couple of chairs away from the crowd so they could talk without raising their voices. Always direct, Lillia asked, 'What made you go into nursing?'

'It is something I wanted to do.'

'As simple as that?'

Ruth nodded. 'I didn't need to work for a living. My family expected me to do the social round, get married and have a family one day, but that wasn't enough for me. I have always had a need to be useful, to help people, and nursing was a way I could do that.'

'Do you enjoy it?'

'I love it.' Ruth's smile was brimming with enthusiasm. 'It isn't always easy, of course, and some girls give up because they can't handle some of the distressing things we see. I wouldn't want to do anything else because at the end of each shift I really feel as if I've helped someone. I don't need to ask what you are going to do with your life. I have heard so much about you and your brother's talent that it is obvious music will be your road in life.'

'We hope so, but that is some way off now Lester intends to stay at the academy. I'm finding it so hard without him...' Her voice shook with emotion. 'We had such plans, but they have now been thrown into disarray.'

Ruth put down her plate and took hold of Lillia's hand. 'Would it help to talk about it? I'm a good listener.'

'Well ... if you don't mind hearing other people's problems it would be a relief to talk to someone. Now my brother isn't with me all the time I don't have anyone to discuss things with. Letters are not the same. We have never been apart before...'

Seeing her distress Ruth stood up. 'Let's find somewhere more private. You can talk freely to me. I never repeat anything said to me in confidence.'

James watched the girls leave the room and

nudged his friend. 'Wonder where they are going? About to discuss the latest fashion, I expect.'

'No, my sister is upset about something.' Lester made a move to follow them but James stopped him.

'I forgot you are aware of each other's feelings, but if she's worried about something, my cousin is a wonder at dealing with problems. That is what makes her such a good nurse.'

'I ought to go to her.' Lester struggled with the feeling of distress coming from his twin, surprised she hadn't come straight to him. Things were changing now they spent less time together. They mustn't be so reliant upon each other, and that was something they were very aware of. He took a deep breath and waited, his thoughts centred on his sister. Gradually he felt the tension ease and a sense of relief sweep through him. She was all right. He turned his head and smiled at James. 'I think you are right about your cousin.'

'She's a marvellous girl and you can trust her. Ah, here comes Mother with your tutor. I don't need to be a mind reader to know what they are after.'

'Nor I.' Lester laughed, completely at ease now. The look of eagerness on the professor's face was all too familiar.

'Emma wondered if you and Lillia would give a concert one evening,' the professor said immediately. 'I told her that of course you would.'

'Only if you would like to,' Emma said hastily. 'You are our guests and we want you to enjoy this time with us, so please don't feel under any obligation to do so.'

'We would be delighted to.' Lester was having difficulty keeping his amusement under control. The professor was almost dancing with excitement.

'That is very gracious of you. Would you mind if we invited a few more friends?'

'Not at all. When would you like us to entertain your guests?'

'Would New Year's Eve be all right?'

'Perfect.' Joshua beamed. 'That will give us time to prepare a programme.'

'Why don't we use the ballroom, Mother?' James suggested. 'We will be able to get more people in then.'

'It would be more suitable, I agree, but the piano in there is not good enough for Lester.'

'We could move the one from the music room.'

'What do you think?' Emma asked Joshua.

'Show me where the ballroom is, dear lady, and I will decide if it is possible. We would have to be very careful with the piano, but I could tune the instrument in the ballroom myself if needs be.'

'Splendid! Your expertise will be gratefully accepted.'

The boys watched them hurry away and James smiled at his friend. 'That is very kind of you. Mother will be absolutely thrilled to fill the house for your concert.'

'We have been apart for months and it will be wonderful to perform together again,' Lester said with a smile.

Chapter Nine

Sara didn't think it was possible to pack in another person. The Andersons must have invited the entire district. Joshua had been working with the twins all day preparing the programme for tonight, and was clearly relishing the chance to have his favourite pupils perform to such a large gathering.

At last the doors were closed and Alex came to sit beside her. 'We have managed to get everyone in. News of your children's talent has spread and every invitation has been accepted.'

'Where have they all come from?'

'Emma and George seem to know everyone,' he laughed. 'But from what I have seen of your children, I don't believe this will make them at all nervous.'

'They won't be,' she replied confidently, 'but I am.'

'You don't need to be. They are exceptional musicians. I have never seen Joshua so excited and I have known him all my life. He adores his twins – as he calls them.'

'It is lovely to see him so happy. He has been horrified by the thought that he might lose them.' She turned to face Alex. 'Thank you for being so kind to my son at the academy. Music is life to him and if he couldn't play then I don't know what he would do.'

'A talent like that shouldn't be stifled. When I heard him play it was difficult to understand what he was doing at the academy. I believe it was his father's wish?'

'My husband arranged it and would not be persuaded to change his mind. He felt they were too isolated from real life and too dependent upon each other. It was hard to see my children parted for the first time, but they are coping well.'

'They are, and if it is any comfort to you, your son will make a fine officer. He has good leadership qualities and is popular with the other cadets.'

'Thank you. Ah, I think they are about to begin the concert.'

Alex sat back and relaxed, looking forward to the evening ahead. He had spent a good deal of time with Sara, and from their conversations he had the impression that her marriage was not a happy one. When she spoke about the twins, she always referred to them as her children, never theirs. He had come to like and admire this elegant, dignified woman, and to think of her as unhappy made him sad.

Joshua stepped forward and the room fell silent. His introduction was brief, but the love and pride he felt for his pupils was evident.

The programme was varied and included something for all tastes. Alex had been aware that these youngsters were good but, as he listened to them this time he realised just how talented they were. Now he could fully understand Joshua's distress at seeing the boy set on a path away from music. He still had the girl as a pupil, of course, and her voice was glorious, but there was something extra

92

special about the boy. He watched him closely, noting the total concentration as he played, the smile he gave his sister in the lighter moments. Alex was struck again by the feeling that Lester looked familiar as he sat at the piano. Who did he remind him of? A name just wouldn't come to mind though.

When the concert came to an end the room erupted in rapturous applause, and as he turned to congratulate Sara on her children's talent, he caught a glimpse of tears in her eyes. It was clear to him that this was what she wanted for her children. He could almost feel the pain, and his heart went out to her. There was something very wrong about this family, and he suspected it all rested on her elusive husband. He wished they had been able to get to the bottom of this mystery, but they hadn't unearthed any information at all and had almost given up. They would have to keep trying, because if he could do anything to help this lovely woman then he would.

The few days with the Andersons had been filled with laughter; they had played games and eaten far too much food. Lester and James had even gone out running one morning in order to keep fit. Lillia watched as the boys ran round a large field at the back of the house. It had turned into a race with them doubled over and laughing at the end. She was happy her brother had found such a good friend, but it was hard to see him moving away from her. That was selfish, of course, and going their separate ways would have been inevitable sometime in the future. It was difficult to accept, though, because it had always been just the two of them, but not any more. Her twin was happy and she had no right to interfere.

'I'm so pleased James has found such a splendid friend.' Ruth came and stood beside her.

'I was just thinking the same thing. They get on well together.' This was all very new for both of them. They had been close, even being tutored at home, and their whole attention on learning and music. She could see now that it was right for them to come out of their own sheltered world and meet other people. It was going to be good for both of them, for they must certainly go in different directions with their careers, and their desire to be musicians hadn't changed. It would never change, no matter what detours they were forced to make along the way.

'I know twins can have a special bond, so does it upset you to see them together?'

'No, but what does upset me is seeing all that talent going to waste. I have a voice, and with more training I should be good enough to achieve my ambition of one day singing opera on stage, but my brother is the real musician. He is special and, I believe, meant for a great career as a concert pianist.'

'I agree that he is an accomplished pianist, but you are underestimating your own talent. You already have a glorious voice with so much feeling in it that it brought tears to my eyes. I am sure you will both achieve your desires for musical careers. In the meantime it won't do any harm to see what else there is in the world to enjoy, will it?'

'You are quite right, of course.' She smiled at

the girl she had become quite friendly with in just a few days. 'How did you become so wise?'

Ruth pursed her lips as she thought about that. 'I'm not sure I would class myself as wise, but nursing makes you face all aspects of life.'

'Perhaps that is something I should do. What do you think?'

'From what I've seen of you over the last few days I believe you have the qualities needed for the nursing profession. It would have to be your own decision, though. Don't do it if it is only to fill the void of your brother moving out on his own. Think about it carefully.'

'I will.'

'May I offer a few more words of wisdom?' Ruth asked.

'Please do. I need all the help I can get.'

'James has told me you are both in this situation because your father has insisted Lester attend the academy. Trust your brother. I understand he is highly thought of. He is intelligent and showing good leadership qualities. Everyone is convinced he will make a fine officer.'

She shook her head, not willing to accept that for her twin, and Ruth caught hold of her arm. 'No. Don't dismiss it so easily. Think, Lillia. You know your brother better than anyone. Would he throw away the life you have always wanted? Why is he doing this?'

There was silence as the question ran through her mind and she began to glimpse the truth. 'No, he wouldn't throw away our longed-for careers, but we need to mature enough to strike out on our own, to become independent ... and he's protecting our mother,' she whispered softly. 'That is what we both want, but I didn't realise what he was prepared to sacrifice to do that. We've always been so close and able to read each other's thoughts at times. When we were young we even used to finish each other's sentences.'

'You are older now and perhaps that rapport you shared as a child isn't quite so strong. Not only do you have different talents, but you are male and female, and that means, of necessity, you will walk on different paths in life.'

'We will always be in tune with each other, but what you are saying is that I must let him go.' She pressed her hands against her heart, trying to ease the pain that realisation caused. 'How can I do that? He is a part of me.'

'You'll do it because you must. Your brother will make his own decisions, and you will do what is right for you. But remember, whatever you both do in life, that bond between you will always be there. Don't think you are losing him, because I don't believe that will ever happen.'

Lillia's sigh was ragged. 'That is going to be so hard, but I know you are right. I will try and be sensible. Thank you for talking this over with me. It has helped to clear my mind.'

The next morning everyone was preparing to leave. Lester was staying with the Andersons and going back to the academy with James the next day. Brigadier Stansfield was escorting Joshua, Sara and Lillia to their homes.

After thanking their hosts for a lovely holiday, Lillia headed for her brother. He was the hardest to say goodbye to, but she was determined not to cry and worry him. The talk she had had with Ruth made a lot of sense and she had spent a sleepless night running everything through her head. Decisions had been made and that was a relief. She had mapped out a path to take. It might not be the right one; only time would tell, but at least she would be doing something.

'You be sure you practice as much as you can when you aren't playing soldier.'

He held her away from him, laughing. 'The professor has already given me a pile of musical scores to master. Keep on with the singing. Your voice is maturing beautifully.'

'I'll do what I can between studying to become a nurse.'

'You've really decided to do that?' he asked in astonishment.

She nodded. 'I've had a long talk with Ruth and thought I would give it a try. It will keep me busy while you are at the academy, and do you know, I really feel as if it is something I would like to do.'

'That's excellent!' He guided her to some chairs and when they were seated he reached out and took hold of her hands, serious now. 'We need to get through the next couple of years, and then we will be old enough to make our own decisions, especially if we are both earning money of our own. This isn't the end of our dreams; we are merely travelling on a small detour until we can make our own way in life.'

'I understand, and it will be sensible for us to both have another profession to support us while we try to establish ourselves as musicians.'

'Exactly. It could take some time and we will need to be exceptional to be successful.'

'We are already exceptional,' she teased, making him chuckle.

'Such confidence, and I think the professor would disagree with you.'

'Well, we have to believe in ourselves or else we might as well give up now. Just you remember that.'

'I'm sure you will not allow me to forget.'

'You can be certain of that,' she told him sternly. 'The brigadier seems to be an understanding man, but if he doesn't allow you enough time to practice you are to come straight home.'

'I can't do that, as you well know.'

She nodded. 'It's so sad, and I don't understand why Father is so against us pursuing a musical career, or why he appears to dislike us.'

'It's a mystery, I agree, but I am certain Mother knows why and she is giving in to him to protect us.'

'But what from?'

Lester shrugged. 'One day we shall find out, but for now we must navigate the road we have been forced to take. We will get through this together.'

'Of course we will.' She hugged him, holding on tight for a long moment, and then stepping back. 'I must go.'

He stood outside with the Andersons and watched them leave. Once they were out of sight James asked, 'Are you all right, my friend? It is hard to say goodbye, isn't it? I have seen how close you are to your delightful sister.'

'It is tough being separated, but we have accepted this is the way it must be.' Lester grinned at James. 'Come on, we had better pack our kit ready to return to the academy tomorrow.'

The festive season with the Andersons had been the most enjoyable time Sara had ever had, but as they had toasted in 1911 the worry for her children came back. Lester appeared to be happy at the academy, and knowing he would be there for some three years or more, Lillia had decided to become a nurse. With these decisions, the pursuit of their musical careers had been set aside. It was a source of great concern to her, but they were adults now and she must respect their wishes, however much it troubled her. She was proud of the way they had taken charge of their lives, and from now on she would support and encourage them in any way she could.

Chapter Ten

April 1914

'Have you had a good day, darling?' Sara asked her daughter when she arrived home from the hospital.

'Busy, as always, but those years of study have been worth it. It's good to feel useful.' She removed her cape and gave her mother a worried look. 'Have you heard the news?'

'So much has happened. What news are you

talking about? Is it to do with the miners' strike?'

'No. The suffragettes have bombed Yarmouth Pier and destroyed it. Did you know they were going to do that?'

'I certainly did not.' Sara was clearly shocked.

'I know they are fighting to win the vote for women, and I agree with that, but I am uneasy about some of the things they are doing. The authorities are arresting them, and I don't want you to end up in prison.'

'That won't happen unless I chain myself to some railings,' she joked.

'Mother, this isn't something to be taken lightly.' She raised her voice. 'The last years have been hard for me and Lester, but we have done what Father wanted and made different lives for ourselves. And it has done some good. Father has become more agreeable and his business appears to be prospering. Items are no longer disappearing from the house, and he has even allowed Lester to come home when on leave. You are the steadying influence in this house, but have you considered what would happen if you were not here? Father could do whatever he wanted to.'

'Don't raise your voice like that. You are not in a concert hall.'

'And I'm never likely to be. I love nursing and I am very pleased Ruth talked me in to the profession, but it isn't what I planned to do with my life. Lester is happy in the army...' Her voice faltered, 'but he has a huge talent going to waste. He told me this would only be a detour, but how are we to get back on the right road after all this time?'

Sara gathered her troubled daughter into her arms. 'Don't give up, darling.'

'I thought we would be back together again by now. Please don't get arrested and put in prison. We need you.'

'I promise to stay out of any militant action. In fact, I will tell them I cannot help for a while. Will that ease your concern?'

'Yes, it would. Thank you.'

'Good. Now we shall go for a walk in the spring sunshine.'

They went to Hyde Park and walked in silence, enjoying the warmth of the sun. Sara's thoughts drifted over the last few years. Her daughter was quite correct. The atmosphere at home had improved. She had no idea what Gilbert was doing, but they saw little of him now. He did appear to be more affluent and that had improved his disposition, but she still kept a close watch on him. Nevertheless, even the improvement in their home life had not calmed Sara's fears. The plight of her talented children was a constant worry. It had seemed so simple when they were youngsters – a musical career for both of them was their destiny. Then overnight that had changed and now her son was a lieutenant in the army and her daughter a nurse. Careers neither of them had really wanted, and deep in her heart she had never believed they would have to walk this road. And all because of one domineering man who insisted on having his own way. The question was always there – could she have done more to protect them from Gilbert? She had tried and succeeded while they were growing up, but as Lester matured, Gilbert's hostility towards him had become more apparent. However, he was her husband and in this case she had given way knowing she would not win and would probably cause more trouble for her children. She had watched the twins struggle with their new lives and was proud of them. Lester, always the strong one, had adapted well, and Alex had helped at the academy by allowing her son to play the piano as much as possible. He was a fine man. For her sensitive daughter, however, it had been more difficult, but she had settled into nursing now with a certain amount of pleasure.

Lillia's laugh cut through her thoughts.

'Look at those squirrels chasing each other,' she pointed out. 'They move so fast.'

They watched their antics for a few moments and then continued their walk. No matter how many times she told herself the children were doing well, she was still deeply concerned for them. Both were committed to their new careers, but she knew their hearts still longed to pursue their dream. They needed to change course, and soon. But how? She had no answer to that problem. Lillia had always relied on her brother to make the decisions, and she knew they had both been waiting for him to find a solution. She sighed deeply and resolved to talk to him very soon. She had to know what he intended to do. If he was set on remaining in the army, then she must help her daughter launch her career without her brother at her side. That would be hard for her, but it might have to be that way. And as much as she agreed with the suffragettes' aims, it was time to distance herself from them and concentrate on her children. Oh, my lovely boy, she cried inwardly, what are you doing? Why have you left it so long, and what do you intend to do? You must talk to me. I have to know.

It had taken two weeks to arrange a visit to her son, and Sara asked him to find a quiet place where they could talk in private.

'Will this do?' he asked, casting his mother a concerned look.

She nodded. The small garden area at the back of the officers' quarters was suitable and she sat on a wooden bench. 'Sit down, Lester. We need to talk.'

He listened while she explained how upset and confused his sister was. 'We assumed that when your studies at the academy were over, you would return to continue with your music studies. We did not expect you to immediately go in to the army. How long have you signed up for?'

'Three years.'

She faced her son, astonished. 'Why didn't you tell us?'

'I did tell you I was going in to the army,' he protested.

'But not for so long. Is this the end of your dreams of a musical career?' If her husband had made her son turn away from music and waste his huge talent, then she would not remain silent any longer. 'Is the army to be your life from now on? Tell me truthfully, because if that is so then I must do all I can to help Lillia achieve her ambition.'

'Don't be so upset.' He grasped his mother's

hand. 'I didn't take this decision without a lot of heart searching, but in the end I decided that this was the way for me to go. Father is still hostile towards me, although he has tolerated me when I have been on leave, but I know that would change if I returned home permanently. Things could have become nasty again, and I was not going to be the cause of more unhappiness for you.'

'Oh, my boy...' Tears filled her eyes. 'The last thing I want you to do is sacrifice your life's ambition for me. I'll do anything, endure anything, to see you and Lillia happy.'

'We know that, but how can we be happy knowing life is difficult for you because of us? We are still young, and we are both supporting ourselves now. By the time my enlistment is over we will be mature enough to make our way in life without depending upon anyone.'

'Does that mean you haven't abandoned your career as a pianist?'

'Of course I haven't. Do you really think I could do that?' he asked. 'Music has been our whole life and I could never walk away from it.' He smiled at his mother. 'I like army life; it is helping me to grow, but this is only temporary. Explain that to Lillia and tell her to continue with her studies, and if she gets a chance to turn professional she must take it. I'll catch up with her later.'

'I'm so relieved we've had this talk.' Sara grasped her son's hand and smiled. 'You have put my mind at ease, and even though I don't agree with your reasoning, I can understand why you are doing this. You have always been the clearest thinker in the family, but I do wish you had told me this before you joined the army for three years. We have all been worrying that you were going to give up your music career.'

'Never.'

Sara sighed with relief at his emphatic response. 'If you had decided to make the army your career then I would have accepted your choice. You know that, don't you, darling? You are both exceptionally talented, but if at any time you told me you were no longer passionate about music, that would be all right with me. All I've ever wanted is for you both to be happy.'

'We know that.'

'Good morning, Sara. What a pleasant surprise to see you here.'

At the sound of the familiar voice Lester hastily rose and came to attention. 'Sir.'

'My apologies for intruding upon you and your son, but I could not leave without greeting you.' Alex smiled at Sara. 'I trust you are keeping well?'

'I am, indeed. Are you stationed here now?'

'No, I had to attend a meeting.'

Lester glanced anxiously at the large clock over the door of the officers' quarters. Brigadier Stansfield didn't appear to be in any hurry. 'Mother, I am on duty in thirty minutes. That will just give me time to walk you to the station.'

'Perhaps you will allow me to escort you, Sara? It will give us a chance to catch up on what has been happening since we last met. My business here is finished and we must not keep the lieutenant from his duties.'

'That is kind of you, Alex.' She turned to her son and kissed his cheek. 'You take care of

105

yourself, my dear.'

'Make sure you do the same, and tell Lillia and the professor that everything will be all right in the end.'

He saluted the brigadier and watched them walk away, already deep in conversation. How much happier they would be if someone as kind as the brigadier was their father. He turned sharply and marched back to the barracks. There was no point in wishing for the impossible; they had to deal with the situation they were faced with. As young children they had not been aware of their father's dislike, but the older they became, the more his hostility increased – not only towards them but their mother as well. That could not be tolerated, and he was dealing with it in the best way he could. He desperately hoped he was doing the right thing by holding back the musical career. His sister's last letter had indicated that the atmosphere at home was more agreeable, and that gave him some peace – for the moment.

As he marched along, his mind and hands longed for a piano, but he had made his choice, for good or bad, and he now had duties to carry out. They were already gaining independence from their father, and that, hopefully, was making life easier for their mother. Even if their mother and the professor were convinced of their talent, the road ahead wasn't going to be easy. But they would make it when the time was right.

'Ah, good, you're back. Did you have a successful day?'

Alex tossed his hat on the desk and sat down.

'The meeting was a waste of time, but the rest of the day was fine.'

'Did you see any of your ex-pupils?'

'Yes, and they are doing well. Sara Holdsworth was there talking to her son. He was about to return to duty so I took his mother to lunch and then drove her home.'

Bob sat up straight and asked eagerly, 'Did she invite you in?'

'She did, and I had the chance to look round. It is a fine house that has been in Sara's family for several generations. The music room has the most beautiful piano I have ever seen and the tone is exquisite. No wonder the son was unhappy when he arrived here. It must have been a wrench to leave that behind, and it is a testament to his strong character that he settled in so quickly.'

'I'm glad he did because he could have a good career in the army.'

'I don't think that is his intention,' Alex said. 'James believes his service will be short. For some reason he is biding his time until he can launch a musical career. That doesn't make sense, though, because in my view he is good enough now.'

'We will have to wait and see what he does. Did you get a chance to meet General Holdsworth while you were there?'

'Unfortunately not. It was puzzling. There were pictures everywhere of the twins and their mother, but not one of her husband. I wish we had been able to find his army records.'

'We did confirm that some records were lost in a fire, and it is likely his information was one of them. The only general we found by that name was too old, so he might be a past relative of his.'

'You are quite right.' Alex sighed. 'It's frustrating, though.'

'Meeting Sara Holdsworth again appears to have unsettled you.' Bob grinned. 'Are you attracted to her?'

'Don't be ridiculous. I am too old for romance – and certainly not with a married woman.'

'If you say so, but you are only forty. That isn't too old and you are still a handsome man.'

Alex laughed and stood up. 'I'm forty-two actually. Come on, you can buy me a drink.'

Chapter Eleven

The sound of someone running across the empty parade ground made Lester stop and turn. James was heading towards him, waving his arms about to catch his attention. What was the matter with his friend? He must be mad, running like that in the early August heat.

James skidded to a halt, and took several deep breaths. 'Have you heard what's happened?'

'No, and you look as if you need a drink.' He began walking towards the officers' mess, but his friend caught his arm.

'Will you stand still for a moment? This is important. Germany has declared war on France!'

'Oh, damn! I was afraid of that after Archduke Ferdinand of Austria was assassinated in late June. That set off a dangerous series of events:

Austria–Hungary declared war on Serbia – the French socialist leader was then murdered in Paris and Germany invaded Luxembourg.'

James nodded grimly. 'Looks as if we are heading for war too.'

'I hope not. Let's get that drink. I need one now.'

The noise from the officers' bar hit them as soon as they opened the door. Everyone seemed to be talking at once, each giving their own opinions on what was going to happen now.

'What do you want?' James shouted.

'A cup of tea.'

'What? I know you never drink more than a small beer, but surely you want something stronger today?'

'Tell them to make the tea strong.' Lester turned and studied the men in the room. There was an air of excitement as they discussed the recent events; some appeared concerned and a few were silent as they wondered what the future would bring. If they did go to war, then his own future was going to be in disarray – again.

'Lieutenant.' The duty officer pushed his way over to him. 'Would you play some soothing music, please, to try and calm everyone down?'

'That's a waste of time,' James said as he handed his friend the tea. 'No one will hear in this racket.'

'It will help to settle my concerns.' Lester drank his tea quickly and walked over to the piano.

The moment he began to play his whole attention was focused on the music and he became oblivious to his surroundings. Playing one of his sister's favourites he reached out to her. 'Are you

109

listening? It looks as if we are going to have to take another detour, but remember that we will eventually get back on the right road. Whatever happens we are in this together. Nothing can change that.'

When the words – 'together as always', came into his mind, clearly and strongly, he knew she had picked up his thoughts, and he relaxed.

James sipped his second beer and nodded. It had only taken a few minutes for the noise to abate and the room settle down. When they had entered it had been chaos with everyone standing around talking at the top of their voices, now most were seated and talking quietly, while others were silent, listening to the music. His friend certainly had the ability to soothe with his music.

The duty officer nodded his approval as he noticed the difference. 'I swear, Holdsworth has magic in his hands. It's tragic to think we might have to send men like that onto the battlefield.'

'He's a good officer, sir,' James pointed out. 'Do you believe we are heading for war?'

'I fear we are, but we will have to wait and see what tomorrow brings.'

The next day – 4th August – Germany invaded Belgium, and Britain declared war on Germany.

'My father has already been recalled for duty,' James said. 'I expect your father has as well. They are going to need all the experienced soldiers they can get.'

'No doubt.' That was one piece of news that heartened Lester. If their father was recalled then it would be good for their mother as well as the general. With him out of the way most of the time, then harmony might descend on their home.

'You'll stay in the army now, won't you?' James looked hopefully at his friend. 'I know you signed on for three years, but I've always had the feeling you might try to buy yourself out after a while.'

'Did you?'

'Yes. It's obvious where your heart is, and it isn't with the army. I was surprised and delighted when you joined up with me, but I believe it is because you have serious problems at home.' James held up his hands and said quickly, 'That is none of my business, and I'm not prying. I'm just pleased you are here. You haven't answered my question, though.'

'I always intended to stay for the three years, but now there will be no question about leaving until the war is over.'

'That's great, but I bet the war will be over in a year.'

'Really? How do you know that?'

'I heard some officers talking.'

'Then I believe they are being overly optimistic.'

'I expect you're right. Nevertheless we are in it now and I'm glad we have been posted to the same camp. That was a bit of luck.'

'I don't think luck had anything to do with it,' Lester remarked dryly. 'I suspect your father had a hand in that.'

His friend grinned. 'Well, I did tell him how much I hoped we could stay together.'

'I'm pleased you did. I wonder what the girls will do now. They are both nurses and medical care will be needed.'

'That has crossed my mind as well. Ruth certainly won't stay on the sidelines. I expect she is already finding out if she can take an active role in caring for the injured. What do you think your sister will do?'

'The same as your cousin, I expect, but all this is speculation. This war is only a few hours old so we will have to wait and see how things work out.'

James nodded. 'We had better get along to this briefing and, hopefully, find out where we are being sent.'

'I've applied to work at a military hospital, and Ruth has done the same,' Lillia informed her mother.

'Do you know where you will be sent?' Sara tried to keep the sadness out of her voice. Both of her children would soon be involved in this war, and it was a worrying thought.

'Not yet, but it could be outside London, and that means I might have to live away from home. I hope you don't mind?'

'Of course I mind, but you must do what you can. We all must.'

She smiled at her mother. 'I knew you would feel like that, and that's why I put in my request without discussing it with you first. There is a big recruitment going on – do you know if Father has been recalled for duty?'

'He hasn't said so, but I've hardly seen him for the past four weeks. He pops in for a couple of days and then is off again. Goodness knows where he goes or what he's doing.'

'Hmm. Well, if he hasn't been approached then it is very strange. With his rank I would have thought he would have been one of the first to be contacted.'

A servant entered the room and handed Sara a calling card. Her face lit up with pleasure. 'Please send him in.'

Alex strode in and greeted the two women. 'Forgive my unannounced visit.'

'You are welcome here at any time. Would you care for some refreshments?'

'No, thank you. I am not able to stay long. I would like a word with your husband if he is at home.'

'I'm sorry. He has been out all day and I have no idea when he will return. Please sit down, and at least have a cup of tea with us – unless you would like something stronger?'

'Tea will be fine, thank you.' Alex settled in a chair and smiled at Lillia, still in her uniform. 'Are you enjoying nursing?'

'I like it very much.' She poured tea and handed the cup to him. 'I was just telling Mother that I will be going to work at a military hospital.'

'That is excellent. You will be badly needed.' He turned his attention back to Sara. 'I have been moved from the academy and given the task of contacting ex-army officers. We have been unable to find General Holdsworth's records. Can you tell me where he served and his regiment?'

'He has never talked about his army career. All he said was that he moved around a lot and spent some time abroad.'

'Do you know where?'

She shook her head. 'I am sorry. He is not very communicative.'

113

'Well, when he returns would you tell him I called and ask him to contact me here.' He handed her an address.

'I will do that.' She took the paper and placed it on a small table.

'Thank you for seeing me.' He stood up. 'If you will excuse me, I have another call to make.'

'I am sorry your visit was fruitless.'

'Not at all. It has been good to see you again. I would be interested to know which hospital you go to,' he told Lillia. 'Would you both be kind enough to write to me occasionally and let me know how you are getting on?'

'It would be our pleasure,' mother and daughter replied together.

He smiled, bowed slightly and left.

'What a charming man he is,' Lillia said the moment the front door closed. 'I am surprised he asked us to write to him.'

'These men have a grim task ahead of them, darling, and letters from home will be very important. He doesn't have a wife or children who will write to him.'

'Of course. I never thought of that.' She pursed her lips. 'I wonder why they can't find Father's army records.'

'They must have an enormous amount to go through and they might have been lost or filed in the wrong place.'

'Yes, it would be easy to misplace records.'

It was past midnight when Gilbert arrived back. 'You are not usually up at this time of night,' he remarked, heading straight for his study.

114

'I have an urgent message for you.' Sara nearly bumped into him when he stopped suddenly. 'Brigadier Stansfield called today wanting to see you. They have been unable to find your army records, and he asked that you contact him at this address.'

He took the card she was holding out and tossed it onto the desk. 'If they can't find any records then how did they know about me?'

'He was the head of the academy you sent Lester to, so your name would have been on the application, but he has now returned to active duty. There is a great need for experienced officers like you. Do contact him as a matter of urgency.'

Her husband muttered something under his breath and turned away. Surprised by his reaction, she remained standing while he seated himself behind his desk.

'Was there anything else?' he asked sharply.

'No, but do get in touch with him. He called especially to see you.'

'I'll do what I have to! Now, leave me, I have things to do.'

Taking his reply to mean that he would contact the army, she retired. Much to her surprise she slept soundly and her daughter was already at breakfast when she came downstairs.

'Good morning, Mother.' Lillia hastily drank her tea. 'Cook said Father left at six this morning. Perhaps he's gone to see the brigadier. How did he take the news that the army was looking for him?'

'Hard to tell, but he wasn't overjoyed.'

She laughed. 'That doesn't surprise me. He has never talked about his army career, and that

115

makes me think it wasn't a happy experience. I expect he'll find a way to avoid being recalled. He doesn't look too healthy, so he could probably use that as a way out.'

'I thought he would be eager to return to duty, but after seeing his reaction last night, I'm sure that isn't so.'

'Oh, look at the time!' She kissed her mother. 'I must rush.'

During the next four weeks Sara didn't see her husband, although Adams informed her that he was in and out during the night. He never appeared at mealtimes, and she began to notice things missing from the house, including two landscapes which were particular favourites of hers. She was angry. The agreement they had made had lasted well, but he was obviously in financial trouble again. This could not be allowed to continue. If he was in serious difficulty then he must discuss it with her. She would not have her family home drained of sentimental items. She never entered his room, but that unspoken rule was about to be broken as she hurried up the stairs.

The door was locked so she knocked and called out to him, but there was no reply.

'Can I be of help?' Adams hurried up the last few steps to join her.

'I am concerned that I haven't seen my husband for a while. This door is locked. Do you have a spare key?'

He searched through the large bundle of keys he carried on a chain, found one and unlocked the door.

Sara walked in and looked around, but there was no sign of her husband. A quick inspection showed that all of his private possessions were there.

'Is there a problem?' Adams asked.

'It seems not. When I found the door locked I feared my husband might have been taken ill and be in need of help. He doesn't usually lock his door.'

'Most unusual.' Adams prowled the room, his eyes taking in every detail. 'Everything appears to be as usual. Shall I lock the room again?'

'Yes, please. Did he let you know where he was going and when he would be back?'

'We haven't seen him for some days. Cook is a light sleeper and told me she heard him arrive in the early hours of the morning, staying for a short time and then leaving again before dawn.'

'I know at times his business does require him to work strange hours.' She was puzzled by his recent behaviour, but kept that to herself. 'If you see him before I do would you say that I would like to discuss something with him when he has a moment to spare?'

'Certainly.' Adams locked the door. 'Is there anything else I can do for you, madam?'

'No, thank you.' She smiled and headed back down the stairs. Once in the sitting room she gazed out of the window. They had never been close as a husband and wife should be, but over the years she had become accustomed to his ways – but disappearing for so long wasn't normal. What was he up to?

Chapter Twelve

December 1914

The letter was quite short, telling Alex that Lillia had left to help in one of the many auxiliary hospitals set up around the country, but it was Sara's last remark that made him frown. She mentioned that her husband had been given his message the evening of his visit, and hoped he had contacted him as requested. He surged to his feet and called for Bob, who had been transferred with him to Aldershot.

The captain appeared immediately. 'Sir?'

'Have we received anything from General Holdsworth?'

'No, and I still haven't been able to find his file.'

'Then I don't think we are going to. I saw his wife weeks ago and she gave him the message the same day.'

'Well, we can't force him to return to service, but if we knew what his experience was he could, possibly, act in an advisory capacity. However, there is a real question mark hanging over this man.'

'If he hadn't sent his son to the academy we wouldn't have known about him. I suppose he could be using a rank he isn't entitled to. That wouldn't be unusual, and if so, then that could account for his reluctance to meet any of us.'

'That's a possibility, but surely his wife would know?'

Alex shook his head. 'I am certain she honestly believes him to be a general, but anyone can see it is not a close relationship. I'd love to find out more about him, but where do we start?'

'I have already tried to get hold of his birth certificate while looking for more information, but without success. Do you think Mrs Holdsworth would let you see what papers she has?'

'I would be uneasy asking her for such personal documents. The only way would be if she was to confide in me about her marriage, and that is most unlikely.'

Bob pursed his lips in thought. 'Tell you what, leave it with me a while longer and I'll continue to see if I can unearth anything about him.'

'All right,' he agreed reluctantly. 'I don't see what else we can do, and we have already wasted enough time on this matter.'

'By the way, did you know that quite a few of the ex-academy boys have been transferred here?' Bob said, changing the subject. 'I've seen a few familiar faces around camp. They will be on their way to France soon, I expect.'

'Is the Holdsworth boy here?'

'I wouldn't be surprised.' Bob grinned. 'If he is I hope they have tuned the piano.'

Alex was immediately on his feet. 'I'll see who I can find. They were a fine crowd of youngsters, and I hate to think what they are going to have to face in this war. They are little more than children still.'

He strode out of the office and was nearly at the

officers' mess when he heard his name called.

James hurried towards him, all smiles and saluted smartly. 'Brigadier. Good to see you again.'

'And you. How many of you are here?'

'Six from our class and a few others have been sent elsewhere.'

'Is Holdsworth here with you?'

'Yes, we've managed to stay together and Lester's off to see if he can find a piano.' James laughed. 'I told him he won't be able to fit one in his kitbag when we're on our way to France.'

'He'll have a good try,' Alex replied, joining in the joke. 'What did he say to that?'

'He said that if there was a piano within ten miles he would find it. Did you know his sister and Ruth are at the military hospital here?'

'No, I didn't. I'll go along and see them when I have a chance. I had a letter from your father to let me know he was back in the army.'

'They wouldn't be able to keep him away, though he is concerned that they might give him a desk job because of his age.'

'Everyone is going to be needed regardless of their age. There is a piano in the mess, so I'd like to go and see if our musician has found it. Are you free to come with me? You can get me up to date with the family news.'

'I'm not on duty for a while.' James glanced at the tall man beside him. He had known him all his life, and while off-duty they talked without the army formalities.

When they walked into the mess they saw Lester with his head in the grand piano, and James groaned. 'Oh, he's found it and is tuning it. Hey, come out of that instrument and see who's here.'

He looked up and snapped to attention. 'Hello, sir. I didn't know you were here.'

'I was sent here three weeks ago. James tells me your sister and Ruth are working at the hospital. Have you seen them yet?'

'I went straight over there, but they were busy. They come off duty at six o'clock so I'll see them then. We are off-duty so I thought I'd come and see what shape this piano is in.'

'And what is it like?'

Lester shrugged. 'Not bad. At least it's playable.'

When she saw her brother she ran and threw her arms around him in delight. 'What a bit of luck you being posted here. It's so good to see you.'

James greeted his cousin, Ruth, and then said, 'Hey, don't give him all your hugs. Save some for me!'

Amid gurgles of laughter it was hugs all round.

'Can we go to the canteen and get something to eat and drink?' Ruth asked. 'We haven't had time for food.'

'They keep you busy, do they?'

She nodded to her cousin but said nothing.

'Are you here permanently?' Lillia asked as they settled at a vacant table.

'No, we are waiting for orders, but before they tell us where we're going, we have seven days' leave. Guess who we saw today? Brigadier Stansfield.'

'Mother told me he was coming here, but we haven't seen him yet.'

'Oh, how did she know he had left the academy?' Lester asked.

'He called to see Father, but he wasn't at home – as usual. They are trying to contact as many ex-officers as possible. With their experience they might be able to help in some way.'

That was the first he had heard about the visit. 'Do you know what happened?'

Lillia shook her head. 'Mother gave Father the message, but she hasn't seen him since. You know he can disappear on business quite often.'

'Of course.' He grinned at James and Ruth who were listening intently. 'Our father keeps very unpredictable hours at times. I've been away from home for so long I had forgotten.'

'When does your leave start?' Lillia asked.

'Next week and I'm looking forward to seeing Mother. Is there any chance you can get some time off?' he asked his sister hopefully. 'It would be lovely if we could spend Christmas together.'

'No, sorry. Casualties are coming in all the time from France and keeping all of us busy. Let me know next time you're on leave and I'll see if I can arrange something.'

'I will.' Brother and sister looked at each other and they didn't need words to know how unlikely that was. It wouldn't be long before he was in France; the hope of meeting up was slim.

They sat with the girls for a couple of hours, laughing and joking about anything but the war.

The following week, he dropped his kitbag in the hall and gazed around. It was good to be home. How he wished his sister had been able to be here as well.

'Lester!' His mother ran and hugged him, and he lifted her off her feet, smiling with delight. 'Why didn't you let me know you were coming?'

'I thought I'd surprise you.'

'And what a lovely surprise it is. Adams, ask Cook to send in some refreshments. I expect my son is hungry.'

'At once, madam.' Adams gave a smart salute. 'Welcome home, Lieutenant.'

'It's good to be home.' He followed his mother to the sitting room and sat down in his favourite chair with a sigh of relief. He was desperate to get his hands on his piano, but he couldn't rush to the music room the minute he arrived. Spending time with his mother was more important because he knew she was lonely with them both away.

When the tea had been served and they were alone, he said, 'Lillia told me Brigadier Stansfield had been here and left a message for Father to contact him. Do you know if he did?'

'He hasn't mentioned it.'

'Is he home now?'

Sara nodded. 'Adams told me he arrived in the early hours of the morning, but I haven't seen him yet.'

At that moment the door swung open and Gilbert strode in, stopping abruptly when he saw Lester. 'What the hell are you doing here?'

Already on his feet, Lester was now taller than his father. He spoke calmly. 'This is my home and I am here to see my mother. What are you doing here when the army is desperate for experienced men?'

123

'That's none of your damned business, and how dare you address me in that disrespectful manner.'

Lester took a step forward. 'I merely asked a question. Brigadier Stansfield is looking for you. Have you contacted him as requested?'

'No, I bloody well haven't.'

'Well, if I were you I would do so. There is a war on, but perhaps you haven't heard.' He took another step forward. 'And watch your language when a lady is present.'

Sara's first instinct had been to rush in and protect her son, but she soon realised he didn't need help. The beloved children she had fought so hard to shield all their lives were now adults. With a supreme effort she remained seated and watched the confrontation, heart hammering uncomfortably. Her son had grown into a tall, strong and confident person who would no longer bow down to her husband. The exchange was heated, but she no longer heard the words. Gilbert was backing away from him.

'Sara,' he shouted. 'Do something about your son. I will not be spoken to like this.'

She jerked back to the present and managed an innocent smile. 'Lester is a man now and neither of us can tell him what to do. Those days are gone. You have always treated him abominably, so you can hardly expect respect from him now, especially as you are clearly shirking your duty as an ex-army officer.'

Without another word, Gilbert turned and slammed out of the room.

'I apologise. I didn't want to upset you, but that

scene was long overdue.'

'You did not upset me. I was relieved to see you stand up to him like that, and it has lifted a great weight from my shoulders. His domination of this household is at an end, and I could see in his expression that he knows it only too well.'

'He obviously hasn't any intention of replying to the brigadier's request, and that is strange. Do you know anything about his army career?'

'He has never talked about it.'

'We've always found it difficult to understand why you married him.'

'I didn't have a choice.' She paused and took a slow breath before continuing. 'I had been showing too much interest in a man I could not possibly marry, and as a result it was felt that no man of breeding would ever offer to marry me.'

'That is hard to believe.' He smiled affectionately at her. 'You are still lovely and must have been very beautiful when you were younger.'

She laughed and changed the subject quickly. 'Such a charming compliment, and has my handsome son found a beautiful girl of his own yet?'

'There is one I am attracted to, and you already know her. It's Ruth, but this is no time to form lasting attachments.'

'She's a lovely girl and so sensible. She has been a great help to Lillia.'

'I know, and I have a feeling that James is quite in love with my sister, but like me, we would like to get the war over with before we think about the future.'

Sara's face clouded with worry. 'Please be careful, darling.'

'Don't be concerned,' he told her lightly. 'Your children have a dream to fulfil, and no war is going to stop that.'

Chapter Thirteen

September 1915

'I wonder what this is about.'

James shrugged. 'They've probably decided what to do with us at last. We are the only two remaining from our squad. The rest have been shipped out quickly, and that seems strange.'

'I thought so as well.'

Waiting for them was the station commander, Brigadier Stansfield and Captain Eaton, who they had only seen once before.

'At ease. I expect you are wondering why you are here?'

'Yes, sir,' they answered.

'You have been receiving special training to ascertain your suitability for a certain career change. You have done well in the technical skills and have shown the ability to think quickly and make decisions in difficult situations. Today you are going to undergo a test which will be given by Brigadier Stansfield and Captain Eaton. They have convinced me that you are suitable candidates, so don't let them down. Off you go.'

They saluted and marched out of the room.

'What was that all about? Go where?' James

whispered once the door was closed.

'No idea, but we'd better wait here and ask the brigadier when he comes out.'

The officers came out almost immediately and the captain grinned, emphasising his boyish looks. 'Don't look so puzzled. Come with us and you will see what we have planned for you.'

The boys followed them to a waiting car and got in as ordered, glancing at each other and shrugging. They said nothing as the car turned out of the camp, but this was intriguing. They had been left behind when everyone else they knew had been shipped out, and that had been hard to understand.

'Lovely day for what we are about to do,' Alex said.

'And what would that be, sirs?' James looked hopefully at the officers.

'Stop teasing them, Alex,' the captain laughed, turning round to face them in the back seat. 'The mystery will soon be revealed, and believe me it will be worth the wait.'

'They might not think so. Alan is so besotted with this he thinks everyone is going to feel the same.'

'Of course they will. I bet you five shillings.'

'Before you go throwing your money away, sirs, you should know that if it is anything to do with water, I can't swim,' Lester told them, highly amused by the informal chatter.

That sent them into peals of laughter, making the boys even more confused, and the rest of the journey was made in silence. When they finally reached their destination, James gripped his friend's arm and muttered under his breath, 'Bloody hell!'

Lester was speechless as he got out of the car and gazed around. This was the last thing he expected.

'Beautiful, aren't they?' Alan said, looking at the aeroplanes on the field. 'How do you feel about flying one of those? We need pilots desperately for the Royal Flying Corps. We'll take you for a ride to see if you can handle being in the air. James, you come with me, and Lester will go with Alex.'

'You're a pilot?' Lester asked the brigadier in astonishment.

'I learnt to fly three years ago. Let's get you into more suitable clothing.'

In no time at all they were tightly strapped in the two planes. James waved and grinned at his friend as they taxied for take-off.

Once in the air they dived, turned and spun until Lester didn't know which was the right way up. It was the most frightening and exhilarating thing he had ever experienced. When they levelled out and flew straight, he sighed and looked around. Everything on the ground was so small, and above – it was breathtaking, giving him the same feeling he had when he played a beautiful concerto. At that moment he knew this was what he wanted to do.

'Well, what did you think of that?' Alex asked after they had landed.

'Fantastic, sir. I would like to learn to fly.'

Alex was clearly pleased by his response. 'I knew you would be the right choice. Let's go and see how James got on.'

'Captain Eaton said they want us to train as pilots,' James told Lester the moment they reached him.

'I know.' He grinned at his friend's animated expression. 'I've already told the brigadier that I would like to learn how to fly like that.'

'Oh, I say, this is very exciting.'

'I take it you are both volunteering to join the RFC?'

'Yes, sir!' the boys chorused.

'Good. You will be transferred here at once to begin your training. When you have flown solo you will be judged on your ability. If we don't think you are good enough you will return to your regiment. Is that understood?'

'Yes, sir.'

'You should also understand that this isn't going to be a joy ride. If you become qualified pilots you will be asked to fly dangerous missions. You are going to need to be very good pilots.'

'We will be, sir,' Lester replied confidently, while James nodded enthusiastically.

'Right then. Return to camp and collect your gear. I will expect you here at dawn tomorrow to begin your instruction.'

'How long will the training take?' James wanted to know.

'That depends on your ability and how many planes you break while learning to land,' he added dryly. 'Watch this one coming in now. It's his first solo flight.'

They turned their attention to the plane. It was wobbling from side to side.

'Straighten those wings,' the captain muttered.

And as if the pilot heard he levelled out just in time and hit the ground with a thud, bouncing three times before coming to a halt.

'My word,' James gasped, 'that was a rough landing, but at least he's in one piece.'

'We've seen worse.' The captain looked across at Alex and smirked. 'Haven't we?'

'Much worse.' He chuckled. 'I ran out of grass and ended up in a hedge.'

The boys looked at him in astonishment, and Lester remarked, 'You obviously got it right, because you are a superb pilot now, sir.'

'My instructor pulled me out, sat me in another plane and told me to damned well go round again, and without crashing this time. Fortunately I did or I wouldn't have qualified and I doubt he was ready to give me another chance. Ah, here's our transport.'

The captain was based at Hendon, so they saluted smartly and headed for the car. Their minds were whirling with the unexpected opportunity to learn to fly.

Once back in camp, Lester was able to catch the brigadier on his own. 'May I ask, sir, did you ever hear from my father?'

'He hasn't contacted me yet, but that is his choice. He doesn't have to.'

'Nevertheless, he should at least have had the courtesy to send you a letter. Mother told me you haven't been able to find his army records.'

'That's true, but if we had more information we might be able to track them down. Do you know anything about his army career?'

'He's never talked about it with us. I wish I

could help.'

'Captain Bob Andrews has carried out a thorough search without success. He did say that if he could see something like a birth certificate that might give him more information. He hasn't been able to obtain a copy of that. It looks as if documents have gone missing over the years.' He studied the tall boy, and hesitated a moment before saying, 'I didn't like to ask your mother if I could see any personal documents she had.'

'I'm sure she wouldn't have minded. Would you like me to do that for you, sir?'

'That would be appreciated. The captain is working on contacting all ex-military, though most of those are coming forward without being asked. Only a few are proving difficult to trace.'

'Father should have contacted you. I'll write to Mother tonight and ask her for any documents she has that might help.'

'Thank you, and please give her my apologies for the unusual request, but it is our last hope. If some of our records are missing we need to find out what has happened to them. The more information we can gather, the better. Any documents your mother sends us will be given to the captain and kept in the strictest confidence. I will no longer be in charge of that section after today, because I am transferring as a temporary instructor to the RFC.'

'Really, sir?' Lester's face lit up with pleasure. He had always liked this man and was delighted to know he would be based at Hendon as well. 'That's wonderful. James and I are very excited about learning to fly.'

131

'Enthusiasm is what we need. I believe aeroplanes are going to play a vital part in this war, and in the future. Go and pack your gear and I'll see you at Hendon tomorrow.'

'Sir.' He saluted and marched away to find his friend.

'I say, where have you been?' James was already packed. 'We've got to see the girls and tell them we're leaving.'

'I've been talking with the brigadier. Do you know he's transferring to the RFC to be an instructor?'

'That's terrific. I wouldn't mind him as my instructor, but that is unlikely because he is friends with my family and is like an uncle to me. You might get him, though.'

'We'll have to wait and see.' He began collecting his belongings together. 'Let me pack and then we'll go across to the hospital. Hope the girls will be free to see us. If not we will have to leave a message.'

They were in luck. The girls were just about to have an hour's break.

'Let's get a cup of tea, I'm gasping.' Lillia slipped her hand through her brother's arm, happy to see him.

'We've got news,' James blurted out the moment they were settled at a table. 'We are leaving in the morning. You'll never guess where we are going and what we shall be doing.'

'Let me see.' Ruth gazed into space. 'France.'

'No.'

Lillia drew in a silent breath of relief, but said nothing. They were dealing with casualties from the war and she feared that her twin might become one of them. The longer he stayed out of the front line the better.

Ruth continued with the guessing game. 'You're going into the cavalry?'

'No,' James was laughing with excitement. 'You'll never guess, so I'll tell you. Tomorrow we are being posted to Hendon to train as pilots.'

'What?'

Ruth's cup crashed back into the saucer and Lillia grabbed her brother's arm. 'Tell me you are not doing this as well.'

He squeezed her hand. 'Don't worry. We went up today and it was exhilarating. The brigadier was my pilot, and he's very good.'

'I didn't know he could fly a plane, did you?' Ruth asked her cousin.

James shook his head. 'He kept that quiet.'

'He most certainly did. Just wait until I see him. I expect he's responsible for dragging you two into this.' Ruth began wiping up spilt tea, and then looked up. 'Can you refuse the posting?'

'Refuse!' Both boys exclaimed in horror.

'We can't, and we wouldn't want to,' Lester told them.

'You mean you want to do this?' Lillia was horrified. 'But it must be horribly dangerous.'

'No more dangerous than being on the ground.'

'I suppose so, but please be careful. I hate to think of you flying around up in the sky.'

He sat back and winked at his sister. 'It's wonderful. I'll take you up when I'm a qualified pilot.'

Feeling his excitement she smiled. 'We'll see. It might not be as easy as you think to learn to fly.'

133

'Oh, we'll do it without any trouble,' James told them confidently. 'At least, without too much trouble – we hope.'

The boys looked at each other and burst into laughter.

'What's so funny?' Ruth wanted to know. 'Come on, tell us.'

'The brigadier told us he ended up in a hedge when he was trying to land after a solo flight.'

'That doesn't fill me with confidence,' she scolded her brother, then her expression softened and she grasped his hand across the table. 'But I can see this is something you really want to do, so good luck. I know you'll make a skilled and safe pilot. You both will.'

'Wonder how long the training takes?' Lillia said, as they made their way back to the ward.

'No idea. Why?'

'I've been thinking that this might not be a bad thing for the boys to do. It will keep them out of the fighting for a while longer, and I thought they would have been sent to France some time ago. They have obviously been holding on to them for this very reason.'

'I had the same thought myself. When you are dealing with the injured all the time it's difficult not to imagine how you'd feel if the person in the bed was someone you love.'

'I know, but all we can do is help the poor devils as much as we can.'

'And that's exactly what we are doing.' Ruth held the door open. 'Back to work and I'll see you when our shift finishes. We can talk about this then.'

Chapter Fourteen

'How do you feel about going solo?'

'I would like to try,' Lester answered calmly. 'That is your decision, sir. In your opinion, am I becoming a good pilot?'

Alex studied the young man sitting at the other side of the desk. He had come to know him well during the training, and he was impressed not only with his sharp mind, but with the methodical way he had approached the task of learning to fly. He guessed that his musical training had a lot to do with that. His concentration was superb. He could make changes when necessary without being told. Two days ago the engine had cut out and Alex had been ready to take over, but it hadn't been necessary. Lester had restarted the engine without fuss or panic. He sat back in his chair and said, 'Yes, I do believe you will make a good pilot. We have been lucky to have fine weather to fly in. Winter is not the best time to train, but you have done well – you both have. You are going to be welcome additions to the RFC, and will be ready for active service by the spring. The moment we get a calm, clear day, you can make your first solo flight.'

'Thank you, sir.' Lester was elated. He was surprised just how much he loved flying and was eager to get up there by himself. Then he remembered the letter and pulled it out of his pocket.

135

'Mother said she could only find the marriage certificate and has copied out the details for you. We hope this will be of some help to the captain.'

'Ah, thank you. I'm going to see Captain Andrews tomorrow. He'll be pleased with any information. The weather forecast is bad for the next few days so you might as well take some time off.'

'Thank you, sir.' Lester stood up, saluted and marched out of the office to find James waiting for him with a huge smile on his face.

'How did you get on?'

'Fine. The brigadier thinks I'm ready to go solo, and if we pass then we could be sent to France in the spring of next year.'

'Me too. I say, that is going to be an exciting year.'

'Going solo isn't the end of our training,' he pointed out to his excited friend. 'We've got to learn how to navigate or we won't know where we are. Once that is completed I suspect it could get even more exciting – and dangerous.'

'And they want us to be able to take photographs from the air as well. Pictures could be very useful to the chaps on the ground.'

'I imagine so,' Lester agreed. 'I've got some time off now, so I'm going to have another go at tuning that wreck of a piano in the mess, though I suspect it is beyond hope.'

'It sounds all right to me.' As his friend started to walk away, James called out, 'You tuned it two days ago.'

'And I'm going to have another go.'

'Mrs Holdsworth could only find a marriage certificate and sent these details for us.' Alex handed over the sheet of paper. 'I'm only here for the day and have to return to Hendon by tonight. Will you be free for us to have lunch together?'

'Of course. Thanks for this, now I've got some checking to do. See you for lunch.'

'One o'clock all right? I've got a meeting to attend this morning. Those two boys are going to make first-class pilots and their transfers need to be made permanent.'

When his friend nodded agreement to meeting at one o'clock, Alex headed for the door. There was a lot to do while he was here.

The morning went smoothly and he found Bob already waiting for him. He sat down. 'Have you ordered?'

'No, I waited for you. Did you get your business settled?'

'Yes, their transfers are going through. How did you get on? Was that information any use?'

'Well, I'm not sure how to tell you this, but the details Mrs Holdsworth copied from the marriage certificate don't make sense. I'm expert at tracing information, but in this case I would swear that no such person as General Gilbert Holdsworth exists.'

Alex sat bolt upright in the chair. 'Are you saying that the details Sara sent you about her husband are false?'

'That's my opinion, but I can't prove it, of course. I would love to get a close look at that certificate. I've had experts working on it and we have found a birth certificate for Sara Kirkby, as

137

she was, but not for Gilbert Holdsworth.'

'I really don't know what to make of this. We should have been able to find something.'

'I'm sorry, I know you are friends with the family, but we've always had a suspicion that something wasn't right. There might be a perfectly good reason for this mess, though, so don't give up. I expect something will turn up and solve the mystery.'

He was stunned and didn't know what to believe. Was the man using a false title, and they were looking in the wrong places for him? If Sara had any suspicion that there was something wrong with her husband's name, she wouldn't have sent them all the details from the certificate. 'Let's hope there is an explanation. Whatever has happened here she is innocent and so are her children. The question remains. Who the hell is he?'

'Not an ex-army general, that's for sure.'

'I can't tell his family that we suspect he's a fraud.'

'If I were you I would just thank her for giving us the information and that we appreciate her helpfulness.'

'I'll do that, but what are we going to do about the bogus general – for all the evidence is pointing that way?'

'There isn't much we can do. If he is masquerading under a false name and title, it will only cause the family trouble if we dig any deeper. I suggest this is no longer the army's concern and we should cross him off the list of the men we are trying to contact.'

'Just forget it, you mean?'

Bob nodded.

'I hate to walk away from this, but you are right. We could destroy three lovely people if we continue with the investigation. And we don't really know what the truth of the matter is, do we? This is all speculation. Right?'

'There isn't one piece of evidence that he is an impostor. It just appears that way, and for the sake of his family we keep our suspicions to ourselves.'

'That's for the best,' Alex agreed. 'You won't mention this to anyone?'

'You have my word, but if you ever meet him will you let me know? Just out of curiosity.'

'I will. That is unlikely, though. He's done a good job of avoiding us, hasn't he?'

'He certainly has, and we can't waste more time on this – we have a war to win. I expect to be deployed soon and this office is being closed down. I'm not much of a sailor, so I hope the sea is calm.'

Alex knew exactly what his friend was saying. He was off to France. 'You take care.'

'And you. I'll wave if you fly overhead any time.'

Alex laughed. 'I'm an instructor, remember, but you might see the two youngsters.'

Three days later the weather was clear with little wind, and Lester and James waited anxiously to see if they would be given the chance to go solo. They had been up once already with the instructors who had disappeared the moment they had landed.

'Do you think they are discussing us?' James asked. 'I'll be devastated if they say I'm not suitable for the RFC. I really want to do this.'

'We're already in.'

'What?' James spun round to face his friend. 'How do you know?'

'The brigadier hinted that our transfer was already being processed.'

'Both of us?'

'Of course. Don't get too excited,' he warned. 'When we go solo we will need a smooth take-off and landing.'

'No problem.' James slapped his friend on the back. 'We'll show them we can handle a plane like experts. After all, we have been taught by the best.'

'Here they come, and they are smiling, so we might get our chance.'

'Come on,' the brigadier ordered Lester. 'Let's make the most of the good weather. You sit in the front.'

He settled in and waited while his harness was checked. Then instead of getting in the brigadier jumped down and stepped back. 'Right, you're on your own. I want to see some good flying. Make two circuits of the field and a smooth landing.'

'Yes, sir.' He started the engine, feeling the thrill he always had as he taxied to the end of the field. He was going solo!

'I'm going to let Anderson go solo if Holdsworth does well.' Alan came and stood beside Alex, both men watching the plane closely as it gathered speed for take-off. 'This is always an anxious moment.'

Alex jammed his hands in his pockets and held his breath as the plane left the ground and climbed smoothly. 'Nicely done,' he breathed softly.

'He's flying like a pilot with a good few hours logged,' Alan remarked as he watched the plane fly round the field. 'Let's hope he can land without any mishaps. Here he comes.'

They waited, noting every move and then the captain laughed. 'You can breathe again. That was a landing even I would have been proud of.'

'And me.' Alex removed his hands from his pockets and ran them through his short dark hair. 'I knew he was going to make a good pilot, he has a feel for a plane and his concentration is superb, but allowing him up on his own was nerve-racking.'

'You'll get used to it.' He watched James running out to greet his friend as the plane came to a halt. 'Now it's my turn to sweat. Anderson is more excitable so I wouldn't expect his flight to be as smooth, but he's got the ability to make a good pilot and loads of enthusiasm.'

'Let's hope we can find more young men as competent as these.'

'There's plenty eager to try, so we are going to be kept busy.' The captain strode across the field to his pupil.

'How did I do, sir?' Lester asked the moment he reached Alex.

'Very well. Now we have to teach you how to navigate over territory you have never seen before. You are now officially in the Royal Flying Corps.'

'Thank you, sir.' Lester smiled, pleased he had done so well. 'Do you know if James is going solo today?'

Alex nodded. 'Any minute now. Let's watch

and see how he does.'

'He'll be fine, sir,' he said confidently. 'Like me, he loves to fly.'

James didn't disappoint those watching, and managed as smooth a landing as his friend.

Before Lester dashed off to congratulate him, Alex said, 'I shall be in London this evening and will call in to see your mother and thank her personally for sending us the information we asked for. I'll also give her the good news about your solo flight.'

'That's kind of you, sir. I am sure she will be pleased to see you. She misses us being around and making all that racket – as our father tells us. It's just noise to him.' He laughed. 'Perhaps he will be at home this time you call.'

'That would be good. Now, off you go and celebrate with James.'

Chapter Fifteen

The house was so quiet without the twins. She should be used to it after all this time – but she wasn't. The book she had been reading held no interest so she closed it. From the moment the children had been born they had been the centre of her life, but they were grown up now and striking out on their own. It was not the route either of them had wanted, but it had seemed just a short delay in launching their careers, until this terrible war had put an end to their plans. No decisions could be made until the war was over. Her children, like thousands of others, were involved in the desperate fight. Her daughter should be safe enough in a military hospital, but she was sick with worry for her son. He was going to become a pilot, and she didn't dare let herself dwell on the dangers he could face. If she lost them now her life would be empty, but she knew she wasn't the only mother with these concerns. Right across the country families were worried about their loved ones.

There was a gentle knock on the door and Adams entered. 'Brigadier Stansfield is here to see you, madam. Are you in for callers?'

'Of course.' The gloomy thoughts were pushed away and she relaxed. 'Have refreshments sent in, please.'

'At once, madam.'

'Forgive me for this unexpected call,' Alex said as soon as he walked in. 'As I was coming this way I told your son I would call in and thank you for sending us those notes.'

'You are always welcome. Was the information of any use?'

'Captain Andrews has still not been able to trace your husband's army records and has concluded that they must have been lost, but he appreciated your help.'

'So, the only one with all the details is my husband. Has he contacted you?'

'Not yet. Is he at home now?'

'No, I am sorry. He is away a great deal.'

'I'm sure he is a very busy man,' he replied politely.

The refreshments had arrived and Alex took a cup of tea from Sara. 'I have good news about your son. He has successfully flown solo and is now attached to the Royal Flying Corps.'

'So soon? I thought the training would take a long time.'

'Not with your son or James. They have taken to flying with great skill and enthusiasm, and are going to be excellent pilots.'

Sara managed a smile. 'I am pleased to hear that. However, the thought of him flying around in the sky does fill me with trepidation. Surely it is very dangerous?'

'This war is full of dangers,' he said quietly, 'but I know where I would rather be – in the air, instead of the battlefield trenches.'

'I had not considered it in that way. What happens now? Will they become involved in the war?'

'Not yet. They still have more training before they are ready for active duty. It will probably be next year before that happens.'

Sara stifled a sigh. 'How long is this dreadful war going to last?'

'I fear it will be some time. There is no end in sight.'

Later that evening, Alex walked into the restaurant and sat at the table with Joshua. 'Sorry I'm late.'

He glanced up from the menu he had been studying and smiled. 'Are you late? I hadn't noticed.'

'I don't suppose you did,' he laughed. 'The only thing you take any notice of is music.'

'Is there anything else?' His eyes gleamed with

amusement. 'So, what has delayed you?'

'I called in to see Sara and stayed longer than intended. Her son flew solo and is now attached to the RFC. He's going to be a fine pilot.'

At the mention of his favourite pupil Joshua immediately became serious. 'You may consider that a cause for celebration, but I do not. He should be seated at a piano, not flying off to danger.'

'There is a war on,' Alex reminded him. 'I know you have high expectations for him, but he would have been called upon to fight, the same as everyone else.'

'I know that, but I am being selfish in my desire to keep him safe. If he is killed the world will have lost a musician of extraordinary abilities.'

'You really believe he is that good?'

Joshua nodded. 'He is as good – no, he is already a more accomplished pianist than Pierre Le Fort.'

'That's who he reminds me of,' Alex declared. 'It's been nagging at me ever since I first saw him. The way he sits at the piano, and the tilt of his head when concentrating on the music.'

'I agree there is a likeness.' Joshua studied Alex's thoughtful expression. 'But most good pianists look similar when seated at a piano.'

'I suppose they do.' Alex thought for a moment. 'Is General Holdsworth Sara's second husband?'

'I don't know. She has never talked about her private life, and I have never asked. The twins bear no resemblance to General Holdsworth and very little of the mother. That family is a complete mystery, but I admire Sara and would not do anything to make her life more difficult. That

145

man she is married to does not deserve such a cultured and charming wife.'

'Then I wonder why she married him?'

'That is another puzzle and I would ask you not to probe in to her life. Please do all you can to see that boy survives this terrible conflict.'

'There is little I can do once he is fully qualified. He will be posted to an active squadron.'

'I know.' Joshua sighed. 'All we can do is pray and hope.'

He picked up the menu. Joshua was already worried about the boy, so he wouldn't say anything about their fruitless search for the general's records. 'I haven't heard anything about that pianist for some time. Is he still alive?'

'I think he was in France when the war started, so I expect he is still there.'

'Ah, then it could be impossible for him to arrange concerts until the war is over.'

'I expect so.' Joshua gave a sad smile. 'I've lost nearly all of my pupils to this damned war, but I grieve over the two most talented. I love the twins as if they were my own.'

'You still see Lillia, surely? She isn't that far away in Aldershot.'

'They've moved her to one of the auxiliary military hospitals they are setting up in country houses. I don't know which one yet, but she is too far away to get home easily. They are also terribly busy; the casualties are appalling.'

'Let's order, shall we, and try to forget the war for a couple of hours?'

They enjoyed the meal by talking about anything but the conflict, and he soon had Joshua laughing about some of the antics the trainee pilots got up to. He avoided telling him about the young pilots who got killed or injured while learning to fly.

Later that night as he tossed and turned, unable to sleep, he kept returning to the conversation he'd had with Joshua. With both of her children away, Sara must be lonely. It didn't appear that her husband was much of a companion so he must try to call and see her more often. That family was certainly a mystery, but whatever secrets she was hiding, he didn't care. He liked her and knew nothing would change that.

He got up and put the kettle on to make a pot of tea. Sleep was impossible so he might as well clear up some paperwork. Every time he closed his eyes he could see Lester at the piano and Joshua standing beside him. The boy's likeness to that famous pianist was striking, but it must be a coincidence; a strange twist of fate. It was none of his business, of course, and he shouldn't be concerning himself with the Holdsworth family, but somewhere along the line he had become close to them, which was not sensible. Making attachments while the war was raging was the height of folly. Especially when he knew that a pilot's survival was counted in weeks. The enemy was more experienced than the young boys he was training. Then there was Lester's twin sister. What horrors was she dealing with every day? Would she ever sing again?

He poured a cup of tea and sat at his desk, staring at the pile of paperwork. All he saw, though, was a mental picture of the twins when they had entertained everyone at Christmas with the Andersons. The joy on their faces had been lovely to see. Now the music had stopped. Would it ever start again for these talented youngsters?

The days dragged for Sara, and she had kept her word to Lillia and severed her connection with the suffragettes, but that would have happened anyway. They had ceased their militant actions for the duration of the war. The London hospitals were busy and welcomed helpers, so she had volunteered and was working three days a week. It helped to fill her days by supplying patients with books for those who wanted to read, taking round meals and helping to feed patients who needed assistance. A good deal of her time was spent talking to patients, and she found this the most satisfying. It also helped to take her mind off worrying about her children. There wasn't anything she could do to keep them safe, and even if Gilbert hadn't forced them to go out into the world, this war would have made them do that. In a way she was now grateful to her husband – because of his actions the children had been much more able to cope with the changes forced upon everyone by the war. The only thing she could do was help where she could and pray that the suffering and grief of so many would soon be over. Moving around the wards had made her conscious that this was no time to be selfish. Help and kindness were needed by so many and not only those she loved, although they were uppermost in her thoughts, of course.

Chapter Sixteen

Spring 1916

'Phew!' James grinned at Lester, his eyes glinting with devilment. 'We are now fully trained pilots of the RFC, and our posting has come through at last. The navigation was the hardest. How many times did you get lost?'

'None I will admit to.'

The boys looked at each other and burst into laughter. James punched his friend on the shoulder. 'You are almost as good a liar as me. We've got three days off now, so let's go and see the girls.'

'They are in Lincolnshire and we won't have enough time to go there. I must go home and see our mother.'

'We could fly up there.'

He faced his friend in disbelief. 'Oh, that's a wonderful idea. We could get court-martialled before we even join our squadron.'

'I've got a plan to avoid that.'

'I don't like the sound of that,' Lester groaned. 'I've experienced some of your "plans" and it always ends in trouble.'

'Ah, but this is a good one. Don't you want to see our girls before we go to France?'

'Of course I do.'

'Then listen to my plan. We could get permission from Alex to do one more training run, land at an airfield, stay overnight, and return the next day.'

'He'll never agree to that. And it's Brigadier Stansfield.'

'Not to me. He's a friend of the family – and yours as well now. He likes you.'

'I like him as well, but I don't like the idea of deceiving him.'

'We won't be doing that. He'll know exactly what we are going to do, and he's quite capable of bending the rules, like he did for you at the academy.'

Lester nodded, but as much as he longed to see his sister again, he was still uneasy about the scheme, although it would be fun. 'All right, we'll give it a try, but if the brigadier refuses then that is the end of it. I'm not going to break any rules after having got this far.'

'Nor am I,' James said, not very convincingly. 'Let's go and see him, and with a bit of luck we might be able to get off this afternoon. I've never been to Lincolnshire. Have you?'

'No. Do you think you can find it?'

'Of course we can. Come on, we're wasting time.'

'Sit down, gentlemen.' Alex watched carefully as they settled. He knew James well enough to recognise the glint in his eyes. They were up to something. 'I thought you would be on your way home by now. Is there a problem?'

James gave one of his winning smiles. 'We've been talking and felt it would be a good idea if we had another flight to somewhere we haven't been before, and we would like your permission.'

'You have already passed the navigation tests, with success I might add. Where were you thinking of going?'

'Somewhere like Lincolnshire. We've never been there before. We could land at North Killingholme Airfield and fly back the next day.'

The urge to burst into laughter was strong, but he managed to keep his expression blank. He looked straight at Lester, who hadn't said a word yet. 'You haven't seen your sister for some time?'

'No, sir.'

'And she is in Lincolnshire, I believe.'

'Ruth is as well,' James said. 'She went there two weeks ago.'

'Really? I didn't know that. And do you expect me to believe that your choice of area was just random?'

'Not really, Alex,' James admitted, reverting to addressing him as a family friend and not his commanding officer.

'I would like to see my sister and my mother before we join our squadron, sir. The only way I can do that is to fly up to Lincolnshire before going home.'

'I understand, but you know I can't authorise a private flight.'

'Of course not, sir. Thank you for seeing us.' Lester went to stand up.

'Stay where you are, we haven't finished this discussion yet.'

Now they were in trouble, he thought, as he sat down again.

'Alex! Sir,' James quickly corrected. 'This was

all my idea. Lester is not to blame in any way.'

He ignored James's attempt to protect his friend and looked directly at Lester. 'And do you believe such a flight would be beneficial?'

'As far as navigation goes it isn't necessary, but it would ease my mind to see my sister and my mother before I leave.'

Their officer was silent for a few moments, then surged to his feet and left the room. He was only gone for about five minutes, and when he returned and sat behind his desk, he faced two worried youngsters. 'As you are both so eager to hone your skills, this is what we will do. Two planes are now being fuelled. You will both be in one and I will be in the other. I will follow you, so I expect you to navigate successfully. We will land at North Killingholme, and you will then be free until the next day. I have business to attend to and will return here this evening. I will expect you to arrive back here by midday tomorrow, and this is officially an extra part of your training. Is that clear?'

'Yes, sir.'

'We take off in an hour, so spend that time working out your route. I don't want you to mess this up because it will be going on your record.'

'We won't, sir.'

The boys broke into a run the moment they were outside and headed for the operations room.

'He hasn't given us much time,' Lester remarked, as he studied the map and began marking their route.

'No, but he's damned good at breaking the rules.' James grinned. 'I knew he'd find a way to do this officially. We must be thorough, though,

152

and not let him down.'

In less than an hour they were ready and they ran out to the airfield, only reaching the planes a couple of minutes before Alex.

'Right. Off you go, and remember I will be right behind you watching every move, so I don't want to see you careering around the sky looking for your destination.'

The weather was clear with only a few high wispy clouds, and they were exuberant when they landed without making one mistake. It had been a textbook flight and they felt confident Alex would not be able to find any fault. They jumped out and waited for the officer to walk over to them. He had been on their tail during the entire flight, making notes, they were sure.

'Not bad,' he told them briskly. 'I will expect you back at Hendon tomorrow, and make sure you are on time. We don't want to have to send out a search party for you.'

'No, sir.' They saluted as he turned to go and check in.

He looked over his shoulder. 'Oh, and when you see your sister thank her for her last letter, and tell her I will write in the next few days.'

Lester was dumbfounded, but the brigadier was already marching away. He looked at James. 'He's writing to my sister?'

His friend shrugged. 'First I've heard of it.'

'But he's twice her age.'

James burst out laughing. 'I don't think it's your sister he's interested in, except as a father figure. It's the other female in your family he's taken a special liking to.'

'Our mother? But she's married. Look. I like him very much–'

'He knows that, and you don't need to worry. I've known Alex all my life and he's a very honourable man. He's offering friendship and support to a family he clearly likes.' He gave his friend a knowing look. 'He's a good man to have on your side.'

'You're right about that. I've often thought how different our lives would be if we had a man like that for a father. I'm still going to ask my sister about it, though.'

'Of course. Now, we had better check in, see where we can sleep tonight and then go to the hospital. Hope we can see the girls for a while.'

The moment they walked in the door a soldier saluted them. 'When you are ready, sirs, there's a car waiting to take you to the auxiliary hospital.'

'We didn't ask for transport, did we?' Lester gave his friend a suspicious look.

'It wasn't me.'

The soldier sprung to attention again when a familiar voice behind them said, 'Don't argue about it, gentlemen.'

They spun round.

'The girls are both off-duty in an hour, so you had better get moving. The ward sister has told them you are coming.'

'Thank you, sir.' Lester was more than surprised as he watched the officer march out to his waiting plane. 'He's laughing – when did he arrange all of this?'

'I told you he was a good man to have as a friend.' James was uncharacteristically serious.

'Whatever happens in the war, he'll look after your family. I reckon that's why he is keeping a close contact with them.'

'I'm grateful to know someone will care about them.'

James slapped him on the back, his ready smile in place again. 'Let's get a move on. The girls are waiting for us.'

'Phew! This is quite a place.' Lester gazed at the imposing building, then at the open parkland.

'It was someone's home, but country houses like this are being commandeered for auxiliary hospitals.'

They walked in the door and found the place a hive of activity as a fleet of ambulances was just arriving, and the boys watched as stretcher after stretcher was brought in.

Lester caught the attention of one of the soldiers. 'Can we help?'

'Thank you, sir, but we can handle this. We are used to it and everyone knows what has to be done.'

Within thirty minutes everything was quiet again in the entrance hall and a sister swept up to them. 'Gentlemen, the nurses you are visiting will be delayed. If you would follow me to the canteen, you will be given something to eat while you wait.'

It was another hour before the girls joined them, and as Lester hugged his sister, he could see how fatigued she was – how weary both of them were. 'Rough day?' he asked gently.

'A long one,' she admitted, and then smiled. 'What a lovely surprise. When did you get here?'

'We flew in this afternoon,' James told them. 'Can you spend a little time with us?'

'We've finished for the day.' Ruth poured tea from a fresh pot just arrived at their table, and eyed the empty plates. 'I see you've eaten, but tell us what you have been up to while we have a meal. Did you say you flew here?'

James launched into the story of how they had managed to persuade Alex to let them come, embellishing the tale and making the girls laugh.

Lester watched the strain ease from their faces, and asked jokingly, 'Oh, by the way, the brigadier asked me to thank you for your letter, and he will answer soon.'

'Thank you. I'll look forward to hearing from him again; he writes such amusing letters.' She looked at her brother and chuckled, knowing what he was thinking. 'Does it bother you that Mother and I are writing to your officer?'

'Mother as well?'

'Yes, he asked us if we would the last time he visited. He's a kind man and we are happy to have him as a friend. Also, letters are so important in this war.'

'I told you so.' James then turned to Lillia. 'I said he was a good man to have looking out for you. And talking of writing, I hope both of you are going to find the time to write to us. We are now qualified pilots and about to join a squadron.'

'Congratulations on completing your training,' Ruth told them. 'Of course we will write to you. Do you know where you will be stationed?'

'Not officially yet, but we have a good idea where we're going. We can't tell you, of course.'

James paused. 'Hope we can fly over – I'm not a good sailor.'

That was enough to let the girls know it would be France, and the subject wasn't mentioned again. They spent a lovely evening together, but didn't keep the girls up late as it was obvious they needed their sleep before facing another hectic day.

When the time came for them to leave, Lillia hugged her brother tightly and whispered, 'Be very careful, my precious twin. Remember we have a destiny to fulfil when this dreadful war is over.'

'I will,' he told her affectionately. 'I intend to be present for your first performance at Covent Garden.'

Chapter Seventeen

The sight of his home brought a smile to Lester's face. Learning to fly had been a terrific experience and their flight to Lincolnshire had brought praise from the brigadier on their return. However, inside that house was his beloved piano, and he couldn't wait to play it again. There had been little time lately to spend on music, but for the next three days he was going to make up for that, no matter what his father said. Within a week he would be in France, and all thoughts of a musical career had been set aside until the war was over – if he survived. He was under no illusions about the risks he would be facing, and neither was his sister.

Visiting the hospital had increased his admiration for the medical staff, the girls in particular. They must have to deal with depressing scenes every day and yet they had laughed and joked with them while they had been together. He hadn't missed the strain and sadness in their eyes in unguarded moments, though, but they hid it well.

'Are you going to stand out there all day?'

He laughed and strode forward to hug his mother, but the laughter died when he saw her expression. 'What's the matter?'

'Nothing.' She smiled and led him into the sitting room. 'I miss both of you so much, that's all. How long can you stay?'

'Three days. It would have been longer, but I went to see Lillia before coming home.'

'Oh, I'm pleased you did. How is she?'

He waited while the maid wheeled in a trolley with refreshments, then sat down and began to tell her about the trip he and James had made. 'We wouldn't have been able to do that without Brigadier Stansfield's help.'

Sara nodded. 'He's a good man.'

'Yes, he is. I understand you are both writing to him.'

'He asked if we would the last time he came here, and we are happy to do so. Letters bring comfort and a sense of normality to those away from home.'

'That is certainly true. Will you mind if I spend some time with the professor? It will be the last chance I'll get for a while. When I go back we will be joining a squadron.'

'Of course I don't mind, my dear. It will be

158

wonderful to hear music in this house again. It is so quiet with you both away.'

'I don't suppose Father thinks it is,' he joked.

'He won't know. He isn't here.'

Lester stopped with a sandwich halfway to his mouth. 'Has he finally returned to the army?'

'No, he's disappeared. We haven't seen him for over two weeks. His clothes are gone and anything of value he could easily carry.'

'Why didn't you contact me?'

'There wasn't anything you could do.' She gave a grim smile. 'You know he never tells us where he's going or what he's doing, but if he intended to stay away for this long, then he should have mentioned it.'

'Have you reported him missing to the police?' He was astonished by this news. 'Didn't he even leave a note to say where he was going?'

'No, he just packed up and left without anyone knowing. I am not surprised, really, because he has been acting strangely ever since Alex said the army would like to see him.'

'You think he's run away because of that?'

She nodded. 'That's what it looks like.'

'But that doesn't make sense. Even if the army were looking for him, he had only to refuse to serve again and that would have been the end of it.' He gave his mother a concerned look. 'Why would he disappear like this?'

'I really don't know, and you mustn't let it spoil your leave. He will probably turn up as soon as he runs out of money. He always does.' She poured them both another cup of tea and said brightly, 'I am looking forward to hearing you

159

play again, and the professor will be delighted to have his favourite pupil for a few days.'

The puzzling subject of his father had been dismissed, and he knew his mother well enough to know she would not talk about it again.

At his mother's insistence he spent the next two hours at his own piano, and the sheer joy he felt made him realise just how much he had missed it. He enjoyed flying, but this was where his heart was, seated at the piano. If it hadn't been for the war he would now be back here with his sister. However, dwelling on what might have been would only bring heartache. They were at war, and until that was over it needed everyone's full commitment. For the next few days, though, he could indulge in his passion. Tomorrow he would see the professor and spend some time with him.

Closing the lid of the piano he stood up, feeling relaxed and at peace, then he joined his mother for a drink before dinner.

After an enjoyable meal they were in the sitting room when Adams came in. 'There are two gentlemen asking to see you, madam.'

Sara frowned. She wasn't expecting visitors, and if it was someone they knew then Adams would have announced them. 'Who are they?'

'Policemen.'

Lester was immediately on his feet, concerned at how pale his mother had become. 'Did they say what it was about?'

'I asked, but they would not say.'

Sara had regained her composure. 'Send them in and let us see what this is about.'

'Thank you for seeing us,' the senior man said

the moment they entered the room. Then he looked at Lester, still in his RFC uniform and nodded approval. 'And sir,' he added.

'What can we do for you, Sergeant?' he asked, noting the man's rank.

'We are enquiring about a man we would like to talk to, and one of his associates gave us this address. His name is Barber – Gilbert Barber.'

'No one by that name lives here,' Sara informed them. 'My husband's name is Gilbert, but he is General Gilbert Holdsworth. It appears that you have the wrong address.'

'Do you have a likeness of your husband? This would only be to eliminate him from our enquiries.'

'I'm sorry, I haven't.' She gave a bright smile. 'I never could get my husband to sit still long enough for a picture of any kind.'

'Is he away on active service?'

'He is retired, but not here at the moment.'

Lester listened to the questioning with growing concern. Their father had never told them what his business actually was, and who he dealt with in his everyday life. 'Do you have a description of the man you are looking for?'

'Yes, sir.' The constable removed a small notebook from his top pocket, flipped a few pages, and then read out, 'Around five feet eight, stocky with slightly greying hair, a moustache and short beard.'

'That could fit half the population of London. Do you have anything else?'

'No, sir,' the sergeant replied this time. 'We would know if we saw him, though.'

'Can you tell us what you want him for?'

'We can't do that, sir.'

'I'm sorry we can't be of more help,' Sara told them.

'Well, thank you for answering our questions, and our apologies for disturbing you.' The sergeant smiled at Lester before leaving. 'Good luck to you, sir.'

'Thank you, Sergeant.'

'That was very strange,' he said the moment the policemen had left. 'Why would someone give this address for the man they are looking for?'

'I have no idea. It must be a mistake.'

He studied his mother and couldn't detect any sign of concern on her face, but he was puzzled by how little they knew about his father.

'It must have been distressing to marry a man you knew nothing about.'

'I had no choice, dear. My parents insisted, and arranged marriages were quite common when I was a young girl.'

'Even so, it is hard to understand how they could have done that to their child. I can see now why Father tried to do the same to Lillia.'

'Ah, but she could fight back – I couldn't.'

'Why?'

'Because of something I had done they disapproved of. It was either marry Gilbert or be disowned.'

Lester was finding this hard to understand, and sad that his mother had been treated so cruelly. 'What could be so terrible that they would disown their daughter?'

'In their eyes it was unforgivable, and the only

162

way to avoid a scandal was to do as they said. Within a week of being introduced to Gilbert, we were married.'

'Did you even like him?'

'No, my dear. He had the title of general but I saw at once that he was no gentleman. He has gained a touch of polish over the years, but there is still a rough edge to him – as you well know.'

'We visited our grandparents many times before they died, and I remember them as happy times.'

'They adored you both, and in the end they did apologise for what they had done. I understood and did not bear them any ill will.'

'Will you tell me what you did to make them treat you so harshly?'

'I fell in love with the wrong man.' She smiled at her son. 'And I do not regret that for a moment.'

'Was he of working class, then?'

'No, he was a cultured man of good breeding.'

Lester shook his head, confused. 'Then what was the objection?'

'He was betrothed to another, and my parents would not permit our association to continue. He wanted to break off from the other girl, but that would have caused a scandal that would discredit both of our families.'

'Did you ever see him again?'

'No, but he did send the piano as a gift. I have never seen or heard from him again.'

'My beautiful piano was a gift from the man you once loved?' Lester could hardly believe what he was hearing. 'Why did he do that?'

'It was his way of apologising for the trouble and pain he had caused me.'

'I would like to thank him one day, so will you tell me his name?'

She smiled sadly and shook her head. 'It was such a long time ago and I have already said more than I intended. I will tell you the whole story, but not until you are both here. It wouldn't be right to tell one before the other.'

'I understand, but thank you for talking so frankly with me about a very painful episode from your past.'

'You are grown-up now and easy to talk to. A sympathetic ear has been sadly missing from my life, but there has always been a kind of inner quietness about you. Even as a young child it was there; Lillia was the more volatile and emotional one. Many times I have seen you reach out and touch her, and she calmed immediately, the bright smile back on her face.'

'She has steadied a lot since she's been nursing. I saw that the other day at the hospital.'

'I do believe that is true, thank goodness. I never worried about you. I knew you would cope with whatever you had to face, but after you were parted I had many sleepless nights about Lillia.'

'You didn't need to.' Lester grinned. 'She didn't let Father push her into a disastrous marriage.'

'She was determined not to allow that.' Sara laughed. 'And I do believe she began to have more confidence in herself after that, and I am so pleased she made friends with Ruth. She is a good influence on her.'

'She's a fine girl and they get on well together. James and his family are good people.'

'They are, indeed.' She gave her son a studied

164

look. 'Does Ruth know how you feel about her?'

'No, and I won't tell her yet. We don't know what the future will hold.'

'I pray the future holds the realisation of your dreams for musical careers.'

'Amen to that,' Lester said with feeling. 'And talking of music, I must go and see the professor.'

'Adams will send someone with a message for him. You must make the most of the few days you have here.'

A cloud of sorrow briefly crossed Lester's face, and he nodded. 'I don't think there will be much time to play once I join my squadron.'

Sara's insides clenched with anxiety, but she said nothing.

Chapter Eighteen

'Did you enjoy your leave?' Alex asked when he saw Lester.

'Yes, sir. It was lovely to see my sister and mother again. Thank you for allowing us to do that trip to Lincolnshire.'

'It was my pleasure. And how was your mother?'

'I think she's lonely with both of us away, and our father hasn't been home for a while. He isn't much company for her, I'm afraid.'

'Oh?' That remark caught his attention. 'Is he away on business?'

'We really don't know.' Lester shrugged. 'He never tells us what he's doing. It was a shame he wasn't there because he could have answered the policemen's questions and shown them he wasn't the man they were looking for.'

'Policemen called at your house?'

'It was obviously a mistake. They were looking for a man by the name of Barber and had been given our address as his residence. The description was vague and could have been attributed to half the men in London. They apologised and left.'

'Did the enquiries upset your mother?'

'Good heavens, no.' Lester laughed. 'They were polite and it was obvious they had the wrong information.'

Alex pursed his lips in thought. 'I will be visiting Joshua tomorrow and I'll call in and see your mother.'

'She would be pleased to see you. I am concerned that she is alone so much now.'

'It's on my way.' Alex noted that the boy seemed unconcerned about the strange episode, but he wasn't. He had always felt there was something not right about this man, and had an uneasy feeling for the family he had become far too attached to. He pushed this aside for the moment. 'I see you and James are ready and packed.'

'Yes, sir. We leave at dawn tomorrow by ship, and James isn't looking forward to the journey.'

'I don't suppose he is.' Alex chuckled. 'He only has to look at a boat and he's sick. How about you?'

'No idea, sir. I've never been on the sea before so I'll soon find out.'

'You'll be too busy looking after James to succumb yourself. If I don't see you in the morning, have a smooth trip and a safe stay in France. Keep in touch and let me know how you are getting on.'

'We'll do that,' James declared, bouncing into the room. 'Do you know what it's like over there?'

'I'm not going to gloss over conditions,' he told them seriously. 'It's rough, and you will need all your skill and luck to stay alive. You are excellent pilots, though, and that will increase your chances. I will expect you both back here in good health once the war is over. Is that understood?'

'Yes, sir,' they answered smartly.

'You take care of yourself as well,' James told him. 'Watch those trainee pilots and don't let them crash with you in the plane.'

They all laughed, remembering some of the dicey landings they had all made in training.

'If I survived you two, I can manage anything.' Alex shook their hands instead of saluting. 'Good luck, boys.'

The next day Alex went to see his friend Captain Bob Andrews, who was still at Aldershot.

'Good to see you and you're just in time for lunch. What brings you here?'

'I have news about the elusive General Holdsworth. It might mean nothing, but I can't get the uneasy feeling out of my head. I'm pleased your deployment has been delayed because I need to talk this over with you. It might help to clear my mind.'

'I'm intrigued. Come on, you can talk while we eat.'

Over lunch, Alex told him about the police visit

to Sara's house, and his friend listened with great interest.

'I agree that it is strange, but it might just be a mistake, as young Holdsworth said. The police can receive a lot of false information and they do have to check on everything, however unlikely, before eliminating it.'

'I know that only too well from my father who is still in the police force. That's why I came to you with this. Is there any way you can find out about this Barber fellow?'

'Well, I could try.' Bob studied his friend with concern. 'Are you sure you want to pursue this? It could unearth things it would be better to leave buried.'

'It could also prove to be a mistake, but whatever happens, I like this family and I'm worried about them. I must know.'

'Excuse me for saying this but aren't you getting too close to them?'

'I am, but it's too late to walk away now. See if you can find out anything, please.'

Bob nodded. 'I'm not making any promises, but I'll try.'

'Once again I must apologise for calling unexpectedly,' Alex said when he was shown in to the sitting room, 'but I am on my way to see Joshua and thought I'd come here first.'

'You are always welcome.' Sara greeted him with real pleasure. 'I was sitting here brooding about my children, but your visit has brightened my evening. Are you dining with the professor?'

'Yes. I see him as often as I can. I've known him

168

all my life and he was my very first, and only, music teacher. By the age of ten he told me that I would only ever be competent as I didn't have the soul of a great musician. After listening to your son I now know what he meant.'

'Yes, he can be very forthright in his criticism.' Sara laughed.

'Would you like a drink before your dinner with Joshua?'

'No, thank you. As you know, Lester and James should have arrived in France by now. I watched them leave this morning and they were in good spirits.'

'Looking forward to the adventure, I expect.' She smiled sadly, fearing for her son's safety.

'I have no doubt they are excited, but they are also aware of the seriousness of what they are about to do. They are both excellent pilots; you can be confident on that point.'

'They have had the best training, and I am grateful for your care of my boy.'

'He's grown into a fine man.' He paused before changing the subject and asking, 'Is there any chance of meeting your husband?'

Concern crossed her expression briefly before answering. 'I am sorry, he is not here, and hasn't been for some time. I expect business is keeping him away.'

'Did he not inform you where he was going?'

'He never does. Usually it is only for a day or two, but it is longer this time. I do wish he was more forthcoming about his activities. It would save a great deal of uncertainty.'

Alex leant forward. 'You must be concerned.

Forgive me if I appear presumptuous, but if there is ever anything I can do for you, please do not hesitate to ask.'

'That is so kind of you. I used to be able to talk over my problems with my children.' She sighed. 'I do miss them so much.'

'Talk to me, Sara, as a friend and in strict confidence. Will you do that?'

She nodded, clearly touched by his kindness. 'I fear something may have happened to my husband.'

'Have you reported him missing to the police?'

'Not yet. I was tempted to when the policemen called, but I keep expecting him to walk in as usual.'

'What did the policemen want?' Alex gave no indication that he already knew about the situation.

'They were looking for someone named Barber, I believe it was, and had been given this address by mistake.'

'Ah, that does happen,' he said casually. 'Is there anything you would like me to do about your husband? I do have family connections to the police force.'

'No, no. He will turn up any day now, quite unconcerned about the worry he has caused.'

'Very well, but do contact me if you need help at any time.'

'Thank you. It is a great comfort to know there is someone I can turn to if needs be.'

'Have you seen Sara lately?' Alex asked Joshua.

'I go there every week. She has asked me to look after the piano while Lester is away. That room used to be alive with music and laughter – now there is silence. It is sad. We are sending our young men off to get killed or maimed. It's barbaric. When is this bloody war going to end?'

'I can't see an end in sight.' Alex was concerned; Joshua was very down, and that wasn't like him.

'Do you know that all of my older pupils have gone into the forces?'

Ah, that was what had made him sound so depressed. 'It will end one day and then you'll have some, if not all, of your pupils back.'

'But in what condition, and will they even be interested in music any longer after what they have been through? My delightful Lillia must be facing unimaginable horrors each day, her glorious voice silent. And you've sent my talented boy to get shot at in the air.'

'Josh!' he said sharply. 'Stop this morbid talk. We are all caught up in this mess and are doing the best we can to end it, and that includes the twins. I know they are special to you, but have you thought how Sara is feeling – how every mother is feeling? They are dreading every knock on the door, and I didn't send that boy anywhere. He was offered the chance to fly and took it willingly, and he's a damned good pilot. Would you rather he was in the trenches? Do you know the survival time of a young officer there? No, of course you don't, but I can tell you it is frighteningly short. He has a slightly better chance with his skill as a pilot of surviving longer.'

Joshua was looking at his family friend in astonishment. 'Good heavens, I have never heard or

171

seen you so angry. I do apologise for pouring out my selfish misery to you, and thank you. I needed to be shaken out of my troubled mood, and you have certainly done that.'

'We have got to remain positive and believe that those we love will come out of this war relatively unscathed. If we let all hope disappear, then we are finished.'

'You are absolutely right.' Joshua's expression cleared and he smiled. 'When peace is finally declared the world will be hungry for music, and I shall be able to get the twins back where they belong. I will have a lot of work to do to bring them back to the standard needed for success. Let us enjoy a pleasant meal and push aside all thoughts of death and destruction for a while.'

Relieved to see Joshua back to his normal, cheerful self, they left the house.

'What do you think about the visit Sara had by the police?'

'You know about that?' Alex asked.

'I was there the other day and Cook told me. She said they were looking for a criminal and had been given that address. There was a lot of gossip among the staff, of course, and I don't know how much of it was true. They don't like the general, so that might have made them think he was up to no good. I've never had anything to do with him, but Sara is from a highly respected family, and the twins are fine youngsters. The police were obviously given the wrong information, which is a shame because it has caused unwanted gossip. That charming lady has enough to cope with without this.'

'Yes, she has,' Alex agreed. 'I'm going to see if I can clear things up.'

'Ah, I thought you might. Will your father help?'

'I'll ask when I see him. He might already know something about this man they are looking for.'

Joshua nodded. 'It would be good to get the whole story and put an end to the speculation.'

'I'll do my best.'

'You're a good friend to them.' Joshua gave Alex a concerned glance. 'I hope that is all you are. That family is fragile enough without you adding another complication.'

'Surely you know me better than that?' he answered sharply. 'I do not pursue married women.'

'Of course you don't. Forgive me but I am uncommonly fond of them.'

Alex took a deep breath. 'Then they have two friends who are concerned about them.'

Chapter Nineteen

'Are you replacement pilots?' A harassed officer rushed up to them the moment they arrived.

'Yes, sir,' James told him.

'Where are the others? I asked for six.'

'We were the only two on the ship, sir.' Lester studied the man carefully and concluded that he could only be the same age as them, but the lines of strain on his face made him look older.

He swore under his breath, and then smiled apologetically at them. The transformation was surprising as the age dropped off him. 'My name is Colonel Preston, though we are very informal here and the pilots usually call me Preston. I run this station. You are badly needed and a welcome addition to the squadron.'

'Thank you, sir. My name is Lester Holdsworth and my friend is James Anderson.' They handed over their papers.

'Sergeant!' he called and the man appeared immediately. 'Take these gentlemen to their quarters, and make sure they know where everything is.'

'Sir.'

'I'll see you when you have settled in, and–'

The sound of a plane coming in caught their attention, and it was clearly in trouble. Without anyone needing to issue orders there was sudden activity all around them as men and vehicles rushed to the landing field. Lester and James ran with them as well, and everyone waited with bated breath as the plane dipped and swung from side to side, smoke pouring out of the engine.

'Can you tell who it is?' Preston asked the sergeant.

'Jimmy Eldrich, I think, sir.'

'I can't see any sign of the other two.'

The sergeant scanned the sky. 'They might have landed somewhere else.'

'Let's hope so.'

The plane hit the ground with force and tipped onto its side, the wings tearing up and breaking apart.

Preston caught hold of Lester and James as they made to run forward to help the stricken pilot. 'Stay here! The rescue teams know what to do. I don't want you injured before you've even flown a mission.' Then he ran to the plane.

The pilot was pulled from the wreck and loaded into an ambulance which drew away at once.

The officer walked back to them with the sergeant. 'That was only his second flight into the war zone, and I pray we haven't lost the other two as well.'

'Was he still alive, sir?' Lester asked.

Preston nodded. 'I doubt he'll fly again, though. Go and settle in to your quarters and then come and see me. After that I suggest you visit Saint-Omer this afternoon and relax after your journey. It's an interesting place and this might be your only chance for a while. No alcohol though. I need you sharp and ready to fly tomorrow.'

'Understood, sir.'

'Wonder what he meant about this being our only chance to see the town?' James asked as they followed the sergeant.

'We'll be kept too busy I expect, or he doesn't consider our chances of surviving for long very good.'

James grimaced and asked the sergeant, 'How long do pilots usually last?'

'Depends on how good or lucky they are.'

'Give us an example,' James suggested.

'The longest are still flying after nearly two years, the shortest two days.' He turned his head and grinned at them. 'But you seem like a couple of lively pilots and I expect to see you around for a long time.'

'We intend to be because we are good and lucky. Also my friend is the best damned pianist you'll ever hear, and he's postponed his career as a concert pianist to fight this blasted war.'

'Really, sir. I like a bit of classical music myself,' the sergeant told them.

'I'll send you tickets for his first concert.'

'I'll keep you to that promise.' The sergeant indicated two doors. 'Those are your quarters. The dining room is on the ground floor and you can go there any time. They never close.'

'That's good to know because James is always looking for food,' Lester joked.

'Come back to the operations building when you've settled in and had something to eat.'

The rooms were small and sparsely furnished, but the beds were clean and comfortable. They had only brought the essentials so it didn't take them long to unpack.

'Shall we see what there is to eat?' James asked as he wandered in to Lester's room. 'I think my stomach will take something now I'm off that blasted boat.'

They walked down the stairs and Lester gave him an amused glance. 'What did you mean by offering the sergeant free tickets? Are you planning on being my agent?'

'Of course I am. I've got good connections, and I'll be part of your family when I marry Lillia.'

'Does my sister know about this?'

'Not yet. I can't do anything about it until the war is over. It wouldn't be possible with us miles apart, but it's a foregone conclusion.'

'When did you come to this ... er ... conclusion?'

'I knew the moment I saw her.'

'You do realise it wouldn't be a comfortable roses-round-the-door kind of marriage, don't you?'

'Of course I do. She's an artist and that is to be her life, but she will need someone by her side to love and support her, just as you will need Ruth.'

'You are marrying me off as well? Don't I even get a choice?' Lester exclaimed. 'We might not even survive this war. What we are going to do is damned dangerous.'

'We are going to come through this – all four of us. I don't believe in chance or coincidence. Everything happens for a reason, and you and Lillia are meant to have successful musical careers, and the four of us are meant to be together. Nothing can change that, not even the war. Just you hold on to that every time we take to the air.'

Lester shook his head in bemusement. 'Your mind works in a strange way, my friend, but I hope you are right.'

'I am, trust me,' he grinned. 'I am not going to die and leave your beautiful sister to someone else who might not look after her as well as I intend to. And you've got too much talent for it to be wasted in such a senseless way.'

'For goodness' sake, let's get some food in you. I think you are light-headed from that sea trip.'

'It isn't my case.' Alex's father looked thoughtful after listening to his son's account of the visit Sara had had from the police. 'I can't imagine they would visit such a prestigious address unless they were sure about their information. Come with me, I know someone who might be able to shed some light on this.'

Charles Stansfield was well known at the station they went to as he had worked there before being promoted to superintendent. He walked straight in, greeting people on the way to the man he wanted to see.

'Ah, good, you're here, Tony. This is my son and we need your help.'

The middle-aged man smiled at Charles and shook Alex's hand. 'Good to meet you, sir. What can I do for you?'

He listened intently while Alex explained, then said, 'I do know of the case. We have known for a long time that there was a smuggling operation going on, but have only recently received some useful information, and the name of Barber as the head of the operation.'

'What are they smuggling?' Charles asked.

'Up to now, anything that would make a profit, but with the outbreak of war they have changed tactics. We believe they are now concentrating on guns and explosives. There have been several reports of a few missing arms at ordinance depots around the country, though how they got in such heavily guarded places is a mystery.'

Alex drew in a deep breath. 'Inside help, perhaps?'

'That is being looked into. We caught one man breaking in to a clothing factory and he gave us some information about this gang, but not enough to make any arrests, as yet. He told us he was offered a job with them, but turned it down, and it was from him we got the Holdsworth address. We thought it might be one of the servants, but they have all been thoroughly investigated and cleared. That leaves the husband, and we have been unable to track him down. He never seems to be around and we need to question him so he can be eliminated from our enquiries – or not, as the case may be.'

'How reliable is this informant of yours?' Charles asked after seeing the look of shock on his son's face. 'My son is a friend of Mrs Holdsworth and her children. He will attest to their fine character.'

'Indeed, I do. Your informant must be trying to lead you astray.'

'That may be the case, sir, and we have challenged him about this, but he still insisted that the head of the group lives at that address. He said he knows because he followed him there one night to find out who he was.'

Alex shook his head in denial.

'We have to follow up every lead, no matter how doubtful.'

'I understand that, but knowing the family as I do, what I'm hearing is unbelievable.'

'You say you know the lady and her children, sir, but do you also know General Holdsworth as well?'

'I have never met him, and can't vouch for his character,' Alex had to admit. 'I am only acquainted with his wife and children, but this can't be right. He is a general.'

'Is he, sir? I know this is hard for you to understand, but it is the only line of enquiry we have at this time, and must pursue it. No one in that

179

household could tell us what kind of business he is involved in. The only activity anyone mentioned was import–export, and that could mean anything.'

'Have you looked in to that?' Charles asked.

'We have. Before the war Holdsworth did ship in cargoes reported to be tea, spices and many household goods. Now most of the merchant ships are bringing in cargoes needed for the country. There is no evidence that he is still in business, but the name of Barber has appeared as the head of a group dealing in arms.'

'I don't see the connection,' Alex said.

'Neither do I.' Charles pursed his lips. 'If you suspect he is the same person and has just changed his name it is stretching things too far, in my opinion. If they are stealing arms, then who can they sell them to?'

'Only a few guns have gone missing from the depots, and we believe they are now working the docks. We're not sure who their buyers are, but we believe there would be a ready market for them.'

'Again, the docks would be too well guarded, especially where military equipment is concerned,' Charles protested.

'No security is foolproof. At first only small amounts were missing, and it was assumed the manifests were incorrect, but the items have increased. We've got to find these criminals and stop them. There is no telling who they are selling to.'

'Do you have any concrete proof someone at that address is involved?' Charles wanted to know.

'None, and that is why we visited the house in the hope of clearing up this matter once and for all. We were prepared to interview everyone there and then turn our attention elsewhere, but we can't find the man and his wife doesn't know where he is, and that makes us suspicious.' The policeman turned to Alex. 'I must ask you not to divulge any of this to Mrs Holdsworth or her children. I met the son and he appeared to be a fine man.'

'He is. I have had the pleasure of teaching him to fly, and his sister is a nurse at a military hospital.'

'Then we mustn't worry them with something that could turn out to be nothing but a pack of lies. We know our informant is only talking to us in the hope of receiving a reduced sentence, but he won't name any of the other men involved.'

'I would like to take an interest in this case,' Charles told his friend. 'Would you keep me informed of any progress?'

'I'll let you know the moment we have a break in the case. We've got every available man working on this and must get a break soon.'

'There isn't anything else we can do at the moment,' Charles told his son when they left the station. 'All we can do is wait and see what they come up with.'

'You can phone me at Hendon if you hear anything.'

'I'll do that, and don't worry, that informant doesn't sound reliable to me.'

'I expect you're right, but I don't like this at all.'

Chapter Twenty

'Ah, you've seen the notice.' Ruth stood beside Lillia in the nurses' room and they both stared at the noticeboard.

'I've already volunteered.'

'Me too, but our families aren't going to be happy about this.'

'I know, and I don't like the thought of leaving my mother, but I've got to go. Lester is out there and I want to be as close to him as possible. Does that sound silly to you?'

'Not at all. I know how hard it is for you to be apart, but it must be of some comfort to you to know that James is with him. I also believe we can be of more help in France. We've been caring for the injured now and our experience will be useful. We should have a good chance of being accepted.'

At the end of their shift they were called in to the matron's office, and she actually smiled when they walked in. 'You have both volunteered to serve in a military field hospital, and before I accept your offers I want to give you a chance to withdraw your application.'

'I understand the dangers, Matron, and I still want to go,' Lillia replied without hesitation.

'I haven't changed my mind either,' Ruth said.

'Very well, if you are certain, I will accept your requests. You are two of my most capable nurses and I will be sorry to lose you, but the job you will be doing is absolutely vital. The wounded have to be treated before the hospital ships can bring them back. You will be going over on one of these ships making a return journey, and that is not without danger. They are being attacked by U-boats which do not appear to be making any distinction between merchant and hospital ships.'

'We are prepared for the risks.' Lillia glanced at her friend who nodded agreement.

The matron smiled again. 'You will be made very welcome in France. Go and pack your bags for three days' leave, then return here. I am sorry it can't be longer but the ship will be sailing then, and the need is desperate. You will receive a full update on where you are going and what to expect when you get there, then you will be taken to the ship. Good luck to you both.'

'Thank you, Matron,' they said together.

The girls ran to the nurses' quarters, not willing to waste a moment of their precious leave, as it could be some time before they saw their homes again.

When they were settled on the train, both girls gave a huge pent-up sigh, wondering what they had let themselves in for.

'They aren't wasting any time,' Ruth remarked, 'and I'm pleased about that. It gives us less time to worry about it, and the sooner we are on our way, the better.'

'I agree. I wouldn't want to be hanging around, waiting to go. It won't be easy telling Mother, though.'

Sara was delighted to see her daughter, but the

joy soon evaporated when she heard her news. She hadn't considered that her daughter would be going to the war zone as well. Her belief had been that as a nurse she would be needed here. Having both of her children in the thick of the fighting filled her with fear, but she knew this was what so many families were facing.

'I don't want to upset you, Mother, but do you see that I must do this?'

'I understand, my dear, and I'm proud of you and Lester. You will both be constantly in my thoughts and prayers. When do you go?'

'Within the week. They are desperate for nurses out there.'

'They will be getting two of the best.' Sara hugged her daughter. She had changed so much; she was now a mature and confident young girl, but then the demand made by the war was changing everyone. 'Let's make the most of these three days together.'

It was the next day before Lillia realised she hadn't seen her father, and when she asked it was apparent that her mother was concerned.

'I haven't seen him for three weeks and I do admit to being worried. It is not like him to disappear for so long.'

'Didn't he tell you where he was going and how long he would be away?'

'Not a word, though that is not unusual, as you know – what is unusual is the length of time he has been away. I am at a loss to know what to do.'

'Have you checked the local hospitals in case he has been taken ill?'

'I visited three but he wasn't in any of them.'

'I think you should report it to the police. Father has only been absent for short periods before.'

'I know you're right, my dear, but after that visit from the police I do hesitate to tell them about this.' Sara sighed deeply. 'With both of you away I admit to feeling lonely with no one to talk to.'

'Alex is a good listener, so why don't you take him into your confidence?'

'He has shown considerable kindness towards us, and I have mentioned this to him, but I don't like to burden him with our problems too much. He has more than enough to do trying to train enough pilots for the RFC.'

'Something has to be done.' Lillia began to pace the room. 'I now wish I wasn't going away and leaving you on your own.'

'You mustn't think like that. You need to go where your skills can be of the most help, and I accept that. I should not have worried you with this. He will probably walk in one day completely unconcerned about the distress he might have caused. Please, don't worry about me.' Sara smiled at her daughter. 'I am quite capable of looking after myself; I have had plenty of practice over the years.'

'I dare say he will turn up when he runs out of money again, as he always does, but this is not his usual behaviour. Nevertheless, I don't think this should be ignored for much longer. Perhaps you could ask Adams to make some enquiries for you?'

'Definitely not. There is enough gossip amongst the servants since the visit by the police, and I expect half of London knows about it by now.'

'Yes, I can see that it wouldn't be wise to stir up more gossip. Could you drop a casual remark that he is helping the army as an adviser? That might explain his long absence and stop all the speculation.'

'What a good idea. Why didn't I think of that? I'll let that piece of information slip out while I'm talking to Cook.'

Lillia grinned. 'That should have the news circulating with speed, but I still think some effort should be made to find out where he is. Would you prefer me to contact Alex?'

'No, my dear. Talking with you has helped to clear my mind. I am worrying over nothing. Being on my own so much with no one to discuss problems with seems to throw all things out of proportion. As you have said, he will return the moment he runs out of money.'

Alex frowned as he read Lillia's letter. It was brief and apologised for troubling him, but would he call on her mother the next time he was in London, as she was going away for some time and felt her mother was low in spirit and in need of company. His thoughts turned to the police enquiry and wondered if Sara was more worried about the police visit than she had made out to him. He folded the letter and put it in his pocket. He had better see when he could have a day's leave, or more, if possible.

With the urgent need to train more pilots it was nearly a week before he could get to London, and Sara was clearly delighted to see him.

'What a lovely surprise, and your visit is particu-

186

larly welcome at this time. Lillia should now be on her way to France and, with both of my children involved in the war, I am in need of company.'

'She told me she was going in a letter I received from her. You must be proud of your brave youngsters.'

Sara clenched her hands together showing the strain she was under. 'I am, but I am also afraid for their safety.'

'That is understandable. Lillia also mentioned in her letter that your husband has still not returned, and asked me to call when I had time.'

'Oh, she shouldn't have done that. I told her we couldn't burden you with our problems.'

'I would be pleased to help in any way I can, even if it is only to provide a sympathetic ear.'

'That would be helpful, if you don't mind listening to my worries?'

'Not at all, please tell me what has happened.'

'As you already know my husband has gone away and forgotten to tell me where he was going and for how long. I expect he was in a hurry and probably thought he had already mentioned it to me. He has taken two suitcases with all of his personal items.' He had also taken some small items of value, but she didn't say anything about these.

'I see.' He relaxed back in the chair, trying to keep the conversation casual. She was obviously under great strain, but whether that was because of her children or her husband, he was not yet sure. 'And how long has the general been away now?'

'A little over four weeks, but it isn't unusual for him to be away on business.' She didn't look at

187

him while she poured them more tea from the trolley the maid had brought in. She was silent for a moment and then her composure shattered. 'What should I do, Alex? I am normally used to dealing with problems on my own, but in this case I find myself unable to decide what to do.'

'As this long absence is unusual my advice would be to report it to the police. They have the resources to search for him.' He took the cup from her and his feeling of unease was growing. There was something very wrong here, but would she allow him to help? He really hoped so because Lillia had mentioned that her mother didn't have anyone she could turn to for help and advice.

'I hesitate to report him missing.'

'May I ask why?'

'I am afraid.'

She had uttered those words so softly he had only just caught them. Why would this charming, intelligent woman be afraid to report her husband missing to the authorities? 'There is no need to be afraid of the police.'

'I am not, but there is something I should have told my children, and I am afraid it might be uncovered before I can tell them about it. I have tried several times, but have not been able to bring myself to relate the entire story. Lester knows some, but not all. I am a coward. And now they are both away for goodness knows how long, and I must be the one to tell them.'

'You are afraid that this – whatever it is – might be uncovered and they hear it from some source other than you?'

'Yes,' she told him. 'I promised to explain when

188

they were older, but I have been putting it off. As I've said, I am a coward.'

'I don't believe that,' he told her gently. 'You have been trying to protect them, and that is only natural.'

'I have been protecting them from this knowledge from the moment they were born.'

He was not surprised by her declaration. It had been clear from their first meeting that something wasn't right with this family. Whatever it was, though, was not a case of an uncaring husband and father, as he had thought. 'If I could promise you that anything discovered in the search for your husband would not become common knowledge, would you trust me?'

'I doubt you could make such a promise.' She dredged up a smile. 'But, of course, I trust you to give me sound advice.'

'My father is a police superintendent, so will you allow me to tell him about your husband and ask if there is any way he can give discreet help? I can assure you that anything he discovers will be between you and him. No one else will be involved, not even me, if that is the way you want it.'

'Would he do that?' A glimmer of hope crossed her face.

'I can ask.'

She was more at ease when he left an hour later, and he went straight to his father. Luckily he was at their London home while he attended to some police business.

'I need to ask a favour,' he said, the moment he walked in.

His father laughed. 'Again. Is that the only reason for your unexpected visits?'

'I am always pleased to see you, of course,' he joked, 'but in this case it is.'

'Well, at least enjoy a drink with me while you tell me about this favour you need.'

He listened intently to the account of his son's conversation with Sara. 'Hmm, I don't suppose she told you what she was frightened might be uncovered?'

'No, and I didn't ask. Is there any way you can discreetly make a search for her husband?'

'I doubt it. Do you think his disappearance is connected to that visit from the police?'

'Unlikely because he had been away for about a week when they called, so it's more likely this is unrelated.'

'Perhaps, but you must realise that this immediately heaps more suspicion upon him. I'll keep the enquiries as low key as possible, but I can't make any promises. If anything untoward is discovered, I will do my best to contain it from becoming public knowledge. I can't do more than that. What on earth can that delightful woman have in her past that makes her so fearful?'

'I have no idea,' Alex admitted. 'But in an unguarded moment she said she had been protecting her children from the moment of their birth. She didn't say what she had been protecting them from, though.'

'That points to an abusive husband, which wouldn't surprise me. I would say she is afraid of him, and doesn't want society to know he has been mistreating her.' Charles shook his head. 'I know you are fond of Sara and her children, but please be careful, son. I have a nasty feeling that this could get unpleasant.'

'You could be right about him being abusive, and that could be why the children have needed to be shielded from him, but if so she has done a good job. They don't appear to like him very much, but are not afraid of him. The general could also return with a perfectly reasonable answer, and all this speculation will have been for nothing.'

'Let's hope that is the case.'

Chapter Twenty-One

Lester jumped out of his plane and strode over to his friend who had just landed. 'That was nasty. Are you all right?'

'Still in one piece.' His smile was grim. 'We've only been here two weeks and this is the second time I've come back with holes in my plane. Look at this – I can put my hand through it. Did you get back undamaged?'

'A couple of bullet holes, but they can easily be repaired. I saw you careering around trying to shake off that enemy plane and I came in to try and distract him.'

'Thanks, he would have got me for sure without your help. We were lucky this time. Come on, let's get something to eat. I'm starving.'

'There's a surprise.'

The friends were laughing as they sat down, relieving the tension of a dangerous mission by joking about it.

About halfway through their meal, Lester gasped and the colour drained from his face.

'What's the matter?' James was immediately on his feet and grabbing Lester's shoulder. 'Are you hurt and didn't tell me?'

'Lillia,' he croaked, breathing hard and closing his eyes.

A medic was at the next table and immediately came to help. 'Take it easy, sir, and tell me what's wrong.'

When he didn't speak, the man turned to James, who was close to panic. 'Is your friend injured?'

James shook his head. 'I don't know what's wrong. All he's said is his sister's name. They are twins. When one is hurt or troubled, the other one feels it as well.'

The medic nodded. 'I've heard about twins who have a rapport with each other in that way. Is your sister hurt, sir?'

'Dying...'

'Oh, dear God!' James was now as white as his friend. 'She's a nurse and is on a hospital ship coming to France. My cousin is also with her.'

'Let's get you to the sickbay, sir.' The medic tried to get Lester on his feet, but he refused to move.

'I don't need medical help,' he managed to say. 'I'll be all right in a minute.'

'Do you know what's happened?' James asked urgently.

'You know it doesn't work like that. All I get are my sister's feelings. Something bad has happened. Perhaps she's had an accident.'

'Well, if she has then she's in the right place to receive the best treatment.' James tried to sound hopeful, but he didn't doubt his friend's feelings. It was uncanny; he had seen it a few times with them, but never with such a violent reaction. He could feel Lester trembling.

The medic looked equally concerned and beckoned to another man. He scribbled a note and handed it to him without saying a word. The man read it, nodded, and left the room. Then he ordered strong tea and insisted Lester drink two cups.

'Feeling better?' James asked.

Lester looked up. 'I just feel numb now. Perhaps it was a delayed reaction to that scrap we just had. I thought you were finished for sure; for heaven's sake be more careful in future.'

The man the medic had sent on an errand came back and returned the paper. After reading it the medic drew in a deep breath. 'Nothing?'

'Not yet, sir. I'll let you know if anything comes through.'

He nodded and turned back to Lester. 'I still think you should come to the sickbay, sir. You are very pale and in obvious distress.'

'No, but thank you for your concern. Whatever it was is wearing off now. Just give me a couple of minutes and I'll be fine.'

'Very well. Try and finish your meal now. I'm here if you need me.'

'Isn't there a damned piano in this place?' James exploded, still agitated by his friend's bad turn.

'Piano?' The medic was mystified.

'He and his twin sister are musicians. She has a

glorious voice...' His voice broke when he thought of the girl he loved who might be in danger. 'And Lester is the best damned pianist you'll ever hear. Playing is his joy and in times of trouble it is what he needs.'

'Don't upset yourself, sir,' the medic told James. 'I know you have both just returned from a dangerous mission and, as your friend said, this might be a delayed reaction. If brother and sister are as close as you say, it would be natural for his thoughts to turn to her.'

'No,' he insisted firmly. 'He's always calm and in control. It would take more than that dicey mission to upset him like this.'

Lester took a deep breath, lifted his head and drank a glass of water the medic handed him.

'Good, your colour is returning. You are feeling better, sir?'

'Is something wrong with your sister, or are you going down with some illness?' James interjected.

'I don't know. I can't feel anything. She's gone.'

'What do you mean "she's gone"? Don't say things like that, Lester, you are frightening the life out of me.'

'Whatever was making me feel bad has gone – that's what I mean.'

'Lillia, Lillia.' Ruth thrashed about in the water, calling with all the strength she had left. It had all happened so quickly. There had been a huge explosion, and then another and the ship was already tipping onto her side. There had only been time to launch a few lifeboats before the ship went down, and after that there had been no option but

194

to jump from the stricken ship. Had her friend made it? Was she in a lifeboat or the water? She had to find her.

Someone grabbed her. 'Save your strength, Nurse. Let's get to that boat over there.'

'I must find my friend.' She gasped as a wave swamped her and strong hands pulled her to the surface.

'Can you swim?'

She was coughing so much all she could do was shake her head.

'Hold on to me.'

As he towed her towards the boat she could hear people shouting for help. 'There are others in the water. We must help them.'

'We will when we are safely on that boat. Now, save your breath and kick your legs.'

With her strength failing she did as ordered. It seemed ages before she was being hauled on board and finally looked at the man who had saved her. He was one of the doctors. 'Thank you,' she managed to say.

The small boat was already quite full, but the seaman in charge was determined to pick up as many as he could, and three more lifeboats were doing the same. They found some hanging on to any piece of wreckage they could find to keep afloat, but others were already dead.

With tears running unnoticed down her cheeks, Ruth helped all she could, and continually scanned the sea for her friend. The few boats had joined up, and to her dismay, Lillia was not on any of them.

It had become very quiet now and hope was

fading of finding any more alive. The eerie silence was unnerving.

'There are some boxes floating over there,' the doctor pointed out.

When they reached the wreckage it didn't appear as if there were any survivors and they were about to move away when one of the sailors shouted, 'Go closer. I think I saw something.'

The light was fading and it was difficult to see, but when they reached the spot the man was pointing at, they saw three people hanging on to a large packing case.

One of the survivors raised a hand and when they reached out to pull him aboard, he said, 'These two first, they are unconscious.'

'Are they still alive?' the doctor asked.

'Think so.'

'Thank God you came,' the man gasped when they were all safely on the boat. 'We wouldn't have lasted much longer, and my strength was failing. I was trying to keep all three of us above water.'

The doctor and Ruth immediately went to see if the other two were alive, and when they turned the woman over Ruth cried out in distress. 'Lillia, please be alive.'

The doctor was already checking for a pulse. 'She is, but if we are not rescued quickly she might not survive. She's taken a nasty bash on the head and has been in the water for too long.'

Ruth began to try and rub some warmth back in to her friend. 'She's so cold. Do we have anything we can cover her with?'

'We didn't have time to collect such things, and everything in the boat is wet,' the sailor explained.

'All we can do is wait and hope someone got a message out before the ship went down.' The doctor gave Ruth a grim smile. 'There are others in a bad way and I need your help, Nurse.'

'Of course, Doctor.' Reluctantly she left Lillia. She was still alive, but in these conditions there was very little they could do for her.

Once everyone had been made as comfortable as possible, Ruth gathered her friend in her arms to try and give her some warmth. She dozed on and off, and thought the night would never end. Even more worrying was the fact that Lillia showed no sign of regaining consciousness. There was one thing they were all grateful for, though, the blessing that they hadn't been carrying wounded. The thought of what would have happened then was too terrible to contemplate.

It had been daylight for some time when a man on lookout shouted and pointed to a dot on the ocean. Everyone in the boat began to shout and wave their arms. One man took off his white shirt, stood up and began to wave it. The same thing was happening in the other boats near them. The ship was coming straight for them but was still no more than the size of a toy.

'Save your breath,' a sailor ordered. 'They can't hear us yet, but keep on waving.'

Suddenly Ruth felt Lillia move and make a sound. 'Doctor, I think she's coming round.'

They sat her up and, although she didn't open her eyes, she smiled and began to sing, sending a sense of calm over the excited occupants of the small boat.

James was worried. Lester had barely said a word since yesterday and they were about to go on a mission to photograph enemy lines. If his condition didn't change soon then it might not be safe for him to fly. He went and stood beside his friend who was staring out at the airfield. 'I can do this on my own,' he suggested.

'No need.' He turned his head and smiled. 'Whatever happened is over now. I feel fine.'

'Thank God.' James sagged in relief. 'Was it a bad feeling about your sister?'

'I'm not really sure. We were very in tune when we were younger, but as we've got older that intuition, one might call it, has begun to fade. I felt bad and immediately thought it was Lillia in trouble, but it was probably something else that upset me.'

'I hope so! You frightened the life out of me.' He slapped his friend on the back. 'Come on, we've got a mission to fly, and don't you ever do that again.'

Chapter Twenty-Two

For two days, and at great risk to itself, the rescue ship searched for more survivors. While this was going on the crew began to make a list of those rescued, and it soon became apparent that many had died.

'What a senseless loss of life,' Ruth raged in her grief. Nurses and doctors they had worked with at the hospital were among the missing. 'The ship was clearly marked. Why did they attack it?'

'Perhaps they thought it was carrying arms to France under the guise of a medical ship.' Lillia was propped up in a bed, warm, comfortable and already recovering. 'We are alive and that means we will have to work hard to make up for those who have died.'

Ruth nodded. 'I was frantic when I couldn't find you, and when we finally dragged you out of the sea I thought you were going to die.'

'So did I.'

'It was such a relief when you came round. There was a ship coming towards us and everyone was so excited that the boat was rocking dangerously. You started to sing and that calmed them down. I was so happy, but now we know how many were lost, that happiness seems wrong.'

'No, it wasn't. I heard the excited shouting; everyone was happy they were going to be rescued and there's nothing wrong about that. It was a natural reaction.'

'I don't think anyone considered it might be an enemy ship,' Ruth laughed. 'We were desperate to get out of those wet, cramped lifeboats and receive proper help for the injured.'

'You are supposed to be resting,' the doctor scolded as he arrived in the sickbay. 'You are going to be needed when we reach the field hospital.'

'We are already fit enough to work,' Lillia told him.

'Hmm.' He examined her head. 'Do you know what hit you?'

'I think I hit something when I jumped off the

ship. It was at a crazy angle when I leapt over the side.'

'Well, you are doing all right. Another day of bed rest and you should be fine, but tell me if you get headaches or blurred vision.'

'I will.'

He sat on the end of the bed and asked, 'Do you know why you were singing in the lifeboat?'

'I heard all the shouting and being confused I thought I was performing in an opera.'

'Oh, which one?'

'*Madame Butterfly*. It is what I was training for before the war began. My brother used to make me sing it until I got it perfect.'

'They are twins,' Ruth explained, 'and excellent musicians.'

'Really?' The doctor settled more comfortably, obviously interested. 'Is your brother a singer as well?'

'No, he's a pianist.' Her expression clouded. 'I must get word to him. He'll be so worried.'

'I don't suppose the news has broken about the sinking of the ship yet.'

'He might have felt something. If one of us is sick, hurt or troubled in any way, the other usually knows without being told.'

He frowned and began to take her pulse.

Ruth grinned. 'It's quite true. They seem to be tuned in to each other. It can happen sometimes with twins.'

'So I've heard.' He still looked doubtful. 'Is your brother in the forces?'

'He's a pilot in the Royal Flying Corps, and is in France.'

'Do you know where in France?'

'Saint-Omer, or near there.' She frowned, trying to remember the name of the base. 'I think he's at a place called Wizernes Airfield, but I might not have that right.'

The doctor stood up. 'I'll go to the wireless room and see if they will send a message.'

'Would they let you do that?' she asked eagerly.

'I'll say it's important to your recovery,' he joked, giving a cheeky wink.

'My cousin is also there with him. Pilot James Anderson.'

'Right. I'll see what I can do.'

As he strode out of the sickbay, Ruth raised her eyebrows to her friend. 'I do believe our young Doctor Horton has taken a fancy to you. Did I tell you he saved my life?'

Lillia shook her head. 'We were both very lucky, weren't we? If it hadn't been for two courageous men we would have drowned. The man who kept me afloat has popped in a couple of times to see how I am. How do you thank them for your life?'

'By regaining full health and doing the job we volunteered to do. I'm sure that's all the thanks they need.'

'You're right, of course, but they have lost friends and must be hurting. I just wish there was something I could do to help them.'

'You could sing for them. Music is very uplifting. The crew of this Royal Navy ship have had the distressing task of searching for everyone who was on our ship – dead or alive – so we won't be in France until tomorrow. Why don't you give a little recital after dinner tonight?'

Lillia sat up straight, her eyes alight with interest. 'Do you think they would like that?'

'I'm sure they would.'

She began to look doubtful. 'But I'd have to sing unaccompanied.'

'There is probably someone on board who can play an instrument of some kind.' Ruth stood up. 'I'll have a word with the captain. He might know who could join you. Will you do it if he agrees?'

'Yes. I would like to bring a little musical harmony to ease the sadness everyone is feeling.'

'Good. I'll see what I can sort out, but you rest now and leave it all to me.'

Lillia had been asleep and was woken by the sound of voices. She opened her eyes and was surprised to see the doctor, captain, her friend and two sailors standing round the bed.

'Are you sure she is well enough?' the captain was asking.

'I am quite fit,' she replied before the doctor could answer. 'I can't wait to get out of this bed and stretch my legs.'

'I am asking the doctor, young lady, not you,' the captain scolded. 'I'm not having you collapsing while you are performing.'

'I won't do that, sir.'

He studied her thoughtfully. 'I must admit it is a good idea, but can you really sing?'

She grabbed a robe, stood up and glared at him. 'If you are going to insult me then I had better prove to you that I have enough talent to entertain your crew.'

The captain's mouth twitched at the corners

when he saw her reaction, and turned to the doctor. 'That dunking in the sea hasn't dulled her spirit, I see.'

'Not a bit, sir. I believe opera is to be her chosen profession.'

'Ah, eminently suited to that, I'd say.'

'When you have finished discussing me, can we get on with this please?'

The captain inclined his head, openly smiling now.

One of the sailors was holding an accordion and the other a harmonica. She tightened the belt of the robe and asked, 'Do you know any classical music or only the popular tunes?'

'I can play both,' the man with the accordion told her, 'and Fred here is good at improvising. You sing and we'll follow you as best we can.'

This had all the makings of a disaster, she admitted to herself, and these men thought so too. She would just have to change their minds. Any accompaniment was better than nothing. 'All right, let's try one of my favourite arias, and remember we have to impress your captain. I'm a soprano, by the way.'

The sailors grinned, nodded, and waited while she had a drink of water. She began gently, trying out her vocal cords after that spell in the sea, and giving the sailors time to start playing. It was an odd combination, but as soon as she knew they were fairly competent, she relaxed and her lovely voice filled the room. When the last notes faded there was a stunned silence, and Ruth wasn't the only one wiping away a tear.

Suddenly the other patients in the sickbay were

applauding and shouting for more. She smiled and did as elegant a curtsy as possible in an over-sized robe. Then she thanked the sailors, and turned her attention to the captain, waiting for his response. She was quite pleased her voice hadn't suffered too much, but would the captain think it was good enough?

'Good heavens, you should be on the concert stage.'

'That is where I intend to be as soon as this dreadful war is over. Do I have your permission to sing for everyone tonight, Captain?'

'You do, and I will see that as many men as possible can attend.'

'What about us?' one of the injured called.

'We could broadcast it over the ship's system,' a sailor suggested. 'Then everyone will be able to hear.'

'Even the U-Boats will hear a voice like that,' another remarked.

The captain smiled at the man who had spoken. 'By nightfall we shall be docked, ready to disembark in the morning. Save me a front-row seat,' he ordered before turning to leave.

Ruth was practically jumping with excitement. 'This is just what everyone needs – something to take their minds off this disaster for a while. I'll go and set up a suitable place.'

'Grab some chairs,' Lillia told the two sailors. 'We need to decide on a programme.'

'Don't overdo it, Nurse,' the doctor warned, but he was smiling. 'Oh, and by the way, a message is on its way to your brother.'

'That is kind of you, and such a relief. Thank

you so much.'

'My pleasure.' He bent close to her ear. 'That was brave of you to put the captain in his place.' Then he walked away laughing softly.

For the next hour they worked out a programme to include classical and popular songs of the day so everyone could have a sing-song. 'You have been a great help,' she told the musicians. 'I will see you at nine o'clock, but now I must rest.'

Before drifting off to sleep her thoughts went out to her brother. If you were here, what a concert we would give the troubled people on this ship.

'You look lovely.' Ruth took a final look at her friend.

'Liar. I look a mess,' she laughed. 'But at least the ship's laundry has done a good job with our uniforms. I would have thought they were beyond saving.'

'Are you going to be all right?' Ruth was suddenly worried about this idea of hers. 'I wish your brother was here.'

'So do I, but he isn't, so remove that frown from your face. I am quite well enough and looking forward to the concert. Come on, we mustn't keep them waiting. Have you got your introduction ready?'

'The captain is doing that.'

'Oh, goody, that should be interesting. I'm still not sure he is really in favour of this concert.'

The room they had set up was crowded. All the seats were taken and some of the crew were sitting on the floor. The two musicians were waiting for her with broad grins on their faces. She walked to the front, acknowledging the polite applause.

After the introduction, which was surprisingly complimentary, she began with a gentle lullaby and then on to the more classical pieces. At the end she sang popular songs and encouraged everyone to sing along. At the end she received a standing ovation, and although she was exhausted, it did her heart good to see so many smiling faces around her.

Doctor Horton pushed his way through the crowd, wanting to speak to her and took hold of her arm. 'I'm sorry, gentlemen, but Nurse Holdsworth must rest now. She is still recovering from an injury.'

She stumbled as he led her back to sickbay. 'That was wonderful and just the kind of lift we all needed. You gave your all and now you must sleep. You can hardly stand up.'

'I am very tired, but it was worth it to see happy faces again.'

'Ah, there you are. I've been looking for you.' The radio operator sat at the table where James and Lester were enjoying a cup of tea before retiring for the night. 'Where have you been?'

'We went into the town,' James told him. 'What's up?'

'I have a message for both of you.' He produced a slip of paper covered in scribble.

Lester peered at it and shook his head. 'You had better read it to us. That is illegible.'

'I had to get it down quickly as it was Morse code from a ship. The message reads, "Hospital

206

ship sunk four days ago. Lillia and Ruth safe".'

After the initial shock the boys were on their feet hugging each other and slapping the radio operator on the back.

'Does it say how they are?' Lester asked, dragging the man out of his seat.

'No, that's all.' He was grinning now. 'Who are these girls?'

'Lillia is my sister and Ruth is James's cousin, and we owe you a drink. Join us in town tomorrow.'

'Thanks, I'll see if I can get away.'

They were too excited and relieved to sleep so they talked for a while.

'So you did know Lillia was in danger.'

Lester nodded. 'It looks as if the old communication is still working in extreme cases, but I'm glad I had doubts because I would have been worrying until I heard from her. That was terrible news about the ship and a dreadful thing for the girls to experience, but thank goodness they are safe.'

'Agreed,' James said as he raised his cup of tea. 'A toast to our two lovely girls.'

Chapter Twenty-Three

'I received your message,' Alex told his father. 'It sounded urgent. Is there a break in the case?'

'There is, but as you weren't able to be with us for New Year, have a drink with me to toast 1917 before I explain. How are your trainee pilots coming along?' he asked while pouring them both a generous brandy.

'A mixed bunch. Some good, some who won't make it as pilots.' They clinked glasses and Alex waited for his father to explain why he had sent for him.

'They've caught Barber. He was trying to hide away on a ship that would be making a stop to unload goods in Ireland. When he was discovered, the master was suspicious and called the police. No one would run the risk of stowing away on a merchant ship unless they were desperate to get out of the country.'

'They certainly wouldn't,' Alex agreed. 'You know a hospital ship was sunk recently? Ruth and Lillia were on board, but thankfully have survived.'

'I had heard. It's a risky way to travel with U-Boats around, so in view of the dangers, you can understand why the master was suspicious. I believe you have never met Sara's husband?'

He shook his head and studied his father apprehensively. 'You are surely not still connecting the two?'

'Barber's activities are being investigated,' he said, ignoring his son's question. 'He appears to have used a few aliases and been involved in many unlawful pursuits.'

'Such as?'

'Theft and extortion by impersonating the wealthy have been uncovered so far. Most of the time he seems to have been a small-time criminal, until the war. That gave him the chance to move on to more serious crimes, and he must have thought the police were getting too close...' He paused. 'Or the fact that the army had been looking for him made him decide to run.'

'You do think it's the same man.' Alex couldn't believe what he was hearing. His worst fears were being confirmed. 'What proof do you have?'

'None yet. The officers on the case wanted to ask Sara to the station to identify the man they have caught but, in view of the fact that we are acquainted with her, I have persuaded them to let me handle it.' He picked up an envelope from the desk. 'In there is a police photograph of Barber. Have a look at it.'

He studied the image for a moment. 'This means nothing to me. I have never seen this man before, and if you believe it is Holdsworth then his children bear no resemblance to him.'

'Agreed. That also poses another question. If this is Holdsworth – and that is a false name – then his marriage to Sara could also be false.'

'You are assuming an awful lot. You admit there isn't any proof, and yet you are talking as if it is a certainty. Why? There must be something you aren't telling me.'

'When we searched his bag we found several small items of value, but the most interesting were paintings of two children – twins.'

Alex drew in a deep breath.

'Joshua identified them as Lester and Lillia at five years old. He remembers them being painted, and the pictures are worth a lot of money.'

'Perhaps Sara's had a burglary?'

'She hasn't, but Joshua said her husband often took items from the house to sell when he was short of money.'

'Oh, good Lord, that poor woman. Did you show Josh the photograph? He would have seen him over the years.'

'I did, but he couldn't be sure. The general had a beard and moustache, but Barber is clean-shaven and roughly spoken.'

'I still think they can't be the same man, but you obviously believe there is a connection. What are you going to do next?'

'I am going to visit Sara and ask her about the items we found on Barber. If she can identify them they can be returned to her when the case is settled, and I want her to look at the photograph. I want you with me when I do this in case she becomes upset.'

He gave his father an incredulous look. 'Of course she'll be upset. She must already be in a delicate state after nearly losing her daughter. When do you intend to see her?'

'Now.'

'Can't it wait for a few days?'

'No. Barber is scheduled to appear at court in a week's time, and we must gather all the information we can before then. Will you come with me?'

Alex drained his glass and stood up. 'Let's get this over with.'

Sara greeted them when they were shown to the sitting room.

'Forgive the intrusion,' Charles said, wasting no time, 'but the man the police asked you about has been caught. He had in his possession certain items that have raised questions, and we hope you can help us.'

She frowned. 'It is good news he has been caught, but I don't know how I can be of help. Please be seated and tell me about it.'

'Is your husband here? This would also be of interest to him.'

'He is away at the moment.' She cast Alex a concerned glance. 'But your son knows that.'

'I was hoping he had returned.'

Alex watched his father smile to put Sara at ease, but he saw this was a policeman with a case to be solved and not a friend. He was grateful his father had called on him because this charming woman was going to need the support of someone who cared about her. He was certain now that the police were sure of the connection between the general and Barber or they wouldn't be pursuing this line of enquiry so persistently.

'I was relieved to know Lillia and Ruth were safe,' he said, changing the subject to give Sara a chance to recover. She was clearly disturbed now.

'Yes, it was a miracle that both the girls survived. 'What a terrible experience that must have been for them, but I've had a letter from my daughter. She said the navy ship that rescued them was a sad place so she gave a concert to lift their spirits. That was so like her, and very brave, wasn't it?'

'Indeed, and her singing would help everyone forget the grim facts for a while.'

She gave him a grateful smile and turned her attention back to his father. 'I think you had better tell me exactly what is going on with this case. I didn't expect to receive a visit from another policeman, for I suspect you are here in that capacity.'

'And also as a friend to make this as easy as possible for you.'

'Thank you. Please continue with your questions.'

'When Barber was captured he had items in his bag that we believe came from this house.' He listed them.

Sara's lips compressed in a straight line, and she did not try to hide her anger. 'They do sound like mine, for I have pieces like that missing. I will be perfectly straight with you; my husband was often short of money and, with my permission in most cases, took certain items to sell. This man, Barber, could have got them from anywhere.'

'You say – in most cases?'

'The miniature portraits I did not say he could sell. I would never have parted with those and I would like them returned, if that is possible. The other items I am not concerned about.'

'Once this man is tried and sentenced all items belonging to you will be returned.' He removed the photograph from the envelope and held it out to her. 'Do you recognise this man?'

She studied it in silence for some time, then she handed it back. 'There is something familiar about him, but I could not be sure. I have never seen my husband clean-shaven and would need to see this man in person to make a positive identification.'

Alex tensed. She was quite calm now, but his sense of foreboding increased. She wasn't denying that this was her husband, and he had expected an outright denial from her. Indeed, had hoped for that denial so they could walk away and leave her out of the investigation.

'Could you say who you think it might be?' Charles asked.

'As I've said, I can't be sure from a photograph...'

'But?' Charles continued, pushing for an answer.

She looked him straight in the eyes. 'There is a resemblance to my husband, but that is all. As I've said, I would need to look him in the eyes to know for sure. What is this man accused of?'

'The charges are theft, extortion and selling arms, to mention just a few. Would you be willing to come to the station and see him? If you can definitely tell us that the man we are holding is not your husband, we can eliminate him from our enquiries, and you will not be troubled again.'

'That does seem to be the best course of action. When would you like me to do this?' she asked without hesitation.

'Now, if you wouldn't mind. We need to clear this up as quickly as possible, and my car is outside.'

She stood up and said briskly, 'Let us get this unpleasant business over with.'

Alex sat in the back of the car with Sara, who was pale and composed, but he knew she was under tremendous strain. If this man turned out to be her husband, the ramifications could be devastating for her and her children. There was no doubt she was aware of this, but the determined lift of her head told him that she was prepared to face whatever happened. Sitting beside him was a different woman from the one he had first met, and he admired what he saw. There was courage and strength here. He was certain now that she did believe the criminal was the man she had married, or she would not have agreed so readily to see if she could identify him. He wanted to reach out and grasp her hand to give comfort and support, but he instinctively knew this would be the wrong thing to do. She would face this in her own way, but he would be beside her now and in the future.

It was at that moment he realised he was in love with her – and had been from the moment they had met. It had begun with a talented son who had been forced to attend the academy against his will, and when he had seen him with his twin sister his heart had ached for them. They should never have been separated. Music was their life, but that unfeeling man had tried to thwart their ambition, and the war had completed his plan for them.

Their arrival at the police station brought him out of his troubled thoughts and he helped her out of the car.

'You needn't come in,' his father told him. 'This won't take long.'

'I would also like to see this man, if Sara will permit it?'

'Of course you must come in.' Sara gave him a grateful look and put her hand on his arm for support.

He could feel her trembling slightly as they walked in.

Charles didn't waste any time and ordered that

Barber be brought from his cell, and they went to a small room to await his arrival.

He was brought in almost immediately and the superintendent of the station turned to Sara. 'Do you know this man, Mrs Holdsworth? Take your time.'

Alex had been allowed in the room only because of his father's influence, so he was standing by the wall and watching intently. What would she do if it was her husband? The easy way out for her would be to deny it and walk away. He would be tried under the name of Barber without a trace of scandal attached to her or her family.

No one spoke while Sara studied the man in front of her, who had his head turned slightly away. 'Look at me!' she said in a firm voice.

When he did she took a step towards him. 'How dare you deceive my family all these years? Did my father know who you really are?'

He smirked. 'Fooled you and him, didn't I? I got quite used to acting the toff, and I was good at it. Brought me in a lot of money that role did.'

'And now you are going to pay dearly for that.' She turned to the superintendent. 'This is the man who called himself General Gilbert Holdsworth.'

Alex moved away from the wall and his father motioned him to stay where he was. This was police business, and he understood that, but he knew what this must be costing Sara emotionally. He had an overwhelming desire to punch that man in the face for all the heartache he had brought to Sara and her children. It had taken tremendous courage to identify him, knowing as

215

she must the scandal his trial would cause.

'Well, well,' he snarled, 'I didn't think you would have the nerve to denounce me. That was a foolish thing to do because I can make sure your nasty little secret gets a public airing. What are your precious children going to think of you then, eh?'

'My children will be relieved to know that you are not their father.' She spun round. 'Are we finished here, sir? I don't wish to spend another moment in the same room as this odious man.'

'Certainly, madam. If you will come with me there is some information I need from you.'

'Of course.' She didn't look at Alex or his father as she left the room.

When Barber had been returned to his cell, Charles went up to his son. 'That woman has courage. She could have denied knowing him and that would have been the end of it for her; instead, she has opened up a Pandora's box of trouble for herself. She's an intelligent woman and must be well aware of what she faces, but she didn't hesitate to unmask him, and even admitted in front of witnesses that he is not the father of her children.'

'That is something I had begun to suspect, and do you know, I am pleased about that.' Alex pushed away from the wall and took a deep breath. 'She is going to need friends.'

'She has them.'

Chapter Twenty-Four

An hour later they were back in the house with glasses of much-needed brandy in their hands.

'I am sorry we had to put you through that,' Charles said.

'There is no need to apologise. It was necessary because I had to know. What happens now?'

'I have asked them to keep you out of the trial, if possible, but the newspapers could pick up on the story. The next few weeks will be unpleasant and distressing for you.'

'I am aware of the consequences, but they will have to be faced.'

'You could have saved yourself by denying you knew him. I don't think Barber had any intention of admitting his bogus role as General Holdsworth because, once investigated, it could well add more crimes to the list.'

She shook her head. 'He deserves to face the penalty for his criminal activities – all of them – and in a way I am quite pleased this has happened. I am now free of that odious man, and my main worry is telling the children. But once that is done and we have accepted it, we shall be able to get on with our lives without continually worrying what he is going to do next.'

'That is very true and a good way to deal with this revelation.' Alex spoke for the first time since arriving back. 'There is a difficult time ahead for you, and we want you to know that you have our friendship and support.'

'Even though you now know I had illegitimate children? After they were born I urged him to adopt them, but he always found excuses not to do it, and now I know why.' Her expression clouded. 'I tried so hard to save them from that stigma.'

'You have two of the bravest, most talented youngsters I have ever met. That is something to be proud of,' Alex pointed out.

'You are right about that, and I have never once regretted their birth. They have been a constant joy to me, and my only regret is that I allowed myself to be pushed into a disastrous union to avoid scandal. Now it has caught up with me, and there will be an even greater scandal.'

'I imagine you felt alone at that time and had no other choice, but that is not the case now.' Alex leant forward. 'If you would like to leave London for a while we can easily arrange that for you.'

'Thank you for that kind thought, but I have finished running. I am staying in my own home and will weather the storm when it comes.'

'If you change your mind at any time you must contact us,' Charles urged. 'May I ask a personal question? Do not answer if you would rather not do so.'

'I have few secrets now, so what would you like to know?'

'Where did the marriage take place?'

'It was a small church, but I cannot tell you much about it as I was too distressed at the time and seven months pregnant. To avoid scandal, I was told, it was arranged for ten o'clock at night.

218

The man my family were forcing me to marry took care of all the details, and my father was only too happy to leave it to him.' She looked directly at Alex. 'Did you discover anything from the details I sent you?'

'After a thorough investigation the captain working on this came to the conclusion that Holdsworth was not a general in the army, and he could not find any trace of a Gilbert Holdsworth anywhere.'

'And you did not tell me?'

'We had no proof. It was all speculation and I didn't want to worry you with something that could turn out to have a perfectly reasonable answer. It would have been wrong to slander a man without evidence that he was using a military rank he was not entitled to.'

'But now we know the truth of the matter, and when this becomes public knowledge I pray my children will not hear of it. I cannot send letters because a matter as grave as this cannot be put on paper; I must face them with the truth.' Her voice trembled as she turned her face away. 'My poor darlings. Now my shame is going to touch them. For myself I don't care, but they are completely innocent...'

Her earlier optimism seemed to dissolve as she considered the impact this was going to have on her children, and she was clearly distressed. Alex sat beside her and took hold of her tightly clenched hands. 'Now you listen to me, Sara, you have no need to feel shame. You have brought into the world two fine children, and sacrificed your own happiness to see they had every chance of a normal life. I have come to know the twins well, and you are underestimating them if you believe that this tragic affair is going to make them recoil in horror. It doesn't matter a damn who their father is; they have a mother they love and who loves them. Society's condemnation will not bother them at all. No doubt they will be shocked, but I don't believe it will make any difference to their lives. They are involved in this war and are experiencing unimaginable things, and something like this will just be brushed aside by them. So stop feeling sorry for them – or yourself.'

'Yes, Brigadier,' she answered with a shaky smile.

His father laughed. 'You have your orders, Sara. Let's ask the officer if there is any way he can get your youngsters home soon?'

'I wish I had enough authority to order that, but it's not possible.'

'I wouldn't want them to travel on a ship at this time after nearly losing my daughter in that way. I can only hope they don't hear about this until they are safely home.' She smiled at the men. 'I thank you both for your kindness and understanding. It has been a great comfort to have your support.'

'It was the least we could do for you,' Charles stood up. 'My son will not be around all the time, of course, but I'll be here. You won't have to face this alone; we shall see to that.'

'Thank you.' Her voice was husky with emotion. 'That seems a very inadequate way to express my gratitude.'

'I will come as often as possible,' Alex told her as he stood up. 'Please write and let me know how you are coping.'

'I will.'

They took their leave and Sara watched the door close. Unable to control her feelings a moment longer she covered her face with her hands and wept. She cried for the years of deception, for allowing that criminal to drain her family wealth, for her beloved children who would now carry the stigma of being illegitimate, and lastly she cried for herself – for the wasted years in an unhappy marriage. Her parents had been horrified when they had discovered that their unmarried daughter was pregnant, and they had panicked. If they could see the result of their hasty actions they would be ashamed at what they had done.

'I must get back to Hendon.' Alex checked his watch. 'That was good of you to offer to stand by Sara. Things could get nasty for her, and I wish I could be here for her as well.'

'Don't worry, my boy, you have an important job to do, so you can leave this to me. I'll see she's all right, but I don't feel you need to worry. I suspect that her concern is only for her children. I don't think she cares if society snubs her.'

Alex nodded in agreement. 'She has already done everything she could to protect them, and now her only worry seems to be how this will touch their lives.'

'I'm afraid so, but however bad things have been for her she gave those children a stable, happy upbringing. That was quite an achievement in the circumstances. And there's another blessing.'

'Is there?'

'Of course. She told us that Barber made all the

arrangements for the wedding, so there's a very good chance that the marriage wasn't legitimate. If it is then she is free and young enough to start a new life, and one that must be happier than the years spent with that rogue.'

'That's true,' he agreed. 'She will need to get that looked into.'

'Our lawyer will do that for her. I'll pop round there tomorrow and take her to see him. The sooner she disassociates herself from Barber, the better. Now stop worrying and get back to training more pilots. We need them.'

'What the hell do you think you were doing today?' Lester stormed over to his friend the moment they landed. 'You nearly got yourself killed – again.'

'I couldn't resist it. That was the Red Baron. He was impossible to catch, though.' He gave his usual cheery grin. 'Thanks for your help. I don't know where those other two came from.'

'No, you weren't paying attention and were too intent on that red plane. Don't do that again. I want both of us to survive this war, but we won't do that if you start acting like a fool and being reckless.'

James studied his friend with interest. 'I say, I've never seen you so angry before.'

'Of course I'm angry. Here I am trying to look out for my future brother-in-law and he's willing to throw his life away for a little glory.'

'A *little* glory?' James was now laughing. 'Come on, my friend, we need to get that devil out of the skies.'

'I know.' Lester gave a wry smile, his anger draining away as he listened to James's laughter. 'But don't go after him on your own next time.'

'Promise. Let's get a drink, I'm gasping.' As they walked along James did a little jig. 'You called me your future brother-in-law. Does that mean you give me permission to marry your sister?'

'Of course I do. That's if she'll have you.'

'She won't be able to resist me.'

They were both laughing as they walked into the mess.

Four weeks later the weather was too bad for flying and Lester found his friend in the mess. 'Hey, is that an English newspaper you've got there?'

'One of the other chaps received it in a parcel from home and gave it to me when he'd finished with it.'

'Let's have a look,' he asked eagerly, reaching out for it.

James whipped it away from him. 'You can't have all of it.'

'Oh, come on. I'll give it back to you.'

His friend removed one page, folded it and tucked it into his pocket, and then he handed over the rest.

'Why do you want that page? What's on it?'

'There's a puzzle on there I want to do; there's nothing else of interest.'

'All right.' Lester settled back to enjoy reading news from home. An English newspaper was a rare treat.

James let out a slow, silent breath of relief. He hadn't read all of the report, but enough to know it was about his friend's family – and it wasn't good. If any more English papers arrived he would have to get to them first. Lester mustn't start worrying about home; he needed all his wits about him when they flew. He also hoped there weren't any English newspapers where Lillia was. His heart ached for both of them, but whatever had happened in the past, or recently, he didn't give a damn about. They were still his friends and always would be, and his love for Lillia would not be destroyed by any scandal. He would make her happy one day, of that he was determined.

As a beam of sunshine filtered through the window, an officer came over to them. 'The weather is clearing and will soon be good enough to take photographs of enemy lines. Your plane will be ready any minute now.'

The boys jumped to their feet. 'Where to, sir?'

'Messines Ridge.'

'You take the pictures,' Lester said, 'because you're better with a camera than I am.'

'Wonder if the Red Baron will come to visit us?'

'If he does we are getting out of there as fast as possible. We can't shoot him down with a camera.'

'That's true,' James agreed. 'At least I know he won't catch us with you at the controls.'

'Hope you're right.'

They collected the instructions, maps and equipment and hurried out to the waiting plane.

Chapter Twenty-Five

Much to Sara's relief the courtroom wasn't even full, and as far as she could see the case had only attracted mild interest from two reporters. The newspapers were full of what was happening in the war. In peacetime this trial would probably have been front-page news, but she hoped it would be tucked away on about the third page. Even so, the reports so far had still been damaging. Gilbert's list of aliases was now public knowledge, including the account of how he had posed as General Holdsworth, the husband of Sara Kirkby for some twenty years while carrying out his criminal activities. This perfect role had allowed him to remain at large for so many years, and it was humiliating that she had been duped by him. She'd had her doubts about his breeding, of course, but he was the man her father had chosen, so he must be respectable, she had reasoned. Right from the start he had threatened to tell the children they were illegitimate if she didn't obey him, and she couldn't risk their young lives being thrown into confusion. The press had pestered her for her story, but she had refused to say a word. Let them think what they liked, it didn't matter to her. Charles had tried hard to keep her off the witness stand, but to no avail. The prosecution had insisted that her testimony was crucial. She had given her answers without attempting to hide anything. Now they waited.

'It will soon be over, and once sentence is passed the press will lose interest.'

'That will be a relief.' She smiled at the two men, one either side of her. Charles and Alex had supported her right through the ordeal, and her gratitude knew no bounds. She didn't know how she would have managed without them. When it was apparent that she would have to take the stand, Charles had explained what would happen, going through everything, and that had helped calm her fears.

'Here we go.' Alex helped her to her feet as the judge entered.

When Gilbert was sentenced to life in prison she saw him sway with shock. He turned his head to look at her and when she saw the anguish on his face, she felt sorry for him, which was unbelievable after what he had done to her. There were still doubts about the legality of the marriage, but she thanked God the marriage had not been consummated. At least she was spared that shame. What a fool the man had been. He had schemed his way in to a life of ease and position, but he still hadn't been able to give up his criminal activities.

Once outside the two men protected her from reporters and quickly led her to a waiting car. She closed her eyes as they drove away. It was over!

'He got off lightly,' Alex said. 'They could have hung him for treason.'

'Unfortunately the evidence for that wasn't solid enough, but the judge gave him the maximum sentence he could.'

The door of the house opened before they even

reached it, and Adams smiled with relief. 'Refreshments will be with you immediately, madam, and Cook has made you your favourite fruit cake.'

'That is kind of her.' She smiled at the butler as he helped her out of her coat. 'Please thank her, and you can tell the staff that he received a life sentence. I'll talk to you all when I have rested.'

He beamed at the two men. 'Would you like something stronger than tea, sirs?'

'No, thank you.' Alex returned the faithful servant's smile. 'Tea will be very welcome.'

'They have all been so kind,' Sara said when they were in the sitting room and the refreshments had been served. 'I did wonder if some would leave once the scandal hit us, but not one did. In fact, they have done their best to show their support by spoiling me. They said they can't wait for the war to end and the children to come home to fill the house with music again. I pray that day is soon.'

After enjoying the tea and large slices of the special cake, Charles had to leave. That left Alex and Sara to relax after the turmoil of the last few weeks. It was a relief to spend some quiet time with the man she felt so at ease with. His strong, but gentle manner had carried her through the ordeal.

'This really is excellent cake.' He helped himself to another slice from the stand. 'I must thank your cook.'

'She will be delighted, and thrilled to see so much of it has been eaten. I'll take you to see her before you leave.'

'Do you think she will give me the recipe for my mother?'

'That is a closely guarded secret.' She surprised herself by laughing. It was an age since she had felt so free.

'That's better. When you laugh you are more like the enchanting woman I first met.'

'My goodness, it seems a lifetime since I was flattered so graciously.'

'Then it is long overdue.'

'Are you flirting with me, Brigadier?'

'I do believe I am. After all, you are beautiful, intelligent and I must step in quickly before there is a queue outside your door. I must ask Adams to tell them that you are not at home.' He paused. 'How am I doing?'

She burst in to laughter. 'Alex Stansfield, you are allowing your imagination to run riot.'

'We shall see.' He sat back, satisfied he had made her put some of the trauma behind her at last. 'May I ask a personal question?'

'Of course.'

'I know that man continually wanted money from you, so do you need any help financially? I would be happy to be of assistance, if necessary.'

'That is generous of you, but you have done enough. I still have sufficient funds to run the house and pay my staff, and that is all I need at the moment. Once the children are home I will have to see what is needed so they can pursue their musical careers. I do still have some items of value that I kept out of that man's way.'

'I understand, but remember, I am here if you need any help at all.'

'I appreciate your kind offer, but I am sure we shall be able to manage.'

He realised she had too much pride to ask for financial help and changed the subject. 'Are you still doing volunteer work at the hospital?'

'Yes, I'm pleased to say. I thought they might dispense with my services once they knew about the trial, but the matron was adamant that I was welcome to continue. She declared, very forcibly, that I was not a victim and must stop thinking of myself as one.'

'And she is right. Put it behind you now and start again. You have the chance to make a new life for yourself. Take it.'

'I intend to, and shall start this very moment. I have decided that if the marriage was legal then I shall sue for divorce straight away. Everyone has been so kind through this terrible time.'

'Of course they have, and you have much to be proud of in the way you have handled the whole situation.'

She smiled and stood up. 'Come along, and I will introduce you to Cook before all this flattery goes to my head.'

Their laughter reached the servants as they made their way to the kitchen. They looked at each other and nodded, pleased to hear laughter in the house again.

'Messines Ridge again.' Lester handed the camera to James. 'The weather is better today and you should be able to get clearer pictures.'

'I'll do my best. Wonder why we keep getting this job?'

'Because we keep coming back, I expect.'

'Ah, and I thought it might be for my superb

229

photography skills,' James joked.

'That too.' Lester walked round checking the plane before they took off. 'I'll try and get you closer this time.'

'Good idea. If I can get some really good pictures they might let us get back to the fighting again. There are still far too many enemy planes flying around up there.'

They were soon airborne and James kept a sharp look out for enemy planes, but they had a clear run to their target.

'Ready?' Lester shouted, and when his friend replied he dived, levelling off and flying as low as he dared.

All hell broke loose as guns began firing at them, but he held his course to allow James to get his photos, until his friend yelled, 'Get out of here!'

He banked and climbed as fast as he could and there was a thump and the fuselage beside him shattered. Something felt wrong with his leg as he fought to control the crippled plane in a desperate effort to reach safer territory.

'Are you all right?' James yelled.

Lester lifted his hand, unable to speak, and continued the struggle, but it was no use. The plane was too badly damaged and a crash was inevitable. He spotted a field near a large group of trees. If they survived the crash they were going to need cover, for they were still over enemy territory.

The next thing he was aware of he was being dragged from the wreckage by James.

'Can you stand? We've got to get away from here at once. They'll have seen us come down and will soon come looking for us.'

'Set the plane on fire,' Lester gasped. 'That might delay them for a while if they think we are still in it.'

It was soon a roaring blaze, and hanging on to his friend they made it to the woods. They kept going until they were a good way in and found a gully to hide them.

'Let's have a look at that leg. We've got to stop the bleeding.'

'You're hurt as well.' His friend's sleeve was torn and covered in blood. 'I'm sorry. I tried to keep the plane flying.'

'Don't apologise.' He ripped Lester's trouser leg to reveal a deep nasty gash. 'Is it broken as well?'

'Don't think so.' He turned his head away from the mess his leg was in and saw something on the ground. 'Why are you dragging that camera around with you? It's probably damaged and won't be any use.'

'I wasn't going to leave it behind. I got some good pictures and if I can get them back they will be useful. There, press on that until the bleeding stops. Does it hurt?'

He gave his friend a disbelieving look and grimaced. 'Don't ask daft questions. Of course it hurts. How is your arm?'

'Just a scratch,' he said, stripping off his shirt and tearing it in to strips for bandages. He bound Lester's wound first and then his own, which was more than a scratch. He surveyed his handiwork and nodded. 'Not bad, but what we need are a couple of nurses.'

That brought Lester's attention to his sister, and it was something he had been trying to block from his thought from the moment the shell had struck the plane. He didn't want her to pick up on any pain.

James sat back, closed his eyes for a moment, and then said, 'We shall have to travel at night and hide by day. We also need food and water. I think we must get away from the enemy trenches and the only way to do that is to go further into enemy territory before turning to scout round their lines. What do you think?'

'That's a hell of a walk, but I agree it's probably the only way. We can't cross enemy lines to get to ours, although that would be the shortest route. The problem is I am going to slow you down, so you go on your own. You will have a much better chance without dragging me along.'

'Shut up and rest. I'm not going anywhere without you. We are in this together and that's the way it will stay. Where I go, you go, even if I have to drag you all the way.'

Despite the pain in his leg, Lester drifted off to sleep, exhausted from the loss of blood. When he woke up it was getting dark and James was working on something. He pulled himself up to a sitting position. 'Sorry, have I been asleep for long?'

James looked over. 'You needed it. Do you feel stronger?'

'A little. What are you doing?'

'Making you a crutch to take the weight off your leg, and I found a tiny stream. The water seemed clear so I drank some and it's all right. I had a small flask in my pocket and I collected some for you.'

He drank thirstily and handed back the flask.

'Good, now try this.' He hauled his friend to his feet and tucked the crutch under his arm. 'That looks about right. I've used the rest of my shirt to pad the top. How does it feel?'

'It's comfortable. Thanks, this will be a big help.' He took a few steps and stifled a groan. There was no way he could force his friend to leave him, so he must do his damnedest not to slow him down too much.

'Right, if you're ready, we had better get out of here. When we get back, I'll buy us a bottle of champagne.'

'I'll need a double brandy,' he replied as they began to move.

'Done!'

Lester returned James's grin with effort. They were joking, but both were aware of the perilous situation they were in and that they might not make it back to base.

Keeping away from the roads meant walking over rough ground, and although the crutch was helping, Lester was finding the going exhausting and painful. More than once he stumbled in the dark and would have fallen if James hadn't been supporting him.

'Stop,' his friend whispered after about three hours. 'Your leg is bleeding again. We must rest.'

'How can you see in the dark?'

'I've got cats' eyes,' he joked, pushing Lester down against a tree. 'I'll have to bind your leg tighter.'

Lester laid his head back. 'Can we rest for a while?'

'Fifteen minutes only. If we keep going for another two hours and do the same tomorrow night, we could reach safer territory.'

'That's optimistic with me slowing you up.'

'I'm always optimistic.' There was a flash of white teeth in the dark. 'Now, shut up and rest.'

Chapter Twenty-Six

'Nurse! Why are you limping?'

Lillia stopped and looked round at the sharp command. 'I just knocked my leg on a chair. It's nothing.'

'Get it looked at if it continues to trouble you.'

'Yes, Sister.' Trying to walk properly, she hurried out of the ward, hiding her concern. She couldn't tell anyone what she sensed, they would think she was mad. This short break had come just in time for her to calm her thoughts.

'Ah, there you are.' Ruth came into the rest room. 'A hospital train is coming and we are needed to help board the patients. We are also to stay on there until they reach the ship.'

Lillia gulped down a cup of tea she had just poured for herself and followed her friend out.

'Have you hurt yourself? You're limping.'

'No, I'm quite all right.'

'Then why are you walking so badly?' Ruth stopped and caught hold of her arm. 'If you're not fit enough, you mustn't do this trip. You know how busy it is with long hours on our feet. Tell me the truth. How have you hurt your leg?'

She sighed, knowing her friend wouldn't let the subject drop. 'I haven't hurt myself; I think Lester might have. You know we have always been aware of each other's discomfort.'

'How bad?' Ruth had gone quite pale. 'Has he crashed? Is James with him?'

'Just a minute while I contact him,' she said, sighing dramatically.

'Don't mess about.'

'Well, you know full well that I can't tell you. I shouldn't have said anything because now we will both be worrying when we need our minds on what we are doing. All I know is my leg hurts and I haven't done anything to injure it.'

'But you can tell if he's alive, can't you?'

She urged her friend to start walking again, ignoring the question. 'You like my brother, don't you?'

'I adore that handsome, talented man, and have done so from the moment I saw him. I love and worry about both of them flying around in those planes. How much more dangerous can it get?'

'They could be in the trenches.'

Ruth stopped and looked at the scene in front of them. The train was already packed and they were still loading casualties. 'Oh Lord, I take your point. This is going to be a stressful journey.'

Their concerns about the boys had to be put aside as they boarded and began their work.

The train made slow progress. Many times they had to stop to allow armament trains through as they had priority. It took a week to reach the ship, and once the men were all transferred they stood on the dock watching it sail out of the harbour.

'Safe journey,' whispered Lillia, remembering their traumatic voyage on such a ship.

Ruth glanced at her friend. 'Hope we have a quick journey back to base. Er … I haven't asked because we've been too busy, but does your leg still hurt?'

'No, it's fine. The train's about to leave so let's get moving.'

James had been out with his prediction of making it to safety in two days. They had been travelling for three days and Lester knew he wouldn't have made it this far without his friend. He had remained cheerful and continually urged them forward step by step, but they were both exhausted from lack of sleep and very little food, not to mention they both had wounds that urgently needed attention. The sky was just beginning to get light when they stumbled on an isolated farm and crept towards a barn.

'You stay there.' James shut the door of the barn and made his friend comfortable on a pile of hay. 'I'll see if I can get some food and water. We need something more substantial than raw vegetables dug out of a field.'

'What we really need is help if we are to get any further. I can't keep this up. I've told you time and time again to leave me.'

'And I've told you I won't. You've done jolly well and we are now back on safer ground. I'll have a scout around, and if this village isn't occupied by Germans I'll try to get transport of some kind. I suppose push bikes are out of the question?'

'I'll try anything. See what you can do, but

don't take any chances.'

'Not likely.' His usual grin was rather strained by now, but was still in evidence. 'We're getting back to base. I haven't caught the Red Baron yet.'

Lester laughed quietly. His friend was incorrigible and he would never have made it this far without his dogged determination. 'Next time we see him you can have first go at him.'

James slapped him on the back. 'Then the sooner we get out of this mess, the better. Won't be long. You have a rest and I'll see if there's anything to eat around here. Can't remember when I've been so hungry.'

The commotion of people around woke Lester suddenly and he scrambled to get to his feet.

'It's all right.' His friend rushed to steady him. 'This is the farmer, his wife and their son. They are going to help us.'

The son was a tall, strong youth, and he picked up Lester as if he was nothing more than a feather, and the woman hurried along beside them as they made their way to the farmhouse, shaking her head as she studied his torn and bloody trousers. The son dumped him on the huge kitchen table and tore away the rest of his trouser leg to expose the wound. The father was talking rapidly to his wife who was already cleaning his friend's arm.

'What are they saying?' he asked James. 'My French isn't good enough to follow them.'

'I caught most of it. This woman used to be a midwife and they are dealing with animals all the time here on the farm so they can handle our injuries.'

'Oh, good.' He felt like laughing hysterically. 'I

237

didn't know I was pregnant.'

James felt it his duty to translate this for the family, and soon everyone was laughing.

In a whirl of activity and pain, the wounds were cleaned and bound, and they were enjoying a large bowl of stew with chunks of delicious home-made bread.

After the good meal and with his leg feeling more comfortable, Lester was able to follow much of what was being said, although his French was limited and not used for some time.

The boys thanked the family profusely, but this was waved away as they explained that they were going to take them by cart to as close to a field hospital as possible. They would then be able to make it the rest of the way on their own.

'When the war is over we must come back here and see that these kind people are all right,' Lester said as they travelled along country roads.

'Definitely,' James agreed.

The horse trotted along for about two hours, and at the sound of gunfire they stopped. The farmer and his son then explained that this was as far as they could take them, and pointed out where the hospital could be found.

They began walking – Lester still using the crutch – and an hour later arrived at their destination with a great sigh of relief. They had made it against all the odds.

The journey back had still been slow, and the girls were pleased when the train dropped them off at their base, and they hurried in to resume their duties. The hospital was as busy as ever, but

Ruth had never expected to see her cousin in one of the beds.

She rushed over to him. 'What are you doing here? How badly are you hurt? You look awful.'

'One question at a time,' he told her. 'I had a deep gash in my arm. We got here by walking and then in a farmer's cart – and you are not looking too good yourself.'

'What do you mean "we"?'

'Lester's over there.' He pointed across the ward, and just when she would have rushed over to him, he caught hold of her arm. 'Don't disturb him. He's just come back from surgery and he's walked miles with an injured leg. Don't panic. He's going to be just fine.'

'How did this happen?'

'We were on a photographic mission when we got shot down.'

'Oh, I'm so sorry.' She kissed her cousin on the top of his head. 'I must go and tell Lillia.'

'Is she still here with you as well?'

She nodded. 'Like you and Lester, we have managed to stay together. It helps to have a friend with you when things get tough.'

'That is so true. Go and get her because it will cheer them up to be together again.'

Ruth found her friend with some new arrivals. 'Come with me.'

'I can't leave here. What's the matter?'

'You've got to come. It's urgent. Get someone to cover for you.'

She called another nurse over and told her she had been called elsewhere, but would be back as quickly as possible.

'Go and look in the bed over there, but don't wake him if he's asleep.'

Frowning, she walked to the bed and stood still, staring at the man fast asleep.

Ruth stood beside her and said gently, 'He's all right. There is an injury to his leg, just like you felt, and he's exhausted. I don't know the whole story yet, but they have evidently had to walk a long way.'

She was holding her brother's hand and looked up sharply. 'They?'

'James is over there. He's the one waving with his good arm and has a silly grin on his face.'

'Thank the Lord they are both safe, but they look as if they've had a hard time.'

'No doubt about that. You go over and see him while I stay with your brother.'

'Don't worry about him,' James said as soon as she reached his bed. 'That brother of yours is tough, and his skill at flying saved us by getting a damaged plane on the ground without killing us, even though he was injured.'

'Tell me what happened,' she demanded.

James kept the story short, with little jokes thrown in, but there was no doubt they had been in great peril.

'Thank you,' she told him when he had finished. 'You saved his life.'

'We saved each other. That's what friends do, but you can kiss me if you like.'

She laughed and plumped up his pillows. 'I can't kiss patients.'

'Ah, shame.'

'Go back to sleep.' Then she heard the sound

she knew only too well, and headed for the door to help with arriving ambulances.

The first moment she had she checked on her brother's condition and was satisfied that he would make a complete recovery. The relief that both boys were safe was enormous.

It wasn't until later that evening when the girls were off-duty that they were free to spend time with them. They clustered around Lester's bed and talked until lights out.

After a good night's sleep both boys had recovered well from their exhausted state, and began fretting about letting everyone know they were safe.

'That has all been taken care of,' Ruth told them. 'Stop wandering around, James, and don't you dare try and get out of bed again, Lester.'

'I'm all right. I've walked miles on this injured leg.'

'That is obvious, but you are not taking another step until it has healed completely.'

'But I want to go and see my sister.'

'You can't. She's busy – we are all busy, so you two behave yourselves.'

'Is she always this bossy?' he asked James.

'Not usually, but while you were sleeping I had a wander around this place. It is packed, with more injured arriving all the time, and these doctors and nurses are working until they drop. Some of the things I saw made me realise just how lucky we are.' James shook his head. 'I don't know how our girls do this job. When the war is over we must do everything we can to make their lives happy ones.'

'We will, but there's no end in sight, and I'm worried about our mother. She must have been told I was missing and will be frantic. Please see if you can get me a pen and paper so I can write to her.'

'I've already done that.' Lillia swept up to them. 'I can't stay but I was told you two are fretting. Don't worry because you won't be here long – we need the beds for those more seriously wounded. In a couple of days you will be moved. They might even send you home.'

'No!' they declared together.

'We've got to get back to our airfield. I've still got the pictures I took and they must be delivered.'

'So that's why you are guarding that camera.'

James nodded. 'It's important.'

'He wouldn't leave it behind, even though he had to support me all the time. He's stubborn and I'm grateful, because there is no way I would have made it on my own.'

'I know.' She smiled and winked at her brother. 'He's a stubborn darling though, isn't he?' With that teasing remark she turned and left the ward.

'She called me a darling,' James exclaimed, a huge smile on his face. 'She likes me.'

'Of course she does.'

'I'm glad you are both in such high spirits,' a doctor said, 'because I have just received word that an officer is coming to see you.'

They waited anxiously until evening for the visit, determined not to be sent home. When he arrived they were astounded to see who it was. He walked up to them, pulled out a chair and sat down.

242

'What are you doing here, Alex?' James asked, addressing him as the family friend.

'I brought a new plane over, so I thought I'd see the girls while I was here. I was also hoping to get news about you two. I'm relieved I'll be able to tell everyone at home that you are all right. Now, tell me what the hell you've been up to.'

He studied them carefully as he listened to the account of their escapade, before saying, 'You were lucky to get back without being captured. After an ordeal like that I'll see if there is any chance of getting you sent home.'

'Please don't do that,' James pleaded. 'We're going to recover completely, and then we want to return to our squadron.'

'And you are both of that opinion?' When they nodded, he said, 'Very well. I'll see what I can arrange.'

'Thank you, sir. Do our families know we are safe?'

'Not yet. They have been informed that you are missing, and as soon as I get back I will go and assure both families that you are safe.'

With a sigh of relief Lester rested his head back on the pillow. 'That is a load off my mind.'

Alex stood up. 'I can't stay, but be more careful in future. You have caused a lot of worry.'

'We'll try not to get shot down again,' James told him, his ready smile appearing.

'You do that.' He started to walk away and then turned back. 'Oh, and by the way, well done. That was quite a show of courage and endurance.'

'We'll be all right now,' James declared confidently the moment they were alone again. 'As soon as we are fit we'll be back on active duty.'

'How can you be so sure? The brigadier hasn't any authority over us now, and certainly can't influence where we are sent.'

'You still haven't worked him out, have you?' James made himself comfortable on the edge of the bed. 'He's an impressive man, right?'

'No denying that.'

'He's also a very clever man who knows how to handle people – that's why he was at the academy. At this very moment he will be talking to people and dropping hints until they believe it was all their idea. Relax and let that leg heal properly. Orders to return to base will be arriving in the next few days.'

Lester shook his head in disbelief. 'It will be interesting to see if that happens.'

'No doubt about it, my friend. It's a certainty.'

Chapter Twenty-Seven

'I'm sorry to have taken so long to come and see you, but I have been out of the country. The trip was worthwhile, though.' Alex was shocked at how ill Sara looked, but it shouldn't have surprised him. That business with her husband was disastrous enough, and now she was coping with the news that her son was missing. He wasted no time in putting her mind at rest. 'I have good news. Your son is safe and, apart from an injury to his leg, he is fine.'

She swayed with relief and he made her sit down. He opened the door to find Adams waiting, as he always was. 'Could you please see that refreshments are brought in?'

'At once, sir. Is madam all right?'

'She will be in a little while. I have just brought her the good news that her son is safe.'

'Oh, that's a relief, sir.' Adams beamed. 'I'll see to the refreshments. Nice strong tea needed, then.'

'Absolutely right.'

'Tell me how you know,' she asked eagerly when he returned. 'I've not had official notification yet.'

'I delivered a plane to France, and while I was there I went to see Ruth and Lillia, and they told me that two dishevelled, exhausted pilots had hobbled in the day before. It was James and Lester. They both have injuries, but not serious, and they will make full recoveries. They were shot down over enemy territory and had a long hike to get back. But they made it in spite of their injuries, and are now recovering in the field hospital.'

'Oh, thank God.' Her head bowed in relief, and then she smiled. 'And he found his way to his twin sister. Isn't that just a miracle?'

'It is, indeed, and both the girls are well. They are overworked, of course, but seem to be coping extremely well with the pressures they are under. Lillia said she has written to you.'

'Did they tell you what happened to them?'

'I suspect I received only a brief outline of the story, but I'll tell you what I know.' He paused while the refreshments were wheeled in, and then continued. When he'd finished, he smiled and said, 'I wanted to bring a bottle of champagne

245

with me, but I was so delighted to see the boys I quite forgot to get one.'

'We must celebrate with something more than tea.' She rang for Adams, who was still just outside the door.

'Wonderful news, madam. We are all so thrilled.'

'We want to celebrate. Do we have any champagne in the cellar?'

'Two bottles. We have been saving them for the end of the war, but perhaps this is the right time to crack open one of them?'

'Get the two, and give one to the staff. I am sure they would like to drink to my son's survival.'

'Thank you, madam. They will appreciate that.'

Later that evening, when Sara was in a relaxed mood, Alex asked how things were after the trial.

'Not too bad. I manage to keep busy at the hospital.'

'What about friends? Do you entertain or visit them?'

She pursed her lips. 'When scandal hits, you soon find out who your friends are. My past acquaintances soon crossed me off their visiting list, but I really don't mind. They can say what they like, but I know it was an arranged marriage, in name only, though even the name was false. I am glad my parents did not live to see this. They thought to save my reputation and that of the Kirkby family; instead it has done the opposite.'

'What happened to you in the past is of no consequence to those who know you. It is the woman you are now that I admire, and that goes for everyone who met you at the Andersons' Christmas party.'

'That has been made obvious by the kind letters I have received from them. The Andersons have invited me to stay with them; your father has called on me several times, and your mother sent me a charming letter. I count them as true friends and you as my most supportive friend.'

Alex poured the champagne Adams had just brought in and lifted his glass. 'Let us drink to true friends, and the safe return of all those we love.'

He was pleased he had been able to bring her such welcome news about her son. It was clear that apart from her work at the hospital she was leading a lonely life at this time. It was what he had feared would happen. 'My father will be returning to our home in Cornwall next week and would be delighted if you would stay with them for a while. The countryside is beautiful and a change would be relaxing for you.'

'Your mother has very kindly already extended that invitation to me, but I must stay here. Will they now send Lester home as he is wounded?'

'I doubt that,' he told her gently. 'His injury is not severe and both boys are determined to return to flying as soon as they are well enough.'

She couldn't hide her disappointment. 'I miss my children so much. When am I going to see them again? I have nearly lost both of them. They've been lucky, but what if their luck runs out? I am so frightened for them.'

'They've both had narrow escapes, and for their survival we can be thankful, but we must believe that they will come through this war unscathed. They do say that lightning never strikes twice, and if that is true they will return to take up their musical careers. You've always believed that is their destiny, so continue to hold on to that belief.'

'I can always count on sound, comforting advice from you. What have I ever done to deserve such a friend?' she told him.

'Where shall I start?' he joked, making her laugh. 'That's better; you are lovely when you smile. Promise me you will remain positive and keep smiling.'

'I will try.'

'Good.' He stood up. 'I must take my leave. I don't know when I will be able to come again, but do consider the invites you have received. A change could help to ease the loneliness you are feeling with the children away.'

'I'm sure it would, and thank you for bringing me such good news.'

He kissed her on the cheek and walked out to the car. While driving back to Hendon he thought about the visit, and one thing was now absolutely clear: he wanted to spend the rest of his life with her, if that was possible. What timing, he thought grimly. They were in the middle of a war, and her life was in disarray. There was no way he could let her know how he felt. All she needed at this time was a friend, and that was what he must be. After what she had been through, anything else would just be an added complication to her, and she still had to sort out the mess of that arranged marriage. He must wait for the right time, and exercise the patience he was noted for. Once the war was over they could all sort out their lives, but one thing he was becoming impatient about was his application to return to his regiment. The first one had been rejected, stating that he was doing vital work instructing new pilots. He had immediately put in another application and was still waiting for a decision. If that also was denied he would keep on until they damned well got fed up with his requests and agreed.

'We want you to transfer to the RFC permanently.'

'No, sir.' Alex bristled. He wasn't going to let them do that. 'I agreed to train pilots for six months. That time is up and I want to return to my regiment.'

'You can't do that; they are in France.'

'Why can't I, sir?'

'Because you're a pilot, man, and a damned fine one from all I've heard.'

'I can fly planes, but I am a soldier first and foremost. That has been my life from the age of eighteen.'

The general sat back and glared at the stubborn brigadier standing in front of him. 'I can order you to transfer to the RFC.'

'If you do that, then for the first time in my career I will disobey an order, sir.'

'Will you, indeed? Then you could well face a court martial and dismissal from the army. What would you do then?'

'Join the navy, sir.'

General Trent burst out laughing. 'My God, I do believe you would. All right, you can rejoin your regiment, but don't go and get yourself killed. Good officers are badly needed out there.'

'Wouldn't dream of it, sir.' Alex couldn't help smiling as his application was stamped with approval. He had enjoyed his time as an instructor, but he wanted to do more than that, be more involved, and that desire had made him put in this application.

General Trent stood up and handed over the papers. 'I think you're mad to do this. Do you really know what you are letting yourself in for?'

'I am well aware of the conditions and risks, sir.'

'No doubt, but I still think this is foolhardy and the waste of a good instructor. However, I can see you are determined, so now that's dealt with you can buy me a drink, Alex. Wish I could come with you, but they think I'm too old. Absolute nonsense.'

He nodded agreement. That was something he'd half expected to be raised in his case.

'I know what you're thinking.' The general gave him a sideways glance. 'Your age is just a number on the paper. Look at you; you're tall, lean, strong and disgustingly fit, looking ten years younger than you are. How do you do it?'

'I run every day and swim at least twice a week.'

'Humph. You forgot to mention that you play all kinds of sport, as well.'

'When I can.'

'Don't know where you get the energy from. Mine's a double whisky,' he told Alex as they entered the officers' mess.

The boys were delighted to be back at their airfield, and pleased they had at least been able to spend a little time with the girls and that had been a treat. However, Lester had been grounded because his injury needed more time to heal, and then the weather had closed in and they hadn't been able to fly for some weeks. The moment it cleared, Lester had the frustrating time of watching his friends leave without him.

'Hey, have you heard?' James rushed up to his friend waving a letter. 'Alex is back with his regiment. I knew he wouldn't be able to sit on the sidelines for much longer.'

'His outfit is here in France, isn't it?'

James nodded. 'We'll have to waggle our wings when we fly over the battlegrounds. If he's down there he will know it's us because he taught us that trick.'

'When they let me fly again.' Lester rubbed his leg. 'This has healed now and is only a little stiff, but not bad enough to stop me flying.'

'You're seeing the medic tomorrow and they will probably pass you as fit for active service again.'

'Hope so. I don't like seeing you all take off every day without me, and waiting anxiously to see if you all come back. You haven't got anyone to watch your tail.'

'I miss you, but I'm all right. I've got the others with me. Don't you trust me?'

'Not when a certain enemy plane is around.'

James grinned. 'Haven't seen him for a while, but you needn't worry because I'm sure you'll be with us after tomorrow. I've also had a letter from the girls, did you?'

'Yes.' Lester smiled then. 'It was wonderful to see them. What luck to be taken to their hospital.'

'Yes, worth the struggle we had to get there. I didn't expect to get a medal, though.'

251

'Nor me, but they seemed to consider we'd done something that warranted recognition, and you did bring back those photographs they wanted.'

'True.' James sat down, his expression worried. 'I wish we could get you a piano. You haven't touched one for a long time, and I know how much it means to you.'

Lester tried not to think about that; it was almost like a physical pain to be separated from his music, and he knew his sister was suffering in the same way. They both felt as if half of them were missing without it, but this war and all its brutality had to take priority. 'I'll make up for the lost years when I get back home again. The professor will enjoy knocking me back into shape.'

'And I'll hear your sister sing again,' James sighed. 'I hate to think of you both stuck here with your talent going to waste.'

'Hey, what brought on this miserable tone of voice? Everyone is being asked to make sacrifices.'

'Oh, it's just another year gone, and who knows what this one will bring.'

'The end of the war – hopefully.' Lester stood up, flexed his leg and smiled at his grim friend. 'Let's go to town this evening. You need cheering up.'

'Good idea. We could ask if any of the restaurants have a piano we could buy and bring back here.'

'Will you stop that?'

'All right.' He held up his hands in surrender. 'I won't mention it again. We'll have to make do with the wireless, that's if we can get any music out of it, of course.'

'Oh, heavens. Cheer up or you'll have us both crying in our beer.'

His friend grinned, the sombre mood wiped away. 'The first one is on you.'

The next day Lester was declared fit to fly again and as it was a clear day he took to the air with the rest of the squadron. His one desire was to see the end of this long war and the suffering it was causing. They were all finding it harder and harder to cope, as he saw with James last night. It was unusual for his friend to be so down in spirit, and he knew it was happening to him as well.

Once airborne, he took a deep breath of pleasure. He had never lost that feeling of joy as he climbed into the sky. It was a clear, cold day, and he counted himself lucky to be up here and not on the ground, where he would certainly be if the brigadier hadn't given them the chance to fly. His thoughts went out to the man he had great affection and respect for. He was down there somewhere now, and he prayed for his safety, and all the other little dots below him.

Chapter Twenty-Eight

Autumn, 1918

Alex cast his mind back to the previous year, 1917. What a year it had been. It seemed as if the whole world was in turmoil. There had been the revolution in Russia and Tsar Nicholas II had abdicated and America had joined the war. Then there had been terrible, costly battles here. The loss of so many young lives was appalling, and still it went on. Surely 1918 must bring an end to the fighting.

The sound of planes brought him out of his reverie, and he watched as they swooped in to attack the enemy positions.

'That's a welcome sight, sir.'

'It certainly is. We need all the help we can get, Corporal.'

'I wouldn't argue with that. Ah, look, they are breaking off and two are coming this way. Hope they know we're not the enemy.'

'Don't worry; they won't have any ammunition left.'

They swept in low and waggled their wings as they passed, making Alex laugh out loud, and wave frantically. 'Good flying, boys!'

'I've never seen any of them do that before. Why do you think they flew over us like that, sir?'

'They were looking for me. I taught them that little manoeuvre as a greeting.'

The soldier looked at his officer in amazement. 'Can you fly, then, sir?'

He nodded, still smiling broadly. 'I was assigned as a temporary instructor to the RFC, and I know those two.'

'Well, they're welcome here at any time. We might be able to have something to eat in peace for a while now. That attack must have shaken the enemy up a bit. Can I get you something, sir?'

'No, thanks, Corporal. I'll come along in a while.'

When he was alone again, Alex remained where he was, deep in thought. The boys didn't know where he was, so they must be doing that flying past wherever they went in the hope he would see them. It had certainly brightened his day, and he felt quite proud to have had a hand in their training. They were doing the job with skill and courage, and even their crash hadn't dampened their joy of flying. He must write and tell Sara that he had seen them.

'Alex was there. Did you see him waving?'

'I saw lots of soldiers waving to us,' Lester told his friend. 'How can you be sure one of them was the brigadier?'

'He was standing away from the crowd. I'm positive it was him. I'd know him anywhere, even from the air. I'll write and ask him.'

'Talking of writing, have you heard from Ruth lately? I haven't had a letter from her for some time.'

'I received one yesterday.' James gave him a speculative look. 'You haven't upset her, have you?'

'Of course I haven't.'

'In that case you'll probably receive a letter soon. Try turning on the charm next time you write.'

'How on earth can I do that in a letter?'

'You could let her know how you feel about her. Girls like to hear those things.'

Lester's look was incredulous. 'You're an expert in these things, are you?'

'Not really, but I'm doing my best. I think your sister is starting to become fond of me, and I can't wait for the war to end so I can shower her with special gifts. What kind of jewellery does she like?'

'Emeralds.'

'Of course, they will match her eyes. The first thing I'll buy her is a platinum and emerald necklace. I know a good jeweller and he will make it for me.'

'That will cost a fortune,' Lester pointed out.

'I can afford it. I'm rich.'

'Are you?' He'd known his friend came from a good family, but he'd never considered that he might have a personal fortune.

James shrugged. 'My dear old grandfather liked me.'

'And he was wealthy?'

'Very. I don't talk about it in case it attracts the wrong kind of people, but I know you and Lillia wouldn't let something like that influence you. Come on, we've finished flying for the day, so let's get out of here for a while.'

As it turned out the weather closed in and flying was out of the question for nearly two weeks. They were flying the moment it was clear enough to take to the air again, and the demand on all of the pilots was relentless. It was a relief when they had a break and could relax for a day or so. The strain was showing, not only on them, but on everyone involved in the fighting. It seemed never-ending and they were all war-weary.

'Lord, I'm tired,' Lester groaned as he clambered out of the plane.

James was inspecting a hole in his friend's plane and sucked in a deep breath. 'Are you all right?

That was damned close.'

'I know. I could use a drink.'

'Wonder if everyone made it back.'

'Let's hope so.' Lester scanned the empty sky anxiously. 'They call us the lucky duo to have lasted this long. I do remember you telling me that we were going to survive. It's getting to be a struggle, though.'

'Agreed, but we must keep on being lucky, because this can't go on for ever. It must end soon.'

'Can't be soon enough for me.'

'Your piano will need tuning when you get back,' James joked, turning the subject away from a distressing situation.

'It will be fine. The professor is looking after it for me, and he won't let it deteriorate, neither will Mother. It's a very special instrument.'

'I gathered that. Was it already in your mother's family?'

'No, it was a gift to Mother before we were born.'

'Some gift. Who gave it to your family?'

'Mother told us she is saving that news for us when we get home at last.'

James thought about the newspaper cutting he was still keeping carefully hidden, and was concerned that here was yet another mystery. His friend couldn't wait to get home for good, but there was unpleasant news waiting for him and his sister. He was determined to be close by to support them if they needed it.

'Ah, there you are.' Preston handed them a sheet of paper. 'You two need a break, so you are off-duty for two days. That is advertising a concert taking place tonight at the church in town, in honour of the renowned French pianist, Pierre Le Fort, who was killed six months ago.'

'That's terrible.' Lester was studying the leaflet. 'I heard him once and he was very good. I was only eight at the time, but I remember thinking that I wanted to play as well as him when I was older. Thank you, sir. I'd like to go to this concert.'

'I'm coming as well,' James told him. 'It will be good to relax and enjoy some music.'

The church was crowded and they just managed to find two seats at the back. James was disappointed because he wanted his friend as close to the grand piano as possible. Although Lester never said anything or complained, he knew he must be starved of music. After all, it had been his life until being sent to the academy, and once in France he hadn't touched a piano.

'Keep my seat,' he whispered. 'I'll go and see if there is any room down the front.'

Lester pushed him back. 'This is fine. The acoustics should be good in here.'

'All right.' He craned his neck to see the front and nearly gasped out loud. There was a large poster of the deceased musician seated at a grand piano. He looked from the picture to his friend. 'Hey, look, that could be you when you are older. You sit just like that at a piano.'

'So do all pianists. Be quiet now, they are about to begin.'

Lester closed his eyes and allowed the music to sweep through him, releasing the tension that had built up from month after month of flying into danger.

His friend watched him as the concert continued, and saw him relax. He also sat back and enjoyed the music, glad they had come. They had been under a lot of strain lately, and they were all getting touchy, easily irritated. He was worried they might start getting careless, and that mustn't happen. They had survived this long, when many hadn't, and they must continue to be sharp and alert. Preston had recognised this and had arranged an outing for them. He must thank him in the morning.

Having thoroughly enjoyed the concert they had a drink as they weren't flying the next day, and slept soundly that night.

The next day they were eager to tell Preston all about the concert and thanked him for suggesting it. James told him, 'We needed a distraction, and you know Lester is a good pianist, so he really enjoyed it.'

'So I understand. When I saw the leaflet I thought of him.'

'Very good of you, sir. We really enjoyed it. He's got a twin sister who is a nurse at a field hospital and she's a singer. They are very talented, and gave us a concert one Christmas. We packed the house with people who wanted to hear them.'

'He is also a skilled pilot, you both are, or you wouldn't still be alive. In my time here I have seen pilots come and go, but you keep coming back.' He smiled and slapped James on the back. 'See that you keep that up. It would break my heart to lose you now.'

'Not a chance. I promised my friend we'd survive this war, and that's what I intend to do.'

He winked at Preston. 'And I'm going to marry his beautiful sister and help her with her musical career.'

'Congratulations.'

James laughed. 'Thank you, sir, but that's a bit premature. She doesn't know about it yet.'

'Ah, good luck. I hope she accepts you.'

'She will,' he said confidently.

When James came and sat beside him, Lester looked up from the letter he was reading. 'What did Preston have to say?'

'Nothing about flying. I was telling him about the concert you gave us that Christmas.'

'Heavens, that seems a lifetime ago now.'

'It was.' James leant across. 'Who is the letter from?'

'Ruth. She has apologised for not writing for a while, but she's been on one of those trains again, and there wasn't a moment to spare.' He held up the letter. 'Look, she's written pages and pages.'

'I told you she would write soon. When you reply don't forget to tell her how much you are longing to see her again.'

'I will. How are you getting on with my sister?'

'Making good progress.' He grinned. 'We could have a double wedding.'

'You're impossible,' Lester laughed. 'Lillia won't share the stage with someone else; you ought to know that by now. When she marries, if she marries, she will be the star of that day, and no one else.'

'You're right. You can be our best man, and I'll be yours.'

'We'll see.'

Chapter Twenty-Nine

'You are injured, sir. Let me have a look at it.'

Alex glanced down at his torn blood-soaked tunic. 'It looks worse than it is. Just needs a dressing, I expect.'

'Take off your jacket, sir; I'll need to stop the bleeding.'

'I'm all right. You have plenty of other patients after that battle. See to them first.'

'They are being dealt with, but you are the highest ranking officer still standing. The men need you, so remove your jacket, sir.'

'This is a significant breakthrough, and if we can keep this up the war will be over this year.'

'If you don't let me attend to you, you will not see the end of the war.' The medic signalled to another soldier. 'Help the brigadier.'

'I don't need...' Alex swayed and the men caught hold of him before he hit the ground. They sat him against a wall of the ruined house they were sheltering in, and he tried to stand up again.

'Stubborn,' the medic muttered. 'Do as you are told, sir, and sit down. I'm in charge now. Hold him, Corporal, while I see to that wound.'

'Ouch!' Alex glared at the medic as he probed at the gash in his side. 'Where did you learn first aid?'

'I trained at the best teaching hospital in London, and had just qualified as a doctor when I volunteered for this lot. Sit still.'

'That's hard to do. What the hell are you doing?'

'There's something in here. Ah, here it is; a piece of shrapnel, and another. Hope that is all there is.'

'So do I.' Alex wiped the sweat from his face. 'You nearly finished?'

'Just got to clean it and put in a few stitches. You are lucky; nothing vital has been damaged as far as I can see. I suppose it's useless to ask you to go to a field hospital for further examination?' The look he got from Alex gave him the answer. 'Silly request.'

Another soldier arrived with a mug, handed it to Alex and winked. 'Thought you might like a little drop of brandy, sir.'

'Thanks.' He took a gulp and gasped. 'Where did you get it?'

'Found it in the cellar of this abandoned house, sir. We thought it might come in handy.'

He took a more cautious sip this time. 'Are you sure it's brandy?'

'Well, we can't read the labels, but the bottles were still sealed. It's a spirit of some kind and we are calling it brandy.'

'Bottles? How many did you find?'

'A crate full, sir. We've tried one and it's perfectly drinkable. Quite pleasant, really.'

He laughed and drained the mug. 'That's a matter of opinion.'

The soldier smirked. 'Would you like a drop more, sir?'

'I wouldn't dare risk another one of those, and

if you're handing that round make sure no one gets enough to make them drunk. The last thing we need is an inebriated squad.'

'The sergeant has got it under tight guard, sir. At the moment we are only giving it to the wounded.'

'Good man.' Alex gritted his teeth as the medic stitched his wound.

'There you are, sir. Be careful not to tear the stitches or you'll start bleeding again. I still think you ought to get that looked at by the field doctors.'

'Out of the question. You're a doctor and that's good enough for me.'

The medic sighed. 'In that case I want your promise that you will come to me if you get feverish or feel unwell in any way.'

'I'll do that.'

'Make sure you do. Now, try and sleep while there's a pause in the fighting. You've lost quite a lot of blood and need rest. I can give you something to–' When he saw Alex's expression he shook his head. 'Well, I tried.'

The medic hurried away and Alex settled against the wall and fished in his pocket for the letter he had received from his father. It had taken weeks to reach him, and this was the first quiet moment he'd had to look at it. The news from his father was astonishing. Barber had died of a heart attack in prison, and there was no longer any reason to pursue the legality of the marriage, or file for divorce if that had proved necessary. Now he was dead, Sara wanted the whole thing forgotten. She was free.

Relief that this burden had been taken from

her, made him relax and tiredness swept over him. He knew he had to rest while there was a chance. The end of the war couldn't be far off, and he was determined to keep going until then. There was even more reason now to want the war over and return home.

He woke suddenly to the sound of gunfire and groaned as he moved. Someone had covered him with a blanket, and he pushed it aside struggling to get to his feet.

The medic and a captain arrived. 'We've got to move, sir,' the officer told him, holding out a hand to pull him up.

'Easy does it. How do you feel?' the medic asked, frowning.

'I'm fine.' He stood up straight. 'Just a little stiff, that's all. You did a good job, Doc.'

'I want to have another look at your side the first moment we get.'

'Right. Come on, Captain, fill me in on the situation. How long was I asleep?'

'Five hours, sir.'

'Damn! Whatever was in that mug really knocked me out. Why didn't you wake me?'

'It was quiet, and you needed the rest. We sent out a scouting party to get the lie of the land, and as far as they could tell, the enemy is still retreating.'

'That's good news. Let me talk to them. I want a full report.'

Ruth signalled to Lillia that it was time for them to take a break before the next load of ambulances arrived.

'Not quite so many casualties arriving now,' Ruth said when they sat down.

'I hadn't noticed.' Lillia yawned. 'I'm going to sleep for a week when this is over.'

'Me too, and will you stop yawning? You'll set me off and we've got another five hours before we can collapse into bed, and then there's no guarantee we won't be dragged out in the middle of the night.'

'Sorry, I'll try not to yawn too much. I had a letter from James and my brother yesterday. They told me about a concert they had attended.' She sighed. 'It must have been lovely. I do miss music so much.'

'Hang in there. This war will be over in a matter of weeks, and then you and Lester can get back to your studies.'

'Do you really believe it's nearly over?'

'Everyone says so. I wrote and asked Alex for his opinion, but I haven't heard from him for some time.'

'Neither have I.' She had been dismayed when she'd heard he was in France. He had been good to her brother at the academy, and as she had come to know him, she had grown to like him very much. Wherever he was it was probably in the thick of the fighting. 'I do hope he's all right.'

'We'd have heard if he wasn't,' Ruth said without much conviction.

'I don't know about that. News from the front line can get delayed. Every time a new batch of wounded arrive, I scan the faces hoping there isn't anyone there I know.'

'I'm just the opposite. I try not to look, but

we're worrying unnecessarily. A pile of letters will arrive together, I expect.'

'You're right. I received three from James and four from my brother yesterday.'

'Lucky you. I didn't get that many and we do so look forward to the letters, don't we?'

'Yes, everyone does.'

Ruth sighed sadly. 'It would be lovely to see them again. Wouldn't it be wonderful if we were all home by Christmas?'

'Home seems just a distant memory.'

Both girls ate in silence, deep in thought. The general feeling was that the war was in its final stages, but they didn't dare dwell on it too much in case there was a setback. Also, in this often confused situation, rumours flew around and there was no telling if they were true or not.

'Here they come!' Ruth pushed her chair back and headed for the ambulances with her friend right behind her.

Ruth's optimism that they were receiving fewer casualties was shattered. There were more than they could accommodate this time, and as a hospital ship was expected to dock within the next week, the girls were assigned to help out on the next train. Some nurses rode the trains almost continually, but at times extra help was needed when they packed the men on board. The only way they could get them all on was to make up beds on the floor for some casualties. Every available space had to be used.

With the loading finally completed, Ruth gave her friend a concerned look. 'Hope we don't get many hold-ups on the way because this is going to be a difficult journey.'

'We'll manage.' Lillia eased herself along the crowded train to her working carriage. 'See you at the other end.'

Some of the men were so seriously wounded that there were fears they might not make it to the ship, but the medical staff on the train worked tirelessly to see they did.

Lillia went to one soldier who was distressed, delirious and calling out. Her heart ached for him; he was so young. He was waving his arms around so she caught hold of them and held on firmly. 'It's all right; you are not on the battlefield any more. You are on your way home.' She began to sing softly to him, and slowly his struggles ceased, and he fell into a deep sleep.

'Remarkable, Nurse.' A doctor stood beside her. 'Your voice has had a soothing effect on him.'

'Music can do that.' She smiled up at the weary doctor. 'But it would have had the opposite effect if I belted out an operatic aria.'

'You're a singer?'

'I hope to be one day. That ambition is on hold, though, until this mess ends.'

'Hey, Nurse!' one of the other men called. 'I'd like to hear you let rip. From what I've just heard that's some voice you've got there.'

'Thank you, but what is needed on this train is music to sooth and calm.' She was still holding the boy's hands and felt him squeeze gently as if to say thank you.

'You're welcome, Soldier. Rest now and I'll come and sing to you again later.'

'I do believe he is hearing you.'

'Who knows, but in cases like this we must do everything we can to ease the pain and trauma these men are suffering.'

'And you understand that only too well, being one of the nurses from the hospital ship that was torpedoed.'

She gave him a startled look. They never mentioned that and were under the impression no one knew. 'Where did you hear that?'

'I know someone who was on the recovery ship, and he told me about the courage of you and your friend.'

'Courage?' She gave an inelegant snort. 'I was terrified.'

'So would we all have been.' He put his head to one side and studied her carefully. 'Have you got a boyfriend?'

'There is someone who insists he's going to marry me.'

'And is he?'

'I haven't decided yet.'

The doctor laughed. 'When you have made up your mind and perhaps refuse him, my name is Ben Redman. Remember that. I haven't got a girlfriend.'

'Are you flirting with me, Doctor?'

'I think I am. It's nice to do something normal, isn't it? Will you sing to my patients before lights out and help them have a peaceful night without bad dreams?'

'Of course,' she replied, and he winked cheekily before walking away.

That evening she sang gentle songs that seemed to settle everyone down for the night, and even the medical staff stopped to listen. She felt rusty after not exercising her vocal cords for some time, but she didn't need to use her full power, and everyone expressed their appreciation. Evidently it had helped to calm patients and staff as well. At the request of the doctors she did this every evening, and it did appear to help many of the wounded.

Ben was also leaving on the hospital ship, and after all the patients had been settled on board, he kissed Lillia on the cheek. 'It's been a joy meeting you, and I shall watch to see your name in lights one day soon.'

'Have a safe journey,' she told him.

Ruth watched as he walked on to the ship, and then turned to her friend. 'What was that all about? A doctor kissing a nurse is just not done.'

'Just a little harmless flirting.' She laughed softly. 'He was rather nice, though, don't you think?'

'I suppose he was, but don't let James know you've been kissing a handsome doctor.'

'It was only one peck on the cheek, but I won't tell if you don't.'

The girls were in a lighter mood as they boarded the train for the return journey, and when they got back they found a pile of letters waiting for them. There was also an excited buzz around the place that the war could be over very soon.

In their letters the boys were optimistic they would be home for Christmas, and Alex, although more cautious, was hopeful the end was in sight. And when on November 9th Kaiser Wilhelm II abdicated, it looked as if they could be right.

Chapter Thirty

'Gentlemen, stand down, your work here is finished.'

The boys stared at Preston in disbelief, and then at the planes waiting for them on the field.

'You're grounding us, sir?' James asked.

'That's right. You've flown your last mission.'

'But why? What have we done?' Lester couldn't understand why this was happening.

'What you've done is a damned fine job, but it's all over.' He broke into a huge smile. 'You're so tired you don't know what I'm saying, do you? Haven't you been following the news?'

'We've only been concentrating on flying and trying to stay alive,' James told him. 'What's happened?'

'All fighting has ceased as from today, and an armistice has been signed. The war is over.'

'Who won?' James asked dryly.

'We did, and we'll try to get you home for Christmas.'

They felt dazed. They had been flying and being shot at for so long it had become a way of life to them, filling their thoughts and nightmares. It had suddenly come to an end and they were stunned. They had always jokingly told the girls that the war was nearly over, but only to raise their spirits. In truth they had never been able to see an end to it. Now they were being told it had really happened and they were having trouble grasping this fact.

Preston shook his head. 'I expected more reaction than this, but when it sinks in there will be a celebration in the operations room this evening. I'll expect you to be there. Until then why don't you go back to bed and get some sleep? You look as if you need it.'

'Sir.'

They watched the officer walk away and looked at each other. James shook his head. 'Over? What are we going to do now?'

Lester shoved his hands in his pockets and shrugged. 'Shouldn't we be jumping around and shouting for joy?'

'That would be the normal thing to do, I suppose. Heavens, what has this war done to us? I just feel numb.'

'Me too. Let's get a cup of tea and something to eat. Perhaps we will feel like celebrating after that.'

'Good idea.'

When they reached the canteen a couple of the ground crew rushed up and slapped them on the back, grinning wildly. 'It's all over! We won't have to wait anxiously each time wondering if any of you are coming back. Isn't that wonderful? The war is all over.'

A cheer went up from the crowded canteen and it was so noisy they took their food to the lounge the pilots used. It was quieter there and the pilots were more subdued. They had lost so many pilots over the time they had been here, and as their numbers had diminished it had been necessary

271

to fly more and more missions. They hadn't had time to think of anything else, but now those losses were uppermost in their thoughts.

'We made it.' James sat down, still looking slightly bewildered.

'You said we would, but we're not the same as those two boys who first arrived here. We've grown up and are carrying scars, mental and physical.'

'Change was inevitable, of course, but once we get home we'll soon pick up our lives again. You'll start playing your piano, Lillia will be singing, and I'll be looking after both of you. That will be my new mission in life from now on.'

'Are you still set on marrying my sister?'

'I am. Nothing could ever change my feelings for her. Our two girls have been through a lot and must have seen awful things.' Suddenly James brightened up. 'But it's all over. We have a future again.'

Lester yawned, then finished his tea and stood up. 'I'm going to take Preston's advice and sleep for a couple of hours. Perhaps I'll be able to take this all in after that.'

'Good idea. I'll see you for the celebration later.'

Lester slumped onto the bed and buried his head in the pillow, allowing a few tears to trickle down his face. The killing was over, thank God, and he would soon see his mother, Lillia and Ruth again. He hoped the brigadier was safe, as well. His thoughts turned to his piano and the way they had studied day after day, but that life seemed like a dream now and after all that had happened to them it wasn't going to be easy to start over again. He wondered if his sister was feeling the same at this moment. Knowing her temperament, she would probably walk straight in and demand lessons from the professor. He smiled at the thought of being with his twin again and drifted off to sleep.

Refreshed from their afternoon nap they joined everyone else for the celebration. When they walked in they were handed a glass of something. James sniffed his. 'I say, this is champagne. Where did you get it, sir?'

Preston sipped his own drink and smiled. 'I had it put away waiting for this day. Help yourself to food. A local farmer insisted on supplying us with a few treats as a thank you for helping to end the war.'

'What happens now, sir?' Lester wanted to know.

'We start packing up here, and I want to get you two home as soon as possible. You should have been repatriated after you got shot down, but you had other ideas. I didn't expect to see you again, but was delighted when you arrived back, willing and ready to fly again. I couldn't have asked for better pilots, and will be recommending that you both receive medals for your excellent service.'

'Ah, sir, we've already got one medal, we don't need any more.'

James hit his friend's arm. 'Yes, we do. It will impress our girls.'

'I doubt that,' he told him. 'What will impress them is the fact that we are still in one piece.'

'I'll have his medal as well, sir, if he doesn't

want it,' James joked.

'The pair of you ought to be in the music halls. You've been a good double act from the moment you arrived,' Preston told them, laughing with amusement at their antics. Then said more seriously, 'I'm damned glad I don't have to send any more young men out to get killed.'

'You've had a tough job,' Lester agreed.

'We all have, but now it's over. Enjoy yourselves tonight, and for once you don't have to worry how much you drink because there's no flying to-morrow. In fact, if you ever fly again it will be for pleasure.'

'That will be strange. I will have to keep search-ing the sky to see if someone out there is intent on killing me. Still, I might buy myself a little plane when I get home. It could be useful.' James emptied his glass and looked around for a refill. 'Want another?'

Lester shook his head, and indicated his still nearly full glass. 'This will do me.'

'You never have been keen on alcohol, have you? I remember when you were playing you only ever had water, or sometimes tea. I bet you can't wait to get back to your piano.'

'I've been thinking about that, and do you know, I can hardly recall those days. Everyone's excited about going home, but adjusting to that life again isn't going to be easy.'

'It will take a while,' James admitted. 'You can both come and stay with us if you find it hard to settle. Your mother as well, of course.'

'Thanks, but we will have to see how things go at home first. If Father starts being too difficult we might well take you up on that offer. He's never written to us, though we didn't really expect him to, and Mother has never once mentioned him in her letters.'

James didn't comment. He still had the newspaper cutting and dreaded to think what the twins were going to face when they arrived home. It was unlikely to be a happy homecoming, and that was why he had invited them to stay at his home.

'One thing we must do before we leave is go and see that family who helped us.'

'Definitely.' Lester looked thoughtful. 'I hope they are all right. Do you remember where the farm was?'

'Should be able to find it again, but it's quite a way and we will need transport and a couple of days' leave. I expect we can manage that.'

'There are plenty of vans around now with nothing to do. Can you drive?'

'Of course I can.' James called Preston over and explained what they needed and why. The officer readily agreed and they retired for the night, happy to have something positive to do while they waited to be sent home.

They set off early and after careering around the countryside for most of the day, pulled up at a farm that looked familiar.

It was the right place, and to their relief the family were all right and delighted to see them. They stayed the night with them and returned to base the next day, happy they had been able to fit in this visit to thank them for their help. Without them, it was doubtful if they could have gone much further in their exhausted state. It was right to come and tell them how much it had meant to them.

'There's a ship arriving in two days to take the first lot of soldiers home, and I have been given orders that you are to go with them. Clearing up here and moving men and equipment is going to be a big undertaking, and the sooner we start, the better.'

Alex was surprised by the order. 'I am happy to be returning home so soon, but wouldn't I be of more help here?'

'That isn't my decision. My orders are to send all wounded and sick first. You have been wounded, so you are with the first batch.'

'But my injury healed a long time ago, and it wasn't bad enough to take me out of the front line.'

'I understand you refused to leave.'

'We had just lost six officers in the fighting. I couldn't leave. The medic patched me up and I was able to carry on. I'm perfectly fit now, so this order doesn't apply to me.'

'It does, because I say so,' the brigadier general told him. 'Go home, Alex. You can be of great use back at base. You're excellent at strategy and planning. Clear heads are going to be needed to sort out this mess, and you know what it's like out here. Your experience will be invaluable.'

'It's unlikely I will be given such a commission.'

'You never know. Here are your papers. Go home, and then after seven days' leave, report back to Aldershot. And stop arguing with me.'

The brigadier general was a slight man, but

when he gave orders there was no mistaking his authority. 'I wouldn't dream of arguing with a superior officer, sir. I have my orders.'

'Make sure you damned well obey them – and the name is Edward to you.' He reached in the drawer of the table he was using as a desk and brought out a bottle of whisky. 'Grab a mug and have a drink with me before you leave.'

'What plans have you for the future?' Edward asked while they were enjoying the drink.

'I'm hoping to get married and settle down at last.'

'Really? If you don't mind me saying, you've left it a bit late to do that and possibly start a family, haven't you?'

'She already has two delightful children I am very fond of.'

'Ah, she's a widow then.'

He ignored that remark. 'I don't know yet if she will accept me, but I'm hopeful.'

'Will you stay in the army if she does?'

'Not sure. That is something we will have to discuss, but at the moment the thought of retiring is attractive, and there is a business venture I have been considering for some time. However, that is something for the future because there is going to be a hell of a lot to do sorting out the terrible consequences of this war.' Alex ran a hand through his hair, his expression sad. 'So many young men dead, wounded and with mental problems they might never recover from. The scars of this madness are going to be felt for a very long time.'

'I agree. Many homecomings are going to be stressful, but I hope yours will be happy, and that this woman has the good sense to marry you.'

'We shall see.' Alex finished his drink and stood up. After the first shock of being told he was to be among the first to return home, he was now glad and eager to be on his way. 'I had better pack my gear ready to meet the ship.'

Chapter Thirty-One

The day he arrived back, Alex took the train to Cornwall to see his parents. In his father's last letter he had told him that he was retiring and they would be living permanently in their Cornish home. It was a place they loved for its rugged beauty and tranquillity. Neither of them had ever cared for the hustle and bustle of London.

'Will you be stationed at Aldershot after your leave?' his father asked.

'Those are my orders.'

'Are they going to promote you?'

Alex laughed at his mother's question. 'I really don't know, or care. If things go as I hope, then I might follow Father's example and retire.'

'I can understand if you've had enough after the long years of war, but don't make any hasty decisions.'

'Have you ever known me to act in haste?' he asked his mother.

'No, I haven't. So what are your plans? You must have made some.'

'It's all uncertain at the moment, and will take

278

a while to sort out. I will only be staying with you for three days and then I'll spend the rest of my leave in London. Have you still got the house there, or have you sold it?'

'We've kept it, because we will want to go to London from time to time. You've got your own keys still, haven't you?'

'I have, and that will save me booking in to a hotel.' He recognised the speculative glint in his parents' eyes and knew what was coming next.

'You'll see Sara while you're there?'

'That is the reason for my visit, Mother.'

'Thought it might be, and do tell her she is always welcome here. Care to tell us what you intend to do about that family? We know you have become very fond of them.'

He shook his head. 'As I've said, I don't know anything for sure at the moment. I'll be able to tell you more when I know what I'm going to do. I've had a plan in the back of my mind for some time, and I'll have to look into that before I leave the army.'

'So you really are thinking seriously about leaving?' his father asked.

He smiled at the continual questions. They were probing him for answers, but he didn't want to say too much at the moment. 'Thinking about it, yes, and that is all I can say at this time.'

'We shall have to be patient then,' his mother said, and changed the subject. 'I'm so pleased those two lovely children have survived, though it could have been very different for both of them. One on a ship that was sunk and the other shot down. That must have been terrible for them, and Sara must have been frantic with worry.' She smiled at her son. 'I know how worried I was while you were in France.'

'Just about every mother in the country was worrying about some member of their family,' Charles pointed out.

'Well, it's over now, and settling down to normal life isn't going to be easy for a lot of men.' Alex stood up. 'I think I'll go for a walk along the cliff path before lunch.'

'I'll come with you.' His father hesitated. 'Unless you'd rather be on your own.'

'I'd be glad of your company.'

They walked in silence for a while, enjoying the beauty of the countryside, then Charles said, 'While you were away, Sara did come and stay with us for a week, and we like her very much. She has shown courage and dignity in the way she coped with the scandal of that man, and him dying like that saved her from a lot more heartache. She was relieved to drop the investigation into the legality of the marriage, and a possible divorce if that became necessary. I know you are fond of her and suspect your feelings may go deeper than that, but if you'd rather not talk about it, I understand.'

'I didn't want to say too much in front of Mother because she would get her hopes up, only to be disappointed if things don't work out the way I want them to. I am going to ask Sara to marry me, but after all she went through with that man, I'm not sure she will even consider taking such a step again.'

'Ah, but that marriage was forced on her. This

time she will have a choice, and if she does accept, you will also be taking on the twins.'

'That shouldn't be a problem. I am fond of them and I believe they like me but, of course, their acceptance will be necessary for this to work. I would be able to give them a stable home-life where they can relax and concentrate on their careers.'

'You will be taking on a lot, so are you sure this is what you really want? You've waited a long time, and we had given up hope that you would ever marry.'

'I have never found the woman I wanted to spend the rest of my life with until I met Sara.'

'I hope it works out for you.' He looked at his son and chuckled. 'We will enjoy being grandparents to the twins.'

'Alex! You're back.' Sara greeted him fondly. 'Thank heavens that terrible war is over and you are safe. Welcome home.'

'Thank you, my dear. I am very glad to be back and to see you looking so well.' He took her hands in his and bent to kiss her cheek. 'How have things been for you?'

'Very well and even better now I've seen you. We'll also have the children home for good now the war is over. Isn't it wonderful? There have been such celebrations. Have you seen the professor yet? He is so excited and has been making sure the piano is ready for when Lester returns.'

'I'm going to see Joshua tomorrow.' He sat back and waited while the trolley was brought in.

Adams beamed at him. 'Welcome home, sir.'

'Thank you, I'm glad to be here.' He glanced at the trolley and smiled. 'Is that Cook's famous fruit cake?'

'Yes, sir, she knows you like it.'

'I do, indeed, but how did she know I was coming?'

'She's had it made since the end of the war was declared, ready for your visit.'

'Please thank her and let her know I appreciate her thoughtfulness.'

'I'll do that, sir.' Adams turned to Sara. 'Is there anything else you require, madam?'

'Not at the moment, thank you.'

Once the butler had left she said, 'I've had letters from the children and Lester said he expected to be home soon, but couldn't say when. Lillia won't be returning until all the wounded have been repatriated.'

'They will do that as soon as they can.'

'I'm sure they will, and once they are both here I will have the unpleasant task of telling them about their birth, and what has happened to the man they thought was their father. I don't look forward to that, but it will be a relief to me when they know the whole story. I pray it doesn't spoil their homecoming.'

'We could also give them some good news – at least, I hope they would consider it in that way. From the many letters we have sent each other, you must be aware by now of my feelings for you. I think I fell in love with you the moment I saw you, but could not say anything because you were a married woman. I offered you friendship, and thought I had to be content with that, but now you are free and the war is over there is the future to consider.' He stood up. 'I love you very much, Sara, and would be honoured if you would consent to be my wife.'

'Oh, Alex, I do love you.' She grasped his hands and he pulled her out of the chair. 'But are you sure this is what you want? You know my past.'

'That was a long time ago and you have two delightful children. They are a blessing, my dear, and not something to regret or be ashamed of. They have been your life, but they are not children now, and quite capable of making their own decision. It is time you considered your own happiness. Do you need time to think about my proposal?'

'No, I don't need to think about it. You are quite right and it is time I thought about my own future. I would be proud to be your wife.'

He breathed a sigh of relief and took her into his arms. When their longed-for embrace ended, he said, 'Thank you, my dear, you have made me very happy.'

'That makes two of us.' She smiled up at him with joy in her face. This was more than she could ever have hoped for. After years in that dreadful sham of a marriage she had been given a chance of love and happiness at last. 'What a shame we haven't got any champagne.'

'Ah, but we have. I left a bag in the hall with two bottles in it, just in case you did accept me. One is for us and the other for your staff. They will undoubtedly want to stay with you, so do you think they will accept me?'

'They adore you nearly as much as I do,' she laughed, pushing him out of the door. 'Get the champagne while I ask Adams to bring everyone here.'

Sara had been right; they all appeared to be happy by the news, and Cook's face lit up with excitement as she offered to take care of the catering and make the wedding cake.

'That will be appreciated,' Alex told her. 'We haven't had time to make any plans yet, and nothing can be decided until the twins are home.'

'Of course,' they all agreed, the happy mood dulling for a moment as they all thought about the awful news awaiting them when they did return.

Adams handed round the drinks and they were all smiles again as they congratulated them and wished them well.

Once they were alone again, Alex removed a small box from his pocket, took out the ring and slipped it on her finger. 'Ah, good, it fits. It was my grandmother's and she left it to me a long time ago for my future bride when I found one. It has been worth the wait, and I hope you like it. If not we can find something else later.'

'It's beautiful,' she gasped, gazing at the diamond and sapphire ring. 'I will be proud to wear it.'

'I am sure my grandmother would be pleased with my choice. The next thing we must do is find a suitable house. Do you want to stay in London, or move further out?'

'I hadn't thought about it, but don't you want to live here? This house has come down through the Kirkby family for generations.'

'We can live here, of course, if that is what you

want, but I thought you might like a fresh start. You could give this to the children.'

'What a splendid idea. They are old enough now to have a place of their own.'

Alex chuckled. 'I don't suppose you know, but James is determined to marry Lillia, and I wouldn't be surprised if Ruth and Lester had the same idea. If that is so, then they are going to need somewhere to live, and this house is large enough for all of them.'

'My goodness.' Sara sat down suddenly. 'So much is happening; my head is in a whirl, and you are quite right, they will need this house. I don't mind where we live as long as it's within easy reach of London, because the children will have to stay here to continue their studies.'

'Leave it with me. I will find several houses and we can look at them together before making a choice.'

They talked for hours, making plans for the future, but could not finalise anything for the moment.

They had hoped to celebrate Christmas with their families but had not received permission to leave their base until January 1919. The sea had been rough when they had left France, but there was a lull now and it was quite beautiful when a watery sun shone on the surface. Lester leant on the rail and looked out at the large expanse of water. There was nothing else in sight and he tried to imagine what it had been like for the girls when their ship had been torpedoed. They had jumped into the sea, and after the ship had sunk there would have been nothing but water, no longer beautiful, but deadly.

Someone came and stood beside him and he turned his head to look at his friend who was gripping the rail as tightly as he could. 'Are you feeling better?'

'A bit. I saw a medic and he gave me something. What are you doing out here? It's freezing, and it looks as if another storm is coming in.'

'I wanted some fresh air and I have been trying to imagine what the girls went through when–'

'Don't!' James exclaimed. 'I've got enough to cope with without you frightening the life out of me. Do you think those submarines know the war's over?'

'Of course they do.' He caught hold of his friend as he swayed. 'You're not safe out here in your state. Let's go and see if we can get some food inside you.'

'I'll try a cup of tea.' He groaned as the ship lurched. 'Why didn't they let us fly back?'

Lester pointed to the black clouds rolling in at speed as the wind increased in force. 'Would you like to be up there in that?'

'It would be better than this.'

'Stop grumbling. It's only a short journey.'

'Not short enough for me. You must have a stomach made of iron. Once we get home I'm never going to set foot on a boat again.'

They only caught the tail end of the storm and it soon swept away, leaving the sea calm with hardly a wave on it.

James breathed a sigh of relief and some colour began to return to his face. 'I think I might be able to eat something now. Perhaps a cheese sandwich or some toast would be nice.'

'I'll see what I can get.'

Lester soon returned with soup, bread and a plate of toast. 'Take your pick of whatever you think you can keep down.'

His friend thought about it for a while, then picked up a piece of toast and took small bites. Then he finished the soup and the bread.

'Feel all right?' Lester asked when the plates were empty.

'Think so. Whatever that medic gave me must have settled my insides. How much longer before we reach the London Docks?'

'Less than an hour. Will you go straight on to Winchester, or would you like to stay overnight with us?'

'I'll go straight home, but I'll come and see you in a couple of days.' He grinned. 'We've been together for a long time and it will seem strange going our separate ways. That is only temporary, though, because once the girls are home it will be the four of us together at last.' What he wasn't saying was that his friend might need company to get over the shock of hearing about the scandal of the trial. With his sister still away, he wasn't going to let him suffer alone. They had been through too much together for him to do that.

They parted company at the train station and Lester headed for his home, and he agreed with James; it was strange to be going somewhere without him.

When Adams opened the door he put his fingers to his lips, indicating that the butler should remain silent. He nodded and smiled happily, pointing to the sitting room.

Dropping his kit in the hall, Lester quietly opened the door and looked in. His mother was sitting by the fire reading a book, and glanced up when he walked in.

For a moment she just stared and then leapt to her feet. 'Lester! You're home. I didn't know you were coming.'

He wrapped his arms around her and lifted her off her feet. 'I thought I'd surprise you.'

'You've certainly done that. Let me look at you.' She stepped back a little and stared at her son in wonder. He was no longer the boy she remembered. Standing in front of her was a handsome man, but a man showing the strain of dangerous combat over a long period. 'My goodness, you've grown so tall. How are you? Have you recovered from the injury you had after the crash?'

'I'm fine,' he told her, 'and also very hungry. Is there anything to eat in this house?'

A meal was quickly served and they talked while he tucked in to one of Cook's excellent steak pies. He had her laughing about some of the funny antics he and James had got up to, never once mentioning the unpleasant things.

'Your room is ready for you,' she told him when he kept yawning. 'Have a good night's sleep. You must be tired after your journey.'

'I am,' he admitted. After saying goodnight he walked towards the stairs and paused outside the music room. He wasn't ready to go in there yet. Perhaps tomorrow.

Chapter Thirty-Two

'How is he?' Alex strode into the sitting room where Sara and Joshua were, and both turned to him with worried expressions.

Sara greeted him with a kiss when he went to her side. 'He's withdrawn and takes long walks no matter how bad the weather is.'

'He's been home for two weeks and hasn't once been to the music room.' Joshua clenched his hands together with worry. 'When I told him his piano was tuned and ready to use, he just smiled and thanked me, but didn't even go to look at it. I haven't pushed him to start playing again because I feel that will do more harm than good. To be honest, I am at a loss to know what to do.'

'What is worrying him?' Sara asked. 'And what can we do to help?'

'Exactly what you are doing. Treat him with love and affection, and let him know you are happy to have him home again. As for the music, leave him to deal with this reluctance to play.' He gave Joshua a sympathetic glance. 'You must be prepared for the chance that he might never play again.'

Sara gasped, distressed by the suggestion. 'I do wish Lillia was here. She might be suffering in the same way and they need each other.'

Joshua looked furious. 'What has this bloody war done to my talented darling? Forgive my lan-

289

guage, dear lady, but the thought of all that music being locked in him with no way to express it is more than I can take.'

'You know him well, Alex, and you have a better idea of what it was like out there, so could you talk to him?' she pleaded. 'If you could find out what is wrong, we might be able to help. We feel so helpless. Do you know he hasn't even asked why Gilbert isn't here?'

'I will talk to him about this only if he comes to me for advice. This kind of thing is happening to thousands of men returning from the war. They have been facing danger every day, being shot at and watching their friends die. Then suddenly it stops, and when they return home they are expected to carry on with their lives as if nothing has happened. It isn't that easy; it takes time. That is what Lester needs, time to adjust. Give it to him without any pressure to do something he is clearly not ready for yet. He may return to his music – he may not – but you must leave that decision to him.'

'That is hard to do, but I understand what you are saying.' Joshua smiled sadly at Sara. 'I will stay away until I am sent for, and I pray that happens soon.'

'Professor, you have been with us for so long you are considered a part of our family. I won't hear of you staying away, and you will dine with us tonight as arranged.'

'Sara's right,' Alex told him. 'You have been a constant in the twins' lives since they were little more than babies, and Lester is used to seeing you around. Keep it that way; don't go changing the routine of a lifetime, or that could make him even more uneasy.'

'Oh, well, yes, if you put it like that. I thought my being here might distress him.'

'No, quite the opposite. Where is he, by the way?'

'He's out with James,' Sara told him. 'That boy is a blessing and is staying with us for a while. He doesn't appear to have any problems. He's always smiling and joking.'

'Don't be deceived by his ready smile. There's a real struggle going on inside him, but I think I might have the answer to his problems, and perhaps both of them.'

'I hope so.' Sara sighed. 'James told me that he knows about the trial because he'd seen an English newspaper, but had kept it from Lester. I haven't said anything yet because I want Lillia here as well.'

'She'll be home soon, I'm sure.' Alex heard the front door slam and chatter from the boys.

'Alex!' James swept into the room with Lester right behind him. 'Father told me you are retiring from the army. What will you do?'

He watched them warming their hands by the fire, and said, 'As you know, in April last year the Royal Air Force was created by merging the Royal Flying Corps and the Royal Navy Air Service. I think flying is going to be very important in the future, so I'm going to open a flying school.'

They both spun round, their faces glowing with sudden interest.

'I say, what a splendid idea,' James exclaimed, his face lighting up.

'Can we help?' Lester was more animated than he had been since returning home.

'I was hoping you would say that.'

'Tell us all about it,' James demanded. 'When and where is this school going to be set up?'

'I'll be out of the army by the spring, and have already made arrangements to start the school at Hendon. It will be hard work, but we should be up and running by the summer.'

'Just in time for the good weather. That's terrific.' James slapped his friend on the back. 'We'll be able to fly again, only this time for pleasure.'

'You're going to need instructors.' Lester was as interested as his friend now. 'Will we do?'

'I couldn't ask for better.'

Sara watched her son, relieved to see him looking excited about the scheme, but troubled that it might take him further away from his music. However, she had already discussed this with Alex, and if he felt this might help the boys, then she trusted him. He had been out there in France and understood the problems they were having in adjusting to normal life again. The boys also liked and respected him, and she was sure he was in a better position to help them.

'Will you get many people wanting to learn to fly?' Joshua wanted to know.

'I believe so. Flying played a significant role in the war, and flying will become even more popular as aeroplane design advances. I also intend to run a hire service for qualified pilots. I have researched it carefully and have come to the conclusion that it could be a successful enterprise. It will be hard work to build up, of course.'

'I'd like to go to Hendon again.' Lester looked hopefully at Alex. 'They were good days, weren't they?'

'Yes, they were. Tell you what, why don't you and James come with me now? We can make a quick visit and I'll tell you what the plans are.'

'Wonderful! Can I drive your car?' James asked eagerly.

'Don't let him do that.' Lester raised his hands in mock horror. 'The last time I was in a car with him we careered around France, and I don't care to remember how many times he nearly hit something.'

'We got there, didn't we?'

They were grinning now as they remembered trying to find that farm.

'I think I'd better drive. Get your coats. If we hurry we can be back in time for dinner.'

The moment the boys had rushed from the room to collect their things, Alex kissed Sara. 'Don't worry too much. At least Lester is showing enthusiasm about something again.'

'It was good to see him laughing and joking again. Thank you, darling.'

He found them already waiting by the car and they set off immediately. It was a cold day, but the sky was clear when they reached Hendon, and the first thing the boys did was to rush over to have a look at two planes in the field, talking excitedly about the latest designs.

Lester ran his hands over one and turned to Alex, who had followed them. 'This is new, isn't it?'

'Yes, I've already bought these. Why don't you

take them up and let me know how they handle?'

'Can we?' James crawled out from underneath one of the planes he had been inspecting.

'You'd be doing me a favour. I haven't had time to test them yet. They've got petrol in and are ready to go. Just do a couple of circuits to get the feel of them, then see what they can do, and if you like them I'll order another one. Three should be enough for us to start with.'

He watched as they took to the air, and smiled with satisfaction when they began to turn and dive, putting the planes through their paces. Before landing they swooped low and waggled their wings, making him burst out laughing. They were good – very good.

When they landed and walked over to him all smiles, he asked, 'How did they handle?'

'Mine flew like a dream,' James told him. 'I didn't notice any problems at all.'

'The one I was in was a bit rough at full throttle, but apart from that it was good. You need to get that looked at.' Lester shoved his hands in his pockets and gazed around. 'That was good. Have I got time to wander around?'

Alex nodded. 'We must leave in half an hour if we are to get back in time for dinner.'

'That's fine. I just want to have a look at the old place.'

James watched his friend walk away and glanced at Alex. 'He's having a tough time and I'm worried what is going to happen when he hears all the bad news.'

'He's closed his mind and shut everything out at the moment. I was hoping that the chance to fly again might have woken him up, and it did for a while, but it didn't last.'

'I'm afraid not, but it's done a hell of a lot of good for me. Can I come in with you and help run the school? I've got to have something to do, and this is perfect.'

'I'll be glad to have you and Lester as well, if that's what he wants. You are both excellent pilots and just what I need.'

'Is he ever going to play again?'

'I honestly don't know, but if not then I want him to know he has an alternative, something he's equally good at – flying. However, Sara's hoping that when Lillia comes home and they are together again, the love of music will surface.'

'I know it's none of my business, but are you going to marry his mother? I've noticed you are very fond of each other.'

'We do intend to marry, but can't say anything until Lillia returns and they are told what has happened.'

James shook his head in concern. 'It's going to be a terrible shock to them.'

'It is, and there's no telling how they are going to take it, but it has to be done before any of us can move on with our lives.'

'Ah, here he comes.' James had a bright smile on his face as he greeted his friend again. 'Had a good look round? This place holds lots of happy memories, doesn't it?'

'Yes, and this is the perfect place to start your flying school,' he told Alex. 'There's a building over there that would make a perfect office and classroom.'

'I've already made arrangements to hire that, and I'm relying on you two to help me get it up and flying – so to speak.'

'Can't wait.' James rubbed his hands together in anticipation. 'I think I'll buy myself a car tomorrow, and I'll need you to help me choose one.'

'I will, on one condition.'

'Name it.'

'Teach me to drive.'

'Done.'

'Are you sure you know what you're doing?' Alex laughed. 'I thought you didn't think much of his driving?'

Lester smirked. 'I was kidding. He's not too bad, really.'

'Faint praise, indeed.' James shoved his friend in the front of the car with Alex, and then got in the back. 'You can sit there and watch the expert.'

Dinner that evening was a pleasant meal with James and Alex keeping the conversation lively. Alex had to return to Aldershot that evening so he took Joshua home first.

'The boys are excited about your flying school, but it isn't for Lester.'

'I know that, but I hope we've taken the pressure off him by offering an alternative to music. He's a damned good pilot and I would be more than pleased to have him with us.'

'I've watched him carefully since he arrived home, and I've come to the conclusion that he's afraid he won't be able to play to a high enough standard again. He's been away from it for too long,' said Joshua.

'You might be right. All we can do is leave him in peace, and hope when his sister comes home that will help him. Being together will probably help both of them, because we don't know how much the war and what she's been through has touched her.'

Joshua nodded. 'It will be good to see them together again, and I hope she hasn't changed too much.'

'I'm afraid change is inevitable,' Alex pointed out gently.

Joshua gave him a sideways glance. 'You haven't changed.'

'Haven't I?' He gave a humourless laugh. 'Then I'm doing a good job of fooling you. I'm changing my life completely by leaving the army, getting married and taking risks with a new business venture. Have you ever known me be so reckless?'

'Now you mention it, I haven't. The war has unsettled all of us, hasn't it?'

'It has, but given time some of us will sort ourselves out.'

Chapter Thirty-Three

The next morning the boys set off in search of a car for James, and he was hard to please, insisting that it had to have room for four people. He eventually settled on one he liked, and they returned home with it in the afternoon. It was trying to snow and they were eager to warm up by the fire in the sitting room. Sara was there with Joshua and they weren't alone.

Lester stopped as if he had hit a brick wall, and after a moment he reached out and his sister ran to him. Without a word, they wrapped their arms around each other and held tight, then he lifted one arm and Ruth stepped into the embrace.

'Hey, what about me?' James said, emotion making his voice husky.

Lillia reached out and pulled him to join the group. The four friends stayed like that for some minutes and everyone in the room had moist eyes.

'So, the healing begins,' Joshua told Sara.

'I pray to God it does,' she whispered. 'I've got to get a message to Alex.'

'Leave it to me. I'll track him down.' Joshua silently left the room and Sara went with him.

'Is everything all right, madam?' Adams asked as she closed the door softly behind her. 'Shall I order refreshments?'

'Not just yet. They need a little time together.'

Lillia was the first to break from the group, but still held on to her brother's arm. Their mother had told her that he hadn't even entered the music room and showed no desire to play again. This had shocked her, but she understood what he was going through. There was also a doubt in her mind that she would be able to reach the standard and power she had gained before the war. She was home now and they would face this together, as they always had done.

'Are you boys out of the RFC now?' Ruth asked,

keeping her voice as free from emotion as she could. 'I mean the Royal Air Force as it is now called.'

'As good as. We have been given an extended leave and will not have to report back. Our papers will be sent to us,' James explained. 'What about you?'

'I'm staying on for a while, but Lillia has already resigned.'

'I didn't want to waste any more time.' She smiled at her brother. 'We have things to do. It isn't going to be easy starting over again, but we will begin slowly and see how we get on. What about you, James, do you have any plans?'

'Alex is leaving the army and starting up a flying school. He's going to need pilots and we are two of the best,' he told her proudly.

'How exciting!' She squeezed her brother's arm. 'You should continue to fly, because I know how much you love it.'

'Yesterday, Alex let us test two of the planes he's already bought. We really enjoyed it.'

'I'll say we did. It was wonderful to be up there without the threat of someone shooting at us.' James grinned. 'Though I did look for the gun when Lester dived and got on my tail. I'm definitely going to work with Alex, and the other most important thing is to marry you, Lillia.'

They all burst in to laugher, and she said, 'I haven't agreed to marry you, and come to think of it, I don't recall you ever proposing.'

'I will when the time is right, but what we all need now is time. We can't just switch off from all that has happened. I'm sure we all have demons we need to cage before we can settle down to normal life.'

Ruth looked at her cousin in surprise. 'I've never heard you talk like that before. When did you become so philosophical about life?'

'When some nasty sod shot us down,' he declared. 'You get a different view on life then.'

They all nodded, knowing exactly what he meant.

Ruth stood up. 'I must go now and see my family, but I'll be working in London and will be able to see you often.'

'Make sure you do.' Lillia hugged her friend. 'And thank you for everything.'

Ruth then went to Lester and wrapped her arms around him. 'Everything will be all right, you'll see. You and Lillia work through your problems together, but take your time. There isn't any rush, and I'll be nearby, so you call if you need me. Relax and don't push yourself to do something you're not ready for yet. Do you understand what I'm saying?'

'I do.' He nodded and held her tightly for a moment. 'We'll be able to spend some time together, at last, and I'll try to take your advice, Nurse.'

'Oh, it's so good to see you again,' she told him and then turned to her cousin. 'Go and get your things, and then you can drive me home in that new car sitting outside. I'm assuming it's yours?'

'It is, and isn't it a beauty? We bought it this morning.'

'Come along, then; I'm anxious to get home.'

He looked puzzled for a moment and when he

looked at the twins he understood why his cousin had told him to collect his things. Brother and sister needed time together alone. He shot out the door and thundered up the stairs.

After saying goodbye to Sara, the cousins left, promising to come back soon.

It wasn't until they were enjoying a cup of tea after dinner that Lillia asked, 'Where's Father?'

Sara put down her cup and took a deep breath. The time had come. She had wanted Alex here for this, but it couldn't be delayed any longer. 'He isn't here. Lester, do you remember the two policemen who called when you were on leave?'

He nodded.

They listened in stunned silence as she told them about the arrest and trial.

'He's dead?' Lillia gasped.

'Yes, four weeks after he was sentenced he had a heart attack and died. I think the prospect of facing years in prison was just too much for him.'

'We're the children of a criminal?' the twins said together, horrified by the news.

'That is the other thing I must now tell you, as I promised some time ago. When I was eighteen I met a young struggling musician. We thought we were in love, but our families were against us. Pierre's parents had arranged a marriage for him to a wealthy girl, and my parents objected to me being involved with a penniless boy. They tore us apart, much to my distress. A while after this I discovered I was pregnant and hid it for as long as I could, but by the time I was seven months it could no longer be hidden. My parents were horrified and in order to avoid a scandal, they brought home a man they had made an agreement with. He would be given money and a position in society by marrying me. I disliked him on sight, but as it was to be a marriage in name only, I agreed for the sake of my unborn child.' She smiled at them with sadness and affection. 'Then I had twins who have brought me only joy, and when you both showed musical talent at a young age, I was thrilled.'

Lester ran a hand over his eyes. 'Then the general wasn't our father.'

'That's right.'

The twins looked at each other and said, 'Thank goodness!'

'Who is our father?' Lillia asked.

'Pierre Le Fort.'

'What?' Lester was on his feet. 'I went to a concert in France given in his honour. I'm sorry to tell you, Mother, that he was killed in the war.'

Moisture filled her eyes when she heard about his death. 'That is so sad, but I am glad you were there. He would have been proud of you.'

'Did he know about us?'

'I never saw him again after we were parted, and his family wouldn't have told him, even if they knew. As far as I know all communication between the families was cut off completely.'

'You once told me that my piano was a gift from someone. Was it him?'

'Yes, shortly after he was taken back to France it was delivered with a short note saying how sorry he was to have caused me so much trouble. It was a strange gift but he said he couldn't take it with him, and it was the only thing of value he had at that time and he wanted me to have it.'

'He must have loved you.' Lillia wiped away a tear at hearing such a sad tale. This was a dreadful thing to have happened to their mother.

'I think perhaps he did, but with money behind him he became very famous, and I hope he was happy.'

Lester was clearly distressed. 'You shouldn't have had to face the unpleasantness of that trial alone. I should have been here.'

'I wasn't alone, my dear.' Her children were shocked by what she had just told them, but they were taking it better than she had dared hope. They hadn't spoken one word of condemnation for her behaviour as a young girl. 'Alex and his father were with me all the time. Without their support I don't know how I would have coped. The man I married had hidden his criminal activities under a cloak of respectability, and had fooled us all, including the police, for a very long time.'

'Did he know who our father really was?'

'Unfortunately my father told him.'

'Ah, then now I understand why he disliked us so much, and objected to our musical talent.'

'And as you grew more and more like Pierre, for some reason he couldn't bear to have you around. I don't understand why he acted like that, after all, our marriage was a business affair.'

'Perhaps deep down he had come to care for you,' Lillia suggested.

Sara shook her head. 'If he had then he never showed any indication of affection for me. Quite the opposite, I would say.'

'As the general wasn't our father, and Holdsworth wasn't his real name, what name do we use now?' Lester asked, confused.

At that moment the door opened, Alex strode in and went straight to Sara's side. 'I would be honoured if you would use my name after your mother and I are married.'

'Married!' Lillia jumped to her feet. 'That's wonderful, isn't it?' She rushed over and kissed her mother, then gave a cheeky curtsy to Alex, making them all laugh. 'Lillia Stansfield sounds perfect.'

Lester was more subdued than his sister, but he was smiling when he kissed his mother and shook hands with Alex. 'We are very happy for you, sir, and know you'll take good care of our mother. We will certainly change our names to yours, because we need to sever all contact from that criminal.'

'It will be a fresh start for all of us, and you don't need to call me "sir". Alex will be fine.'

'No.' Lillia was shaking her head. 'I want to call you "Father". May I? We've never had a proper father before.'

Alex was taken aback by the request, and quite overwhelmed by it. He'd had a lingering fear there might be opposition from the twins, and this response was completely unexpected. 'I would be delighted if you could think of me in that way, but the choice is yours. Address me in any way you are comfortable with.'

'Thank you.' She gave him a teasing smile. 'Is it all right to hug a new father?'

'Perfectly acceptable.'

When she wrapped her arms around him she whispered in his ear, 'Thank you for loving Mother, and giving her the chance to be happy.'

'I'll do my best to make us all happy,' he told her quietly.

She stepped back and went to her brother's side. 'What astonishing news!'

'I agree, and to find out that Pierre Le Fort was our father is staggering.'

'Amazing, but now we know where our love of music came from. He was almost as good a pianist as you.'

Lester laughed, and with one swift movement picked her up and swung her round, just as he had done when they'd been children.

'Put me down,' she squealed. 'Our new father will tell us off for behaving so badly. He's an officer, you know – a proper one.'

He put her back on her feet, still laughing, and winked at Alex. 'I don't know where you got your talent from, though, because I'm sure Pierre couldn't sing soprano.'

Sara watched the teasing and breathed a sigh of relief. This was how it had always been, and they had taken the news in their stride. She shouldn't be surprised, though, because both of them had nearly lost their lives in the war, and seen things she couldn't even imagine, and that must have changed their outlook on life. They now knew what was important and what to dismiss. The thing that mattered now to all of them was the future.

Alex placed an arm around Sara and nodded. The thing they had both been dreading was over, and there had been no need for concern. The twins were mature and experienced enough to handle such life-changing news. With that obstacle out of the way it was time to move forward.

'I've managed to wangle five days' leave and have lined up a couple of houses for us to see tomorrow. Would you like to come with us?'

'Houses?' the twins said together.

'Yes, there's one I think would be perfect, but your mother must see it first. It is overlooking Richmond Park.'

'You're buying another house?' Lester was puzzled. 'What are you going to do with this one – sell it?'

'No, it's yours and Lillia's now,' Sara told them. 'I will be taking any of the staff who want to come with us, so you will have to employ your own, but I am sure Adams will help you with that.'

'Oh, my. Have you got any more surprises for us?' she asked her mother.

'I think that's enough for one day, don't you?'

'It's good of you to let us have the house,' Lester told his mother, 'but we can't afford to run it. Neither of us has a job at the moment.'

'You don't have to worry about that. I will meet all the expenses and support you while you pursue your musical careers, or whatever you decide to do.'

'But that is too much to ask of you,' Lester protested.

'I am quite capable of doing that, but if it makes you uncomfortable you can come and live with us. We would both be very happy if you wanted to, but we did think you would want to stay in London, and that's why your mother has given you the house.'

Lillia was chewing her lip as she turned all this over in her mind.

'You don't have to decide now, my dears. It will be a while before we move, so why don't you take time to think about it?'

They looked at their mother and nodded.

'Good. Now, I've booked a table for us to have dinner out this evening.'

'I'm very tired after all the travelling,' Lillia told them, 'so why don't you two go and have a nice quiet meal on your own. I need to have a talk with the brother I haven't seen for a long time.'

When the twins were alone they looked at each other, their minds buzzing with everything they had been told.

'What a day!' She sat next to her brother and stared in to the fire. 'We come home to find our world has exploded. Everything we knew has been swept away, and until Alex and Mother are married, we don't even have a proper name. Holdsworth was one of his aliases.'

'I'm going to start calling myself Stansfield now.'

His sister nodded. 'I'll do the same.'

'When I think of all Mother has suffered and done for us, I swear I would throw that man out on the street if he hadn't already died. I'll bet he threatened to tell us about our birth if she didn't do as he said.'

'I'm sure that was the hold he had over her, but he's gone now and Mother can be happy at last. Alex is a fine man and has stuck by her through the unpleasant times, even though he knew about her past. His family and James's have also given their support. It's comforting to know she had people around her who cared.'

Lester sighed. 'I wonder if James and Ruth knew about the trial.'

'I have a feeling they did, but if so, then they kept it very quiet. They are good friends.'

'The best,' he agreed. 'Nevertheless it is only right they know the whole truth about us.' His sister nodded her agreement, and he said, 'This is a new start for all of us and we must do everything we can to see Mother and Alex have a happy marriage.'

She slipped her arm through her brother's. 'The best way we can do that is to show her that we are happy and planning for our future. A future she has paid such a high price to give us. She is worried about us and we must lift that burden. The thought of starting over again is scary, though.'

'That is what I'm struggling with.'

'Well, there's only one way to find out if we are still any good, and that is to try.'

'True.'

Chapter Thirty-Four

The next day they went with Alex in his car and looked at the houses he had picked out. Every one was excellent, but their mother fell for the one near Richmond Park, and the twins agreed with her choice. It was spacious with a large garden, and from the third floor you could see the park.

'Look, there are deer in there.' Lillia was enthralled. 'Isn't it beautiful?'

Sara agreed. 'It feels like a happy, peaceful home, and how lovely to be away from the noise of London. Alex does prefer this one as well.'

'Then this is the house for you.'

'I have already told the agent we will have it.' Alex joined them at the window, and smiled at the twins. 'Are you sure we can't tempt you to move with us?'

'We really need to stay in London,' Lester told him, 'but we might change our minds later, and we will certainly come and stay with you often.'

'We shall expect you to. There's plenty of room here for you. Would you like to take a ride through the park now we've finished?'

'Yes, please, and when we come and stay can I have this room? You can have the one next door,' she told her brother. 'It's got the same view.'

Alex gazed up at the threatening sky. 'We had better be on our way before the weather gets too bad.'

They arrived home to find James and Ruth waiting for them, and Sara told them they could use the upstairs sitting room. Refreshments were brought to them and the friends settled down by a blazing fire to talk.

'Did you know about the trial?' Lester wanted to know.

'We did.' James then told them about the newspaper article and how he had concealed it from his friend. 'I didn't let you see it because it would have upset you, and there wasn't anything you could do so far away from home. I contacted Alex and he assured me your mother was being well-looked-after. I thought it best to keep quiet.'

'I knew because James told me,' Ruth admitted. 'He wanted to make sure Lillia didn't see any English newspapers. In the situation we were all in we felt it would be better if you didn't know anything about it.'

'It probably was, but we don't think you know he wasn't our father.'

'That doesn't surprise us,' Ruth admitted. 'Will you tell us who your father really is, or would you rather not talk about it?'

'We want you to know.' Lester then began to tell them the whole story, leaving nothing out.

'I said you looked like that pianist,' James exclaimed when his friend had finished talking. 'Wow! You must be shocked.'

'We are.' Lillia managed a smile. 'But we are also very pleased that man wasn't our father, and our mother is finally free of him. Now you know the details of our birth, we would quite understand if you didn't feel you could still be friends with us.'

'What are you talking about?' James demanded.

'You both come from respectable families and they might not think–'

'Stop right there.' James surged to his feet. 'You are soon to be part of the Stansfield family, and you can't get more respectable than that. And let me tell you another thing. We don't give a damn about your past. You are our friends and nothing will ever change that. Alex obviously doesn't care what happened in the past either; he loves your mother and that's all that matters.'

'Quite right,' Ruth agreed. 'It's two beautiful twins we love and respect. That's all we know and all we see, so don't you dare mention this again.'

Lester held up his hands in surrender. 'We had to know how you felt and give you the chance to back away if you wanted to.'

'Don't be daft. How could you think we'd do that after all we've been through together? You are not getting rid of us, so you can forget it,' James scolded, then grinned. 'Now that's out of the way, tell us why you've been looking at houses.'

Having cleared up the point they had been concerned about, Lillia launched into describing the beautiful house they had seen. 'It's to be Mother and Alex's home after they are married, and it's perfect for them.'

'What is going to happen to this house?' Ruth asked. 'Is your mother going to sell it?'

'She's given it to us, and we are going to stay here.'

'I say, what a good idea.' James nudged his cousin and winked, then turned back to their friends. 'Can we come and stay sometimes?'

'Of course you can,' Lester told them. 'This will be our home and you will always be welcome. You might have to help with the chores, though, until we employ our own staff.'

'Happy to do that. I can make a good omelette.'

'He can actually,' Ruth laughed, 'and I'm an expert at bed-making.'

'We won't have any problems at all then.' Lillia laughed and they all joined in.

The twins looked at each other and gave a little nod. They had been shocked by all they had been told, but only good had come from revealing the truth. The way was now clear and the past could be put behind them, but what that future would be they were still unsure about. The doubts still lingered that they would be able to pick up where they had left off so many years ago. She was ready to try, but not without her brother. They had to do this together, because without the support of each other the task would be too daunting. It had to be both of them or failure was a distinct possibility.

'What was that?' Lillia sat bolt upright in bed, wondering what had woken her. She tipped her head to one side and listened. There it was; that was the sound that had disturbed her sleep. Reaching across to put on the light and grab her robe, she glanced at the clock. Five in the morning. She scrambled out of bed and shot out of the door, nearly knocking into her mother. They looked at each other and without speaking, hurried down the stairs. Adams was standing outside the music room and placed his fingers to his lips.

'How long has he been in there?' Sara whispered.

'Two hours, madam. He's playing the same piece over and over again. At first it was soft and I could hardly hear it, but he's really getting in to it now.'

Sara put her hand out to open the door, but her daughter stopped her. 'Let me go in alone.'

She nodded and turned to Adams. 'As soon as it's light I want you to send for the professor.'

'Yes, madam. Would you like tea? Cook is already up.'

'That would be welcome.' She sat on a hall chair. 'I'll stay here.'

Lillia slipped into the music room and closed the door quietly behind her. Her brother stopped halfway through the piece, shook his head, and went back to the beginning again. She could see the perspiration on his face and the frustration as he tried to play the piece to his satisfaction. It was vital that she acted normally, so she took a steadying breath, walked over and sat beside him on the wide stool. 'That's good, but you're rushing it,' she told him calmly. 'Try something else and then go back to that.'

He stopped and wiped his face with a handkerchief. 'What are you doing up?'

'The whole household is up. Don't stop playing.'

'It's hard.' He bowed his head. 'I need the professor.'

'He'll be here soon.' When he clenched his hands she laid hers gently on top of his. 'Relax. Let us start with the basics. Play scales for me while I try and loosen up my vocal chords, and we'll take it from there.'

Sara sat outside the door for over an hour, and when her daughter's voice became clearer and more powerful, with her brother playing for her, she struggled to keep the emotion in check. Adams had stayed with her and she was aware of other members of the staff nearby, listening with smiles on their faces.

'I had better go and get ready for the day. Please call me if they need me.'

'Of course, madam, and I've sent for the professor already. He won't mind being woken early for such good news.'

'Indeed, he won't. Brigadier Stansfield will also be arriving early, so ask Cook to prepare a large breakfast. I think everyone is going to be very hungry.'

'She is doing that now, madam.'

An hour later the professor arrived, stopped outside the music room, listened for a while, then opened the door and strode in. 'Stop! Stop!' he ordered. 'That won't do at all. Dear me, we have a lot of work to do, but before then, go upstairs, wash and dress, and after you've had a good breakfast, we will begin to repair the damage.'

'Yes, Professor,' they replied, and tore out of the room, running up the stairs to their rooms, just as they had done as children when their tutor had given them orders.

Joshua came out and smiled at Sara and Adams. 'Thank you for sending for me. This is the breakthrough we have been hoping for, and they are now ready to study again. Quite a day,' he told them. 'Ah, quite a day.'

By the time Alex arrived, Joshua had his pupils hard at work. Normally he would have taken them separately, but he knew this was a difficult time and they needed to be together.

'That's a lovely sound,' Alex said the moment he walked in the door.

Sara greeted him, her face glowing with joy. 'Lester started playing again in the early hours of the morning, and then Lillia joined him. Isn't it wonderful?'

'I'm so pleased, my dear. It was heartbreaking to know all that talent was being wasted. Does Joshua know?'

'We sent for him and he's in there with them now. Come and have breakfast. Cook has made enough to feed half of London.'

While he was enjoying his meal, James and Ruth arrived, and helped him make a dent in the food.

All the doors had been left open so everyone could hear the music, and James sighed when Lillia's voice soared through the house, making him close his eyes in sheer pleasure.

Ruth had wandered out to the hall and was sitting outside the music room, listening with a smile on her face.

It was an hour later when Joshua stopped them. 'That's enough for this session. That was a good start, now relax.'

'How is it going?' Sara wanted to know when he walked into the dining room and began heaping a plate with food from the covered dishes.

'Because of everything they have been through there is now an extra quality to their interpretation of the music.' He could hardly contain his excitement. 'I do declare they are better than ever.'

'Have you told them?' Alex asked.

'Certainly not! I have already told them they have done well. Too much praise is not good for them.'

James rushed out of the room, grabbed Ruth from her chair and they went in to see their friends, who were still in the music room, talking quietly together.

'That was terrific,' James declared, and then he gazed at them for a moment. 'I say, you both look worn out, so how about coming for a drive? You can show us where this house is in Richmond.'

'What a good idea.' Lester stood up and slapped his friend on the back, more at peace than he had been for a very long time. 'A walk through the park would be excellent.'

In April, Alex left the army and opened his flying school, Sara made preparations for their wedding in May, and the twins worked, driven on by Joshua, completely unaware of passing time.

One evening, after a shorter session than usual, Joshua joined Sara and Alex in the sitting room. He took the drink Alex offered and sat down with a sigh. 'They are ready.'

'You are happy with them at last?' Sara asked hopefully. Joshua had moved in to be constantly with his pupils and had driven himself and the twins in an effort to make up for the wasted years. They were now twenty-seven years old and must launch their careers without further delay.

'I know you think highly of them, but do you honestly believe they have a chance?' Alex asked. 'It's a tough business.'

Joshua drained his glass and held it out for a refill. 'Only the most talented make it to the top, and that is where I believe the twins belong. They know it isn't going to be easy and are quite prepared for that.'

'Is there any way we can help, Josh?'

'You are holding your wedding reception at the Andersons', so I have arranged for them to give a short recital,' he told them, not bothering to ask their permission. 'I will be inviting a few gentlemen to that performance. Now, if you will excuse me I must return to my home. There is much I have to do before the wedding in two weeks.'

'What is he up to?' Sara was puzzled.

'I would say he is going to see the twins are noticed as quickly as possible, and has taken the wedding as a good time to bring some interested people to hear them. We can relax and leave this to Josh, for he clearly has plans for his star pupils.'

'That is wonderful, and it will be lovely to have them perform at our wedding.'

Two days later Ruth arrived while Lester was playing alone in the music room, so she slipped in to listen. He was completely different from the tense, troubled man who had returned from the war. The lines of strain had disappeared and he was relaxed and happy.

He looked up and smiled.

'I love to hear you play.'

'That's good, because you are going to have to live with it.'

'Pardon?'

'I practise every day and there may be times when you would like quiet in the house.'

'What are you talking about?' She was confused.

'When we are married you will have to live with

me playing all the time.'

'Are you proposing?' she asked, standing up slowly.

'Do I need to?' He didn't stop playing.

'Well, it would be nice.'

'In that case; I love you very much, Ruth. Would you agree to marry a struggling musician?'

'I will!' She rushed over to him, and only then did he stop playing so he could gather her into his arms.

Chapter Thirty-Five

It was a beautiful spring day and the twins had never seen their mother looking so radiant as she married Alex. After the wedding in London they had a fleet of cars to take them to the Andersons'. This large house was perfect for the reception, and also the ballroom an ideal place for the recital. Cook and her staff had also been moved there so she could oversee the preparation of the food.

On the way Lester asked James how the flying school was going, and he told him excitedly that they had four pupils already and lots of enquiries were coming in. They were hopeful it was going to be a success.

'It sounds exciting,' Lester told him. 'I'm sorry I can't join you after all.'

'We never expected you to, but Alex wanted to give you the option of doing something else if you couldn't go back to your music.'

He nodded. 'Yes, he's a good man, and at least I'll be able to have a free flight now and again. Just to keep my hand in. Won't I?'

'Any time you like,' his friend told him. 'Ah, here we are.'

The guest list was huge, but this splendid house could easily accommodate such a large gathering. Everyone enjoyed the sumptuous meal, and the house was full of laughter.

James managed to catch up with Lillia as they were getting ready for the performance. 'I say, isn't this a splendid occasion.' He kissed her on the cheek and winked. 'I think we should be next to get married.'

She shook her head. 'No, it's Lester and Ruth next – then us.'

'You agree!' He caught hold of her arm and urged her over to her mother and Alex. 'Can I have permission to marry your daughter, please?' he asked both of them.

'Only if it's what our daughter wants. Is it, darling?'

'I think I had better. He's been on about this for years, and nothing has made him change his mind.' She gave him a teasing smile.

'I never will,' he declared.

'Then you have our permission,' Sara told him.

He gave a whoop of delight, spun Lillia round, kissed her firmly, and shook hands with the newly-weds.

The professor broke up the celebration. 'Come, come. It's time for the recital. My special guests have arrived.'

Joshua's introduction was longer than usual, heaping praise upon his pupils by comparing them to famous artists, and then declaring that in his opinion the twins were better.

'I've never heard such high praise from him,' Sara whispered to Alex.

'He's selling them to his guests.' He glanced along the row at the four men in smart suits, only here because of Joshua's reputation as a first-class tutor. They had slight smiles on their faces as if they'd heard it all before, and they probably had, only to be disappointed in the past. They were about to have that amusement wiped from their faces now, he was sure.

Their performance was varied, showing their different talents to advantage, and when Lillia sang a powerful aria, Alex drew in a deep breath. Josh was right, they were better than ever. By the time Lester closed with one of Beethoven's piano sonatas, everyone was on their feet, cheering for more.

When Joshua walked over to his guests he had a look on his face that said, I told you so. Now you must believe me.

The men, Joshua and the twins disappeared to another room, and the wedding celebrations continued. The newly-weds were going to spend a few days at their new house, but couldn't leave until the children reappeared.

'Wonder what's going on?' James couldn't sit still. 'Did I tell you that Lillia has agreed to marry me?'

'Three times,' Ruth remarked, also anxious about what was happening in that closed room.

An hour later the door opened and the men went over to Sara and Alex, shook their hands, accepted a drink and began to discuss something with them.

The twins came back and the friends rushed over to them.

'What happened?' James wanted to know. 'Who were those men?'

'Two were from an opera company, and the other two are connected to a symphony orchestra,' Lester told them, his expression giving nothing away.

'And?'

He draped an arm around Ruth. 'And I'm starving. Let's find some food.'

'Me too.' Lillia slipped her arm through James's.

The cousins could stand it no longer, and James refused to move. 'Never mind the food. For goodness' sake, talk to us. What did they say?'

'Lillia will be joining the opera company,' Lester told them. 'Minor roles at first, but it will give her the opportunity to learn the art of stage work.'

'I say, that's wonderful, my darling girl.' James was excited by the news. 'I knew they would like you.'

'What about you?' Ruth wanted to know.

'The orchestra have engaged me.' He told her. 'I've actually got a job playing piano. Isn't that marvellous?'

'Just wonderful. You won't be such a struggling musician after all,' she teased.

'I don't know about that. We're starting at the bottom. It will take time.'

'We have plenty of time.'

'True.'

The men came over, shook hands with the twins and left. They all rushed over to Sara and Alex, who were still talking to Joshua.

'I say, isn't this wonderful news?' James couldn't stop smiling. 'What a marvellous day this is turning out to be.'

'Couldn't be better,' Alex agreed.

Joshua still had that satisfied look on his face. 'I know you have both struggled to take up where you left off, but you have worked hard and with a determination I am proud of. You've made a start, and what happens after this will be up to you. But one thing is for sure, now the music will continue.'

The publishers hope that this book has given you enjoyable reading. Large Print Books are especially designed to be as easy to see and hold as possible. If you wish a complete list of our books please ask at your local library or write directly to:

Magna Large Print Books
Cawood House,
Asquith Industrial Estate,
Gargrave,
Nr Skipton, North Yorkshire.
BD23 3SE

This Large Print Book for the partially sighted, who cannot read normal print, is published under the auspices of

THE ULVERSCROFT FOUNDATION